A YOUNG MAN'S TALE

A YOUNG MAN'S TALE

SIMON LENNON

Pine Hill Books

A Young Man's Tale

Fiction (Dystopian, Coming of Age)

Published by Pine Hill Books

ISBN 978-1-925446-26-5 (electronic)

ISBN 978-1-925446-27-2 (paperback)

69,000 words

The characters in this novel are fictitious. Any similarity to specific real people, alive or dead, is coincidental.

To my middle-born son

SOMETIME FROM NOW

Springtime was somewhat unconvincing that year, through the throes of England's end. Leaves of every season lay rotten on the ground, where a generation or two earlier, children would've swept them with their feet; childlessness had been a choice that Europeans made and one they'd not realised they were making. Riding his bicycle through Darlington before the rain came, eighteen-year-old Brandon Frewer was the youngest Englishman around.

Recent years had seen the last of the old time and beginning of the death. Older public clocks of revolving hands read fifteen minutes past nine o'clock, as they read every minute every day. Most houses and apartments in north-east England were deep dark and long forlorn, without residents to nourish them. Abandoned cars stood parked at kerbs, where they would always be, making no impression on Brandon as he passed.

Brandon's mother, Hollie, had cut his thick blond hair neater than his father Alec cut her blonde hair. More than just a winter had passed since customers last patronised the shops, or waiters and the waited-upon last occupied the restaurants. Scampering along the sides of empty buildings, rats ate food that larger creatures left behind, much as they always had. The rolling wheels of Brandon's bicycle slipped a little on the leaves, when he wasn't careful.

Other peoples prospered elsewhere, while the people without progeny had aged. Much of Europe once grandiose and grand, a conquering continent, was almost dead. What wasn't dead was no longer European. None of Europe's reasons for not bestowing newborns endured, leaving a young man on a bicycle behind.

Brandon's mother had asked him to meet her and his father at their friend Tarpin Hobbs' apartment; Brandon was never in a hurry to see Tarpin. More often than Brandon's parents had visited Tarpin before the winter, Tarpin visited their home in Hummersknott, when Brandon waited in another room until he left.

Looking out from a corner of Coniscliffe Road, Tarpin's penthouse apartment was unmistakable; he was the building's final resident. Rain began to fall as Brandon reached the building door, in which a key hung from the lock. Inside were his parents' bicycles; if they'd not been there, Brandon would've headed home. He left his bicycle with theirs.

Windows admitted enough daylight through the lashing rain to lead Brandon trudging up the stairs. "That change in accounting standards helped us," he overheard Tarpin saying as he approached his apartment; Tarpin spoke of business as old soldiers once spoke of battles.

Tarpin in his single chair sat facing Brandon's parents in a sofa. Glasses of rainwater stood on the coffee table between them. Sixty-something years of age, tall Tarpin seemed much older than that, with his grey-white hair that could once have been any colour and his skin made rough by outdoors work too late in life. Since then, he'd become increasingly ample. That day dressed again in a suit, jacket, and tie, Tarpin's shirt was ironed as well as he could've ironed it with an iron heated in a fire. Brandon sat in a spare chair near his mother.

"Our results could've been mediocre that year, poor even," Tarpin continued, "poorer than mediocre was poor, but the changed standard allowed us to report good numbers, and do it truthfully."

Brandon leant towards his mother's ear. "Doesn't he know it's over?" he whispered.

"Shush," she whispered back. Lives had become primitive again, without the worlds of wealth and work that gleefully abandoned them. "Memories are all he has."

Brandon looked around the room. Standing on a sideboard was a silver-framed photograph of Tarpin with his business colleague and occasional mistress Valda. It must have been decades old.

Alec puckered up. "We've decided to leave," he told their host. "I'll see you tomorrow."

"We're moving to Cornwall, Tarpin." Brandon's few friends from school who'd headed there were cause to hope that he might find a home. They alone weren't reason to know he would.

Tarpin hesitated, as he rarely did in Brandon's presence. "What happens to me?" he asked.

"You've got Valda."

Tarpin shook his head. "She hates me now."

"We need to find young people for Brandon," explained his father. Brandon listened attentively, with the vested curiosity of anyone in the presence of somebody talking about him.

"Aren't I young?" asked Tarpin.

"We all need more than just the few of us," interjected Hollie, placing her arm around her only child. "We don't know how else to protect him from growing old alone."

"You could stay, while he goes?"

"He's a boy."

"I'm eighteen!" Brandon insisted, before realising he should have remained silent.

"Do you want to come with us, Tarpin?" asked Hollie. Brandon looked horrified at her.

"This is my home."

"We're only leaving so we can eventually come back again. The north of England is our country. We're not giving up on it."

Tarpin pulled his arms around his chest, hugging himself. "You don't understand," he said. "I don't mean that rudely, it's a compliment, but you don't understand."

"Brandon will keep us in his life as we'll keep him in ours," said Alec, "but his relationship with us can't deter him from new relationships."

Alec, Hollie, and Brandon watched Tarpin for a time, before Tarpin again spoke. "However much you recover England, you won't forget how short you are." They again sat silently. "You better go."

Hollie, and then Alec and Brandon, quietly stood up. They moved towards the open apartment door, where Alec paused and turned around. Thus Hollie and Brandon turned.

Tarpin stood up from his chair. He moved towards the glass-panelled balcony door, as if preparing to watch them riding away along the streets below, before again facing Alec and his family.

Alec raised his hand, as much an acknowledgement he had seen him there as a wave of parting. Tarpin raised his hand. Their parting was brief.

"I haven't brought a raincoat," said Brandon.

His parents and then Brandon moved towards the balcony door, looking past Tarpin up at the dark clouds for any hint of how long the rain might last. "We can wait," replied Hollie.

"I don't mind getting wet," said Brandon.

"There's a man in Larchfield House," interrupted Tarpin, looking through the glass. "He watches me from a window every time I use my balcony, every time I climb part way over the balustrade and dangle my foot. He's not sure what I'm doing, but he'll watch me until I go back inside. I don't know if I hate him, or I recognise myself in him. I think he recognises him in me."

"Dying won't help anyone," said Alec.

"Living doesn't always help either," sighed Tarpin, "not the way I lived. Earning money because I could, buying things I didn't like, dating women I wouldn't love, they were proper ways of killing us and ensuring we'd stay dead."

"Being alive is its own good."

"I can help you now," said Tarpin, "Brandon, all of us." Tarpin opened the balcony door, admitting the cooler air and roar of stormy rain.

"Ah," gasped Hollie, as a gust of wind blew a curtain draped near the door.

Alec grabbed Tarpin's arm. "If you die," yelled Alec above the splashing rain, "you die for you."

"I'm already dead," yelled Tarpin. "I've always been. Don't let me kill us too."

The big man pulled himself away, as Hollie rushed into the rain bearing down upon them. She grabbed Tarpin's arm that Alec wasn't holding, but still Tarpin dragged the rain-drenched three against the wind to the wetted balustrade. Brandon followed them, prodding his hands one way and then another, with no space for him between his parents to hold Tarpin too.

Tarpin's hands held the balcony balustrade, while his writhing arms and back pushed Alec and Hollie away. Tarpin raised his foot from the balcony, whereby Alec wrapped his arm around Tarpin's chest. The falling water made him hard to hold and Alec slipped, as Tarpin's leg twisted over the balustrade. That leg pressed rigidly against the outside balustrade, his arms leveraged his unbalanced body over the balustrade while Alec and Hollie wrestled with him, their waterlogged faces red with the commotion.

"You're a fool, Hobbs!" screamed Alec, trying to pull Tarpin back to the safe side of the balcony.

"I know, Frewer!"

What happened next was very confusing, and no less confusing every time Brandon revived it in his mind. A burst of rain might've made it worse, or a gust of wind disorientated them. The balustrade around a balcony so high above the pavement should never have been so low.

"Now and never," screamed Tarpin, releasing a deep breath. Mustering his last resolve, he pushed himself out into the air with Alec and Hollie holding him, but he then wrapped his arms around them, grabbing them to save himself or lift them over the low balustrade with him. Whatever he was doing, he jettisoned them all away.

Brandon rushed forward, his arms stretched out. "Mum, dad," he screamed, but they fell away from him and down. He reached the balustrade and began to fall over it himself, before he grabbed the wet retention and held himself back, staring down at three people unravelling in the air. They fell through rain and storeys towards the rotten leaves. One or more of them were screaming, before they thumped against the pavement.

Brandon barrelled back through the lounge room, swinging around the doorway to the stairs and every corner downwards. The stairs were much too long however quickly he whisked around them, until he threw open that wretched building door and was back inside the rain. "Mum," he said, as he rushed towards her on the pavement.

Amidst her rumpled clothes, among the quilt of rotten leaves in splattered tones of brown, he pushed her hair from her face. "Mum," he cried, holding her wet head in his hand. Against the rain washing down against her eyes and skin, her face was motionless. Blood oozed from her head between the fingers of his hand holding her. "Oh, God!" he wailed.

"My son," groaned Alec, lying near them on his back, "my son."

"Dad," cried Brandon. Carefully, he laid his mother's head back against her hair. "Dad?" he crawled towards his father, placing his open hands against his father's cheeks. "Oh dad, my God, what can I do?"

His father's pained eyes gazed up at him. His blood trickling from him, glowing, he strained his voice to speak. "By right, you succeed us," he whispered, advising or assuring him.

Brandon gently lifted up his father's head, nursing him, taking more blood on his hands but hoping he helped his father breathe. "I can save you," cried Brandon.

"You will," gasped Alec, choking on the blood in his throat. He closed his eyes and died.

Kneeling on the pavement and cradling in his hands his father's face, Brandon threw his head back in the air and screamed a raucous, bilious squeal with his parents in their deaths. The rain was right to lash his face pointed up before it, a choral throng of wailing fears. His scream tortured their dying market town as he too was tortured, blazing between the bleak and barren building blocks in their moribund decay with the strength and rage that youth afforded him and demanded that he vent until, his throat sore and burning, Brandon dipped his head; he'd failed to save them.

Tarpin's head hung upside down over the kerb, his eyes frozen open. Blood flowed into the gutter.

Brandon held his father's head and wept. The rain tried but couldn't wash them all away.

When his father's head became too heavy for his hands, Brandon laid him back against the melded leaves. His head bowed low, he remained in the rain, however long that was. Used to thinking thoughts aloud and hearing his parents' spontaneous replies, he had no reason to speak without anyone to hear. If he spoke, his parents might reply. Kinder than he deserved, he feared how little they might scold him.

The rain slowly cleared. The sky remained overcast. If crows ate Tarpin's body, then something good would come of him.

Appearing with a wheelbarrow, the man from Larchfield House offered to help Brandon bury his parents in the nearest park, amidst the clusters of wooden crosses falling in the grass and slowly levelling mounds. Brandon declined.

In his penance most available, he alone wrapped his parents' bodies in blankets he took from Tarpin's cupboards. His mother first, it seemed to be polite, he lifted and placed in that wheelbarrow. Often pausing for rest, Brandon pushed the barrow between the puddles and the ponds to Hummersknott.

Along another street of once fashionable abodes, with empty trees and nests for birds, theirs was the house from which white paint wasn't peeling from the windowpanes. The flower boxes contained flowers, in spite of the cruel winter, instead of dust and dirt or mud and mire, because his mother had set them there. An ordinary little home, of any mortal man and woman, save only for the presence of a child, it remained curiously peaceful, without the sense of death that empty houses acquired.

Then Brandon brought his father, much heavier to push along the streets, distracting him. Forgetting his father was there became easier, until his arm swung out from beneath his blood-soiled blanket. Brandon pushed it back again, not to disturb his father's sleep. Finally, his parents lay in their garden behind his childhood home.

Few men or women would've risked their lives as they'd done trying to save their friend, of sorts. Brandon hadn't conceded his dear life to save theirs if the choice had been which of them would die that day. Hopes for his future might've martyred them, but the life their son needed to make was much harder left without them, his only company his mind.

Brandon pushed aside wet soil for carrots and potatoes, which seemed suddenly too much. He took a shovel and began to dig their final resting place, dispelling the last energy in him, straining muscles he'd not already strained. His parents lay silently, threatening to speak or sigh. When the light began to fade, Brandon took a candle from the house; he'd become accustomed to firelight in the half year since electricity ceased flowing. Interring his parents in one grave would mitigate his toil, but lying together might also be romantic, if death could be romantic.

Through the low clouds that night, the light from stars was much too weak to reach Brandon's little eyes. If the moon shone overhead, then it didn't shine on him.

Unable to bear seeing them again, their gravedigger son rolled them in their blankets to the earth. He shovelled dirt across them, covering them, without anything to say. In a town with so many epitaphs, there was no point in any more. Only Brandon needed to know that they were there.

With the candle nearly gone, Brandon sat on the patio, in a chair that seemed always to have been there. His eyes closed in deference to a custom, he wanted to recite a prayer, conducting a funeral service he could not imagine for himself, but could not recall well enough his father's words or mother's sentiment. The parents who might've taught him to pray had died before they did. The night should have been colder than it was.

When his eyes opened, the candle had expired. Brandon could've been anywhere, for all the molecules he saw. He could've been facing cliffs that he could never breach, or been trapped inside a crater on another planet's moon.

Brandon didn't need the light; his familial home had long

been familiar to him. He was again so much a child, the only product of that house surviving. The darkness was much deeper than had been night-time around the small boy in his bed, wrapped in sheets and blankets trying to be warm. "Mummy?" he whispered, "Daddy?"

Slowly, he imagined his parents' souls hearing his mortal voice. He would've been more frightened than consoled if they replied.

His parents might've been the last people with whom he would be close, beyond the dark reflections in greying mirror glass of a young man getting older. Life was a privilege they'd reserved for him not yet repaid. They'd given him the only life he knew, although he no longer knew what to do with what remained. Perhaps he could not do anything. His shoulders shivered.

Clouds passed into mist, revealing a weak crescent of the moon, too meek to shine. The lights of heaven were again the only lights at night.

His parents saw faces in the round lunar light, but all Brandon ever saw was the imprint of a hand. That night, the hand was hidden in the shadows.

Sitting there a child, the moon had been near enough for him to dream of being among the stars. The flags and other tiny toys that astronauts had left on the lunar surface were probably still there, in the otherwise lunar void, where Brandon couldn't see them. Another era of humanity might presume that it was clever and return there to discover them afresh. Brandon knew he never would.

With the mist clearing, stars slowly brightened. Soon, they were in their thickening thousands across the long expanding sky. Stellar multitudes in their millennia filled the spaces between brighter stars with litanies of lesser ones. Each tiny light cast by flames almost an eternity away was a universe. Their activity he couldn't remember seeing before that night beguiled him, when all around was still.

He didn't need so many. In the morning, they'd be again invisible.

Electric lights and living once obscured the sky at night, but the night had always been there. The universal sky was that of anytime, the heavens flickering as they'd done before the earth was born. Ancient students of the sky construed constellations in the stars: a little sense of logic in so big and random a sparkling space. New man never found such images of imagination: the lights of Orion and signs of a zodiac waltzing past that reason had dismissed.

Brandon's father taught him to distinguish a planet from the stars because a planet didn't twinkle; a planet reflected the sun's light without emitting light itself. Brandon tried to discern a planet among the stars above him, but couldn't. The only certain planet was the one on which he sat. If he was searching for something more, then he didn't expect to find it.

His family were further from him than were those little stars. The lives they'd shared were further from him still. His abundance of good fortune was ever being alive. His misfortune was coming to be alone, and bound to being so.

The steady light of an orbiting satellite appeared, gliding towards the near horizon. The satellites of distant populations remained at their control, with little call to pass through English sky. The satellite he saw was probably launched long ago at Europe's behest: blasted in a rocket into atmosphere. It might reflect television or telephone if there were anything to send. It might collect and transmit data for weather forecasts that nobody would make.

Trekking around the Earth in its long rhythm, the light cast made Brandon smile, for the short time the satellite passed by. Beyond a rooftop, the satellite disappeared from view. The heavens were emptier than they'd been before it came.

Its orbit would decline and someday end, burning apart. No merchandise that human beings had made would last forever, and a time would come that Brandon would no longer see satellites above. There would be only persevering planets, stars, and phases of the moon: forever every moment. From the vantage of the stars, one man was very small among the grooves and ruts of earth.

Comets would return, in orbits some longer than human lives, shining between the stars as they passed close to Earth. Men and women didn't make what they recognised and mapped among the skies. In another era of a science, astronomers might again recognise the images from old tapestries and name the comets in their honour. The names that later eras gave patterns in the sky mightn't be the names that Brandon knew.

His life and solitude were those of the last Englishman born in Darlington. There was no answer as to why little he was alive. His might be aged England's final family, but nothing more or less was special about his parents' only child.

If Brandon were to choose the only Englishman, then he would not have chosen him. He'd been neither the most brilliant nor diligent. He'd not been the strongest, fastest, or most agile. He'd not been anybody's hero, even if his parents thought so well of him. His life would not make him a hero for ordinary men were not heroic, except that Brandon's parents had been heroic for bearing him.

Trying to fathom why he was born was too draining an indulgence. The converse was no less problematical: why his generation was so few. If there'd been reasons, then he wasn't smart enough to notice.

Brandon had no more reason to be born than other English people of whom he'd been a part, but England's older children aged. Older people usually died before younger people did. His fortune was to have survived thus far by the chance of being the last one left in line, but he too would grow old. He didn't know how good or bad the fortunes his could be, undeserved on him. Such was his fate, that lonely astronaut in an English market town.

His parents were closer than childless Europeans to immortality, but still they died. They would die again if Brandon died, as everybody died, without a child to bury him or mourn him. Deferring England's death only until then, whittled down to one poor person, England would be dead when the last Englishman was dead.

If England was dead, time was burying her. The grave that England made might be all to endure.

2

NORTHALLERTON

In the morning light of a new dead day, Brandon lazily dropped his leg over his bicycle. He braved his anguished memory to return to where his parents died.

Rain had dispersed most of the blood. Only he who knew that stains were there could see them on the leaves.

A private place to rest made resting easier. A private place to mourn made mourning better. A squirrel pranced across his sedate parents' grave.

The white light of cloudy days inadequately lit what had become Brandon's home alone. He'd seen enough not to see inside the house anymore, but still he languished there, in the presence of his reminiscence. His hair becoming messier, he walked outside. He walked in again, where the air was warmer, as he'd done yesterday and days before yesterday. He lay in bed, sat in chairs, sometimes listening to the wind or rain. When his face spiked whiskers so long as to irritate him, he used another of his dulling razor blades to shave.

In one ill-forgotten moment, when the last embers from the fireplace at dusk were brighter than he'd expected them to be, Brandon presumed his parents were still there. "Hello," he called out, before realising what he'd said.

Smoke billowed from chimneys scattered across Darlington,

in which resided people strong enough to collect and chop windblown wood to burn. Sipping their mugs of boiling water, their only illumination was flames in fireplaces they could not allow to wane. Using the grills from their useless kitchen oven, Brandon's father had erected the means for him to boil pots of water in their fireplace, amidst the wavering red firelight sending shadows around the room. With wood that Brandon brought from the pile behind the house, his log fires never quite survived the night.

At every turn, small memories slipped into his head. Brandon and his father had played chess on the chequerboard lying at one end of the dining table. Awaiting them stood two synthetic armies of sixteen white and sixteen black chess pieces pitted before each other. Brandon moved the white Queen's pawn to start a game. The move was elementary and unimaginative. He moved the black Queen's pawn in similar reply.

Brandon continued moving pieces in turn, playing against himself. He tried gambits to be clever, but never outsmarted him. He turned the board around when he needed to see the pieces from the side for which he was then playing. Finally, he took control and lost control. He defeated him.

The solitary man's dilemma was inescapable. He could only win by losing, and only lose by winning. Brandon couldn't make a life alone.

His parents' deaths left Brandon lonelier than he needed to be. All that kept him there was a chequered chessboard and chess pieces pretending to be for two, along with a weathering grave for which Brandon alone cared. The time to mourn could seem so short, but no time to mourn was adequate. Brandon had little else to do but wonder, in his life of final solitude, but wondering alone was simply getting old. His life ought to be more than simply scrounging from the scraps of people who had died. Brandon mourned all his future could afford.

Pressing a small button on the wall had long ceased opening and closing the garage door, but there'd been precautions against a power outage. Grappling with a short rope above the door, Brandon pulled a wooden handle until the rope jolted from its catch. Hauling up the heavy door rolling in its tracks, he opened daylight back before him.

The day ought to have been a pretty day, as clear spring days once were. Unmoved for a long time, Brandon's mother's car gasped for breath when Brandon turned the key trying to ignite the engine. The noise and movement disturbed the vacuum world, before the engine quickly died. Again, he turned the key, trying to coax the engine into life, but it gasped and died again. Several times he tried, feeling stirrings of a life force through his fingers, before the car staggered into life. Brandon clenched his fists, more relieved than proud, and drove onto and along the street.

He turned the car against its axles back and forth until it cut across the little roundabout, pointing its widest frontage from Tees Grange Avenue towards his home, and stopped. He left it there.

Into his father's car, Brandon packed clean clothes, underclothes, and sturdy pairs of shoes for all the seasons sometime coming. His aged stocks of sustenance were some lasting food and beverage. Hand torches and fresh batteries were the little power left, when other technologies were dead. Bars of soap, razors, and shaving foam, he tucked into seat pockets, along with boxes of matches. On a floor he laid his motley pots, crockery, and cutlery. He stuffed the car until his necessities jammed every corner, piled high from the floors and passenger seats, leaving the driver's seat a hemmed-in cubicle.

His tools were in the boot, with plastic flasks of engine lubricant and radiator coolant, two unused car batteries, and packets of spark plugs and other parts for cars. Another fresh battery he affixed into its slot under the bonnet as his father taught him, the grease blackening his soft fingers. To the rear of his car he affixed a rack, into which he secured his bicycle.

With a thick black pen discharging indelible waterproof ink, Brandon stood outside the front door. "*To those of us not about to die,*" he wrote, although the words were barely true, "*I will return.*" He slipped the pin into his pocket like a reason to believe he might use it again.

Brandon closed the curtains across the windows, as curtains

were closed across most formerly residential windows in County Durham. Without fear of theft, he pulled closed the front door with the key left protruding from the keyhole. That invitation to passers-by was also for his parents' ghosts each time they walked around.

Squeezing a rubber mat under the door, Brandon sealed it as he'd sealed every window, vent, and other door. No grubs or insects could intrude.

His possessions were his car and everything stashed in it. Being unable to see from his driver's seat past his booty crammed beside and behind him didn't matter, for there was no other traffic. All Brandon needed were things to use; the only thing he couldn't bear to lose was his means of getting home. Chance and error might teach him some mechanic skills, but his car might yet break down in a sorry, lonely place.

Had England remained as it once was then Brandon might've been at Teesside University that day and slept that night in a flat. Instead, with clouds gathering above, he headed south, trying to make a future his parents wouldn't see.

Country trees were taller than their town brethren; spring had come there sooner than it had come to town. Less thoroughly than they covered streets in town, rotting leaves covered country roads, becoming mulch along the verges. Roads faded into green, between failing fields of mess. Without human hands to reap them, time and the four seasons had turned flat fertile fields of edible crops aplenty into dumps of agricultural litter.

Driving with all the windows closed was like being in a submarine in Neverland. Brandon stopped the car and lowered the window beside him. The vegetables were odorous but not rancid; his time away from countryside might've changed the senses of his smell. The singing and whistling birds might've been healthier among fields than the small birds along town streets.

Only the fields of grass for nestling animals remained unchanged. Open gates and broken fences allowed them to graze across the roads and paddocks. The few tractors lay idle, perhaps where their fuel expired; Brandon expected no better of the cars parked by homesteads. Away from conspicuous decay, the land might've merely been languishing in a well-passed dead of night.

There was more of everything, but people. Devastation had stripped England of Englishmen and women, leaving lesser lives behind. Brown calves becoming cows and lambs maturing into sheep didn't care enough to talk with Brandon. He hadn't come to talk with them.

Occasionally remembering to look for anyone to know, Brandon didn't need to look too closely. Solitary people might never find each other.

A few old people rested in private chairs outside their homes. Some old villagers crept along, shuffling slowly in their graves. Somewhere most villages' last to die lay dead, buried or unburied.

Without people, the countryside was just a pretty scene, a hologram of what a world could be. It made the beauty something sad.

Some horses wore blankets they could not remove. Brandon might need to learn to control them, harnessing them to draw carts if he couldn't procure more petrol. He would be like the Amish, moving overland without the technologies he no longer had. If people weren't there to find, then he didn't need to hurry. He didn't know what he was doing.

When a sign, which only he still read, bid him welcome to a village, Brandon knew where he was. The first large town he entered was North Yorkshire's county town Northallerton, twinned with a dead French town. Each place without people faded away.

He stopped at a petrol station; the car's tank carried enough petrol to take him further south, but not really very far. Holding the bowser handset high, Brandon flexed his fingers on the lever. Nothing dripped from it. The underground storage tank might've been empty; he couldn't know. The pressure of petrol wasn't enough to force the petrol upwards.

Like most abandoned premises, the doors to the station store opened easily. Brandon inspected every item on the shelves and racks, pushing aside anything he didn't want. He opened every drawer and cupboard. Tanker drivers might have carried with them petrol pumps or other tools to extract fuel, but Brandon hadn't seen a tanker truck among the vehicles parked.

Kneeling on the ground, Brandon touched a flat square metal cover that presumably sealed an underground fuel tank, unable to release or lift it. He squeezed his eyes for the imagination to see through steel. Unlike a bottle imprisoning a genie, rubbing it alone would not release the magic.

Northallerton was another quiet town, quainter than most: moribund England in miniature. Leaves and moments of the damp they left behind dotted the ground, but too many trees remained the silver-grey skeletons they'd been throughout the winter. Stick trees without leaves were like pedestrians, who'd paused there while they walked. Too much had died for Brandon to think that shoots of leaves would sprout from ghostly leafless branches. They could be dead.

Dominating High Street, separated from the tightly set fronts of vacant shops, was a dark medieval church, the clock on its square tower stopped. Brandon thought of God and wondered if He thought of him.

Brandon stopped his car, sounding his horn several times. Neither God nor man replied.

According to the noticeboard, the fungi-stained stone church was All Saints, not obviously Brandon's. He wondered whether modern Europe since those gone days achieved anything at all.

With his working torch in the basket on his handlebars, Brandon rode his bicycle along random roads through every part of town as interesting and uninteresting as any other. Sometimes he rode steadily, watchfully, past pubs burrowed in stone storeys among the stone surrounds. Other times he rode rapidly, his hands gripping the handlebars and legs thrusting in the pedals, past rusted railway lines. Intermittently, he rang his bicycle bell, as loud as any sound around, without seeing somebody young.

One woman, as old and young as Brandon's mother, rode her bicycle. Before the afternoon became late and cool, the oldest men and women sat in their acquiescence on public benches around the Friarage Hospital, awaiting helpers comforting the dying to their deaths. People too sick to move lay ready to die at home.

Their antiquity made Brandon feel younger than his years, embryonic even, but was also a contagion that made him feel so old. Their weariness made them alike, variations on a theme, although their only similarities might've been their age and infertility that brought England to her knees.

Riding without direction was no less pointless than doing anything else alone. Brandon turned before becoming lost, marking tortured squares in grids of silent streets, riding a great circle. The people hopelessly too old watching him might've been the same old people who'd always watched him and his youth no longer theirs.

Ambling along Harewood Lane, Brandon slowly discerned the soft dainty childlike melody of a music box: a sense of life. Brandon followed the sweet sound to an open iron gate. Brandon stopped, dismounted, and leant his bicycle against the brick wall surrounding a property.

The music becoming a little more audible, he stepped along a path between green gardens to as beautiful a two-storey home as he had ever seen. A hook behind the door to an eye on the wall held the front door open, where Brandon paused. "Hello?" he spoke into the house, glad for a cause to speak and hear a human voice, albeit his own.

A small white cat, with dirty matted fur, wandered listlessly from the house. It moseyed past him and away.

"Hello?" said Brandon, slightly louder, but not so loud as to frighten anyone. He didn't want to stir the dead.

He stepped through the open doorway, although his first step seemed too loud and the next he made much softer, and another open doorway. In the twilight of a grand entrance hall, fragile cobwebs joined a candelabrum on a table to the wall, creating clouds of mazes that only spiders and their prey negotiated.

Brandon followed the music into a drawing room, lit by daylight from the adjoining conservatory as much as a window. Lying on a table was the open music box, in which a tiny pink ballerina turned slowly with the tune. The back of a large armchair facing the fireplace concealed a person sitting there, but not her legs stretched forward. "The door was open," Brandon explained, stepping closer.

Staring not at the fireplace but at the tiny ballerina was an old woman. "If I don't see you very well," she said in a firm but weary voice, her stare never leaving the ballerina, "then I won't be certain you are young. If you were old, then I would need to insist that you find someone else who is old, that you leave us young people alone. If you are young, then you would want to stay with me, or you would be a very wicked selfish person."

The longer Brandon stared at her face in crooked profile, the more vividly he saw the daylight reflect in dampness in her eyes. On a wall were plaques of public service and distinction; the woman had been a dignitary. Hanging from an empty chair was a taffeta ball gown, the fabric dulled with dust.

The melody finished, the ballerina stopped turning. The old woman did not lean forward from her chair to wind the key.

Brandon stepped slowly backwards and away: another pauper in a dead people's town. He didn't want to age until he'd finished being young.

From his car, Brandon took a tin can of preserved tuna. Resting on a bench outside All Saints Church where a soft breeze blew, he ate. The empty can and opened lid with traces of tuna on them he left on the pavement for birds to take. He licked his fork clean, and returned it to his car.

The Western world dissolved while that church survived, less dead than England died. Higher than any buildings, the little spires around the church roof and tower could have been hands in prayer, reaching up to heaven. There was no harm in taking comfort from any thought of God.

Through a consecrated arch was a dusty noticeboard, with messages Englishmen stopped reading. In a wooden door, the iron ring did not resist Brandon turning it. The church might've been far enough away from thieves, or nothing might've been there that anyone would steal. The door squeaked as Brandon pushed it open.

Tall windows around the walls admitted enough light for him to explore the soft silence of the stone, unchanged for centuries. To the side, on the floor and windowsills, broken weathered carvings lay in exhibition. Among the stone his forebears carved was an ancient face, or two, in muted peace. Wooden mice among the woodwork were also still.

He'd become like ancient man living among the farms. Exposed to the natural world, they'd seen God in the power of sun, storm, and wind.

If the crest with a shield repeated in the leaded lights was a family crest, it outlived the family. If it once was honourable, then honour had gone. If it once connoted riches, then death impoverished it. If it once was important, it had become unknown. Crests were less important than simply being alive.

Between the window crests was gentle Jesus, with a halo around His head and a portion of his flock, watching Brandon. Only God and angels knew that Brandon stood there.

Brandon imagined the last preacher at the pulpit addressing the elderly in the pews. Their pending deaths might've moved them to congregate, working at their faith. If God led them somewhere different to where other people went, a distant place from which they would not return, that place was better than any place in which Brandon stood alone.

He might've been the final mourner at England's funeral. He might've been dead, and the life he lived was purgatory for people not too bad. Brandon knew only that he was not in paradise. He was lost, but knew that he was lost. He wondered whether to hope for a fate akin to that of a preacher in his church. The only places left to see were heaven and a greater hell than loneliness.

Humanity had not saved England. The futility of prayer was another premise lonely Brandon no longer held so fast. Prayer could be no less foolish than other acts. If prayer was asking God for help, then Brandon did not know how to ask. If prayer was conversation, then he was already uttering words within his mind.

His beliefs or none of them was less important than being there. A nothing chance was better than doing nothing. A man alone could not be arrogant.

"Can you hear me?" Brandon asked aloud, without knowing how far his voice might travel. His only answer was an echo.

Brandon knelt down to the floor. He bowed his head. A character in coloured glass, he stared into stone in hollowed day. He was a stranger in a strange play, as he'd always been.

He closed his eyes, placing his right hand across them so no dwindling daylight could pass through his closed lids. He would ask God for something, in that place and chance for doing so. The moment made him clarify his thoughts, as only conversation could.

Listing everything for which he craved could wind him into craziness, believing something of the reason he was there. He wanted his forebears' life. He feared his solitude, becoming sick without anyone to parent him. He wanted light, warmth, and food. He wanted England to survive and not fail herself again.

Greed had already cursed Europe once. Getting anything would be a miracle and Brandon shouldn't reach too far. He needed to choose the most important thing to him, in his hypothetical opportunity to ask for anything. Hopes and fears swelled inside his head, before stumbling into being one in the same: the only purpose clear to him. "Could I please have someone to touch?" he whispered.

Brandon listened for a voice. There was only silence. The darkness in his eyes made the silence more complete.

"Please, God."

Brandon removed his hand and saw the crimson ends of day that his closed eyelids allowed him. His eyes opened, back in church, without another person there. If God had anything to say, Brandon couldn't hear.

He looked up again at the Nazarene, searching for the subtlest of reflexes in answer to his words, but Christ's eyes failed to brighten or lips move. Grand God did not reveal Himself.

If kneeling there so long gave another person time to walk into the church, it wasn't time enough. When his knees and back became sore, Brandon rose again.

Stepping back outside, ambling aimlessly, the cooling air made the church seem to have been warm. Everywhere was silent, but for the birds he'd already heard.

In a wall outside the church was a sundial without sun. Brandon and the dead didn't need it anymore.

Rain readied to fall when a street light flickered, for the first time in Brandon's sight for half a year. The small joy of a single light soon became elation in a resurgent crowd of lights. Brandon's gaze spread to all of them.

Brandon walked around the artificial lights with his arms stretched high, basking in their brightness in his eyes, revelling in the restoration of utility: the return of civility. He spun around and almost danced with the busy glow of England come alive, electric light that human beings had made, basking in human worth.

Someone somewhere could re-ignite a power station many miles from the circuits they supplied; Brandon would've driven there if he knew which site was operational again. The men or women who reactivated the power might be a pittance aside the people England once was, but still be a multitude to him in solitude.

Brandon wanted everything to happen quickly, as his parents once expected things to happen, but young people might take time to return. A finite wait for restitution was more tolerable than having nothing left for which to hope. Aeroplanes might fly again among the birds. The strange saga of his life might be over.

3

ENCOUNTERS

Rain started to fall. Like lighthouses on a storm-swept coast below a raining sky, the wet lights ablaze shone across rain-blown England to anybody lost, but Brandon was the only ship at sail. The lights had made him forget he was the only person there.

Across High Street from All Saints Church, the Porch House was convenient accommodation. Without call to use the lion's head knocker, a ring handle like the one at the church opened the door.

Brandon flicked a light switch on the inside wall, without result. The filament might have failed. He flicked several more switches, without result. The premises might've been connected to a different circuit than the public power supply.

Beside a telephone were listed telephone codes across Britain and dialling prefixes of foreign countries, with schedules of long distance and international tariffs. Brandon picked up the telephone handset from its mount, hoping to hear a dial tone. The telephone was silent.

Inspecting the building for any reason not to spend the night there, he turned a tap, from which a few drops of water fell. He sealed it again. Excited for the resumption of a world without knowing what that world would be, Brandon didn't know the extent of his reprieve.

The kitchen shelves were stripped bare, the drawers and cupboards open. Brandon opened the refrigerator door to know it didn't work.

Darkness grew around him as it grew one day earlier, but for the lights outside his transitory bedroom window. The strange bed was soft, between crisp sheets and blankets slowly warming, but uncomfortable for not being his. At home, Brandon had suffered the comparison with all his life had been. Away, his only knowledge was the life his had become. The lights of High Street were his only certainties.

Sometimes he slept, woke to see the darkness, and slept again. Daybreak woke him from his restless sleep, when he looked from the window for any movement of a people and listened for the sounds of vehicles. The High Street lights that shone so brightly the previous night were dark again.

Lying in a fork in the nearly bare branches of a nearby tree was a bird's nest, crafted from refuse twigs. The turns of light from the distant sky made the nest feel close enough for Brandon to reach out and touch it, but he couldn't see if the nest contained eggs or hatchlings. Sometimes it seemed the first green buds of spring would become worthwhile, but the spring nature intended was not yet blooming.

Brandon wandered outside. He reached into his car and sounded the horn, blaring noise into the air. He sounded it again and then again, beckoning an answer.

The church tower was most likely the first thing anyone would see. If Brandon could climb it and wave his arms from its high point he would do so, but he was confined to earth.

Looking up drew his attention to little covers atop the glass globe street lights. Brandon's heart sank within him, realising that civic architects had probably camouflaged solar cells, rejuvenating batteries feeding power to the lights. Sensors activated them when days became dark.

"Damn it!" said Brandon, thumping his fist against the pole. His had been an idiot's euphoria. "Damn, damn, damn!"

His fist leaning on the pole to support him, Brandon dropped his head. His reprieve had been a hoax he'd been too quick to believe, perpetrated by people who had died. Those street lights would shine every night whether anybody saw them. They would shine longer through the dark months of winter than in the long days of summer, as if anybody cared.

The false hope of his salvation was a torment crueller than hopelessness had been. Another coming cloudy day laughed at him.

In the park behind the church was a coop with several chickens. In the hutch remained a single egg, Brandon didn't know how long would keep. He took it for the protein.

Brandon returned despondently to the Porch House; small hotels and strangers' homes would be his beds until he found people with whom to stay. The only sound was a mouse scurrying along a hollow skirting of the floor. He flicked off the light switches, in a cynical gesture to his morning, and opened a window. The morning dew was unnecessarily damp.

Without firewood in fireplaces, Brandon sat at a table where windows shed most light upon his uncooked egg, which he would discard if he couldn't bear the taste. With him were his salt and pepper shakers.

Brandon gently placed the unprepared egg in the centre of a bowl. With a teaspoon he'd also brought from home, he tentatively tapped the eggshell until it cracked. Brandon examined the crack closely, uncertain what he'd see, before an ugly liquid dripped from it. He'd called it white when it was cooked.

Gently he tapped the shell again, careful not to spill fragments of the shell. From the gaping crack, more unpalatable liquid oozed. He held each end of the egg above the bowl and pulled the halves apart, dropping the thick liquid and dull cream-yellow yoke into the bowl, briefly bouncing before they settled. Brandon examined closely the coarse puddle, unlike any food previously set before him.

In the liquid egg was a small fragment of the shell. Brandon used the spoon to pick away and try to separate them, but the liquid kept the shell within. His spoon grappled with the shell for several moments, before pushing the liquid up the bowl where his fingers drew out the shell. The liquid egg was clean.

With no more reason to delay, Brandon drew a deep, brave breath. His mouth was apprehensive about what his hands were about to do. Brandon collected a small portion of the liquid in his teaspoon and tried to lift it from the bowl, but the yoke and liquid in the bowl dragged the liquid back again. His mouth reached down to the bowl, nervous for the strange taste to which he would soon subject himself. He pressed the spoon against a space of liquid in the bowl, trying to break the liquid as he dragged the spoon upwards against the bowl towards his open mouth. Pulling the unrefined egg white closer to his lips and tongue, Brandon closed his eyes.

The egg was sickly, with a texture like clotting blood would be. It stumbled about his mouth and aging teeth until he swallowed it, rather than taste it anymore.

His condiments would finally exhaust, but he'd earned the right to use them. Brandon sprinkled salt and ground pepper on the raw egg remaining in the bowl, wondering whether he was trying to compliment a taste or replace it. Lifting up the bowl with both his hands, he pulled it to his open lips. Without thought for trepidation, he poured the remaining egg into his mouth. The only tastes he enjoyed were those of salt and pepper, relieving the taste of egg as Brandon quickly swallowed the liquid yolk and white.

His stomach settling, Brandon sat back in his chair. The food he'd consume for the rest of his life would not improve.

He could patronise all the past abodes for their stashes of old food, but the time might come he'd taken everything he could, and still he'd be alone. He might grow old eating meals at tables at which families could've eaten, before he died slumped over one.

Brandon flicked through pages of an old magazine, without reading them. A small red robin landed on the open windowsill. Its head turning in stilted motions, the robin looked around the room, past Brandon sitting lackadaisically at the table. If it entered the room in search of food or materials for nests it could be trapped inside. The robin flew away. Brandon closed the window.

Leaving behind nothing he'd brought with him, Brandon returned ambivalently to his car. Watching him walk was a large ginger-coloured cat, which Brandon in his foolish dreams imagined coming towards him, joining him. It remained where it was.

Brandon's soiled bowl and cutlery he stowed in a last space on a floor in his car. A little technology endured after all, as did the sun. He'd been foolish to have imagined so much from the lights shining one night earlier, but all he'd lost was a chance he never had: a wrong conviction.

Solar cells were a resource left him. Brandon should be grateful for the light. Solar energy would replenish the supply every time he used it. He didn't need to work for it or do anything but let the rays of sun sustain him. With reels of electrical wire and rubber gloves protecting him, he might stumble upon the means of connecting a solar panel and battery to a petrol bowser and restore his source of petrol. He could then drive across his big and little country. He could have almost everything, except companionship.

Contemplating his endeavour, Brandon's eyes roamed around him. The morning sun reflected in an upstairs window of the Buck Inn might have deceived him, but it appeared a figure of a woman stood watching him.

Brandon stared at the figure, afraid to move less he might break the spell. He mightn't previously have looked towards that window, or might've looked and simply not noticed it. Staring might help him remember seeing it, or might make it move. His imagination might've been deluding him, doubting what he knew to be true, just as the street lights shining had meant too much to him. He smiled at her.

She stepped back from the window, to where he could no longer see her. More than overjoyed, he would simply be relieved to see someone, if she was young.

The black inn door to the pavement opened. Atop the three steps, she stood.

The youngest woman he'd seen since his friends from school

set off to Cornwall, she was perhaps thirty years of age. Tall for a woman, almost as tall as Brandon, she was beautiful, although she would've been beautiful merely by being there. The complexion of her skin was paler than his, pure were it against him. Her fair brown hair was becoming long, resting on her shoulders. A loose-fitting cardigan over a white blouse covered her wide shoulders, chest, and arms. Her long white dress hung free around her waist.

Her eyes looked him up and down, before she stepped slowly down to the pavement and towards him. Her dress swung from her hips in a soft breeze that Brandon hadn't previously noticed. Still several feet away from him, she stopped. Her eyes were blue, rich, for an enthralling soul when he might've never before seen one.

Not quite close enough for him to reach out and touch, she might've been ready to run if he moved too suddenly. Should he shake her hands? Her lips were closed, without expression. Shyer than he'd been with the women at school, his shyness made him weak.

"You're young," she said. "School must be out."

"I'm eighteen!"

She laughed. "I'm not."

"Why were you watching me?"

She dropped back her head to gaze into the air. She brushed her hand across her forehead into her hair, raising her hair higher and away from him, before facing him again. "I didn't know if someone who sounded a car horn so much was someone I should meet, and how many you are."

"I am alone," said Brandon. "If I hadn't seen you, were you ever going to show your face?"

"I let you see me," she smiled, "when I thought I might be better meeting you than not."

"How did you know?"

"I saw your face, the way you walk."

"I'm headed to Cornwall. I can remove some things from my car for you to sit there."

"I was thinking about Kent, and I have a car."

"We have to stay together," he said.

"We have to find more people not old."

Brandon took his thick black pen from his car. He looked around, before heading towards the Buck Inn door.

"What are you doing?" she asked.

"I want to leave a message telling people we're headed to Kent."

"You don't know who might read it."

"I can protect you."

"I can protect me too, most of the time, but nothing will save us from enough people wanting to hurt us."

"Don't you want someone to come?" asked Brandon.

"You think everyone is like you, but everyone is not." The conversation that had been about her had become one about him.

Brandon stared self-consciously at her, starting to say one thing but stopping before he did. "What do you want me to say?" he asked. "Don't fear. Hope. My parents never went anywhere without leaving me a note."

Her voice became meek. "Have you ever been attacked?"

"No."

She gently touched the skin around her tender throat, resting her longest finger in the small part of her neck. She slightly arched her shoulders as if trying to defend her, even from him, alluding to a pain that may have never left her. "I don't think he was trying to kill me," she said, "but he didn't care if an Englishwoman happened to die."

She was vulnerable to people to whom Brandon felt no vulnerability. Her experience exacerbated and excused the fears she felt.

"I don't want to be scared that someone might kill me if he finds me alone," she continued. "I want the community we make to be one in which we're safe, not just one in which we have more people to share a load of work, even if they do work."

After watching her for a moment, Brandon walked up to the wall beside the Buck Inn door. "*We will return*," he wrote.

"You get what you want from your car," she told him, before walking through the archway near the inn door.

From his abundance of things, Brandon took very little: the

clothes for a few days he packed into a small bag. Soon appearing from the side street near him was a compact blue car, with only a small boot and no rear passenger doors but front seats that could bend forward for the rare occasions people sat in the short back seats behind them.

She stopped the car near him. Stepping out, she removed a small bag from the front passenger seat, which she placed in the boot. Brandon placed his bag beside it.

"I'm Brandon Frewer."

"Laura Trimm."

She drove them south, through pastures green. Were those times like England that no longer was, he and Laura would have probably never met. If they'd been acquaintances in a crowd in the England Laura lost and he had been denied, they probably would not have paid the other much attention.

The emptiness to which he'd become accustomed in towns and villages was eerie in a city like York. Dogs and cats, like those he remembered trotting around parks in his hometown only a few years earlier, stood watching them rolling along in their mobile, like they were food to eat. Rusting bicycles stood at racks without chains to lock them, no longer reasons to believe their owners were close at hand. Scattered bonfires smouldered in the streets.

Brandon's senses sunk slowly, entranced more by the nothingness than by anything he saw. "Nobody's here," he said. "It's like the end of the world, but we're the only thing that ended."

"Not seeing people doesn't mean they're not there," replied Laura.

God inspired without convicting a small store near the Minster that once sold witchcraft, crystals, and other spells. Sorcery had vanished without sorcerers.

Turning a corner of an empty intersection, ahead of them appeared a figure of a man, standing in the centre of the street. Laura slowed and stopped the car.

The uninviting figure turned towards them. He stood with his legs apart, most obviously in their way.

Brandon leant forward in his seat, studying him. The figure

wore a large coat and held what appeared to be a cricket bat in both his hands. The man rose within his stance. "Is he wearing a balaclava?" asked Brandon.

Laura promptly reversed the car. It careered towards the kerb.

"What are you doing?" asked Brandon, holding himself in his seat by pressing his outstretched hands on the dashboard in front of him.

"Saving your life," she said, as the car stopped at the kerb. She speedily changed gears to drive the car forward, turning the steering wheel back towards the direction from which they'd come.

Brandon looked at the car's side mirror. The man was running after them. Several more men were coming from a building near him. "Why are you going?"

Laura sped her and Brandon away, back around the corner from which they'd come. "You mentioned the balaclava."

"I was wrong," said Brandon. "That was his face."

"I know," said Laura, as she sped back along the streets they'd already seen. "Don't condemn me for caution."

"We could have talked with them."

"By then, it's too late. Giving him everything we own mightn't be enough. I know you don't understand, but can you please believe me, if only for me?"

She drove them north again. "I want to go to Cornwall," said Brandon, "or Kent."

"If York isn't safe, cities further south aren't safe. There is no cavalry anymore, just us. We need a place to think."

"Northallerton has solar power."

"Many places have solar power, windmills, even watermills."

While Laura drove, Brandon gazed through the side window, without more thought for conversation. Outside were the gentle fields and farmhouses of North Yorkshire, home to cows, sheep, and trees, all standing peacefully. Silent sleeping barns stood with their doors left open: the animals' homes through every winter. Large metal cylinders narrowed into cones near the ground, storing grain for feed. Pottering rabbits nibbled their inexhaustible supplies. A goat chewed long grass by a pole. He didn't know for how long a time she would be with him.

"I'll take you back to your car," said Laura. "If you want to follow me somewhere I think we can stay, you can."

"We'll need to conserve fuel."

"I can open the filling station tanks and pump out any petrol. My father taught me how to do it."

Brandon's car remained where he had left it on the High Street in Northallerton. He alighted from Laura's car into free air.

Laura alighted, too. "Do you want your bag of things back?" she asked him.

"You're difficult to know," responded Brandon.

Slowly, she removed his bag from the boot of her car and handed it to him. "When my mother became sick a year ago," she started, her voice gentler than it had previously been, "my father cared for her; he was very good like that. He went to London to get medicines, refusing to believe London is no longer a place for Englishmen. The police found his body in the Thames. My job had gone, so I came home to care for her; I hated her to be alone. She also cared for me."

Brandon longed for anything to say, but said nothing. If she précised the last year in her life for him to do the same, he couldn't.

"Mum passed away a week ago. I knocked on doors of homes of all the people I once knew in Northallerton, but they'd all gone. Then I knew I was alone. My mother had strived to live until she knew that I was safe, but I might never be safe."

Brandon placed his bag in his car. "Do you like me?" he asked her.

"We need each other. This might be the best that friendship can be, in the lives in which we wander."

She'd finished her life thus far with the isolation in which he, the last Englishman born in Darlington, had started his. "Will I find myself alone again?" he asked her.

"I make friends slowly, but I lose them slowly." If her presence helped him forget their predicament, so might his presence alleviate hers.

Trudging along High Street from the roundabout appeared an old man, dressed in a black duffel coat and carrying a head of dirty lettuce. Brandon and Laura watched him approach them until he stopped close to them, swapping his attention between each of them. Whiskers spiked from his cheeks and chin, but they could not conceal the broad smile forming in his face as his eyes widened. "We might have a chance," he said.

Laura looked back at Brandon, without revealing any more of her reaction than he would reveal of his. She turned back to the old man. "Can I carry that for you?" she asked him.

"If you walk with me today, sit with me," he told them, "I will still die alone, and die ashamed for the last days of my life as I'm ashamed for all my other days. You two leave me, and let me lie alone and dream that England might remain when I do not."

He walked around them, behind Laura, while Brandon and Laura watched him. Laura had to turn around to continuing seeing him.

He then stopped and slowly turned back to them. "Be kind to each other," he said. Again he turned and walked away, to All Saints Church.

Brandon and Laura watched him go. Laura turned suddenly back to Brandon, but her feet slipped on a wet rotting leaf. She started to fall, but Brandon rushed closer and grabbed her before she did. He helped her steady. "Why did you do that?" she asked him.

"We have to help each other now," said Brandon. "We always did."

She studied him. "Will we be the last English people?" she asked him.

Brandon let her go. She stood without him.

Her voice became ever more cautious. "Could we be the last Europeans?"

4

THE CASTLE HOUSE

Brandon in his car followed Laura in her car south again. She led them along Allerton Wath Road and then east towards the Moors, turning towards Boltby. Long hedges kept Brandon from seeing much ahead or more than glimpses of the farms by which they travelled. Past the weathered walls of Upsall and along Whinmoor Hill, she turned into a long driveway, winding between trees, hedges, and a low wall up the slow incline of a small hill. Through the trees appeared a tall, curiously clean castle with a square stone tower and parapets, as if England hadn't changed. The walls of neatly cut blocks of rock would have been impenetrable, but for a door and windows suggesting two, three, or even four storeys inside.

The age-old structure was at once foreboding as intriguing. It might've been a hotel or attraction for tourists, but there'd been no signs to advertise it. It wasn't obviously a museum, but exuded England's enchanting past, their past.

Through the entranceway in a stone wall Laura and then Brandon drove into a courtyard, where a medieval soldier statue stood watch from a pedestal in the plants, holding at the ready a spear no longer there. Facing them from the building front was an empty wooden bench. Curtains beyond the castle windows were drawn closed. Above them were two small heart-shaped windows.

Laura stopped her car. Brandon stopped his behind her. Staring upward, he stepped outside.

Brandon couldn't imagine who'd have lived in a castle when houses were available, without thought of an incursion. The castle was incongruous, anomalous, a fortress where the fields of cows did not require it. A stately mansion carved from a castle with dreams of gloried pasts, it was a home of whimsy.

Laura stood beside him. "I used to call this the castle house," she said. "Other castles are more secure, but this is harder to find." If they didn't lie in ruins since long-dead invaders breached them or have decayed since the defenders no longer needed them, castles across Britain that once seemed obsolete had become necessary again.

"You've been here?" asked Brandon.

"Its origins date to the thirteenth century, but most of it is seventeenth and nineteenth century. Sometimes abandoned, other times restored or recreated, it's been modernised where it needed to be."

"You sound like a tour guide." (Brandon had learnt a lot from old films and television he'd never experienced first-hand.)

Laura led them towards the house, where she knocked on the front door, without reply. She turned the tarnished knob and the door opened; a person in the home might have been too frail to fasten it.

Inside the yard-thick walls was a reception hall with a wooden stand for hats and coats, where Laura drew the curtains open. On the floor tucked in a corner were several keys.

Through double doors, she led them into a large drawing room. Brandon drew open more curtains, admitting every light reflected in the polished oak floors, between plaster walls and ceilings.

Across much of the furniture were the white cotton covers rich people used to shield their best furniture from dust, when they went away on long holidays. Brandon removed the cover from an armchair, revealing bright flowery-patterned cushions.

"What's the point of something beautiful if nobody can see it?" he asked. Laura removed the cover from another armchair.

The room was lightly furnished, with modern furbishing in almost modern styles, aside from a grandfather clock Laura uncovered. The clock stood still, until she opened the long door and set the pendulum swinging back and forth. She set the time to shortly after two o'clock; there'd been a clock in her car. She complemented everything around them, as only Englishwomen could.

Beside a fireplace apparently unparched, the iron rods hanging from a stand were probably ornamental. On the mantelpiece was a sword, which Brandon picked up. "I dub thee Lady Laura," he told her, dabbing the sword on each of her shoulders in an investiture, "from this day forth."

"Dame," she said, walking away.

Brandon contemplated laughing, before replacing the sword where he'd found it. Crouched on the floor, he and looked upwards to the chimney, without knowing what he expected to see, to a hole far above him.

Free to touch as museum visitors and potential purchasers weren't, they explored the house as much as inspected it, as new owners might. The modern kitchen could have been seized from any moment of a life, with drawers of cutlery, can and bottle openers, and linen, except that the refrigerator was empty.

"The boiler provides electricity as well as heat," said Laura.

"You know this house well," said Brandon. Her eyes moved away before she did.

Brandon turned a tap over the kitchen sink expecting nothing to happen, but water flowed. Connoting some small amenity he'd become accustomed not to having, he watched it flow expecting it to stop, but the rainwater tank required only gravity to supply the taps. The water was cold against his skin and he quickly pulled his hand away. He turned the tap to stop it, careful to conserve their sudden fortune.

The larder contained hundreds of tin cans and sealed plastic packets of food, along with bottles of soft drink. Thin wooden racks were filled with glass jars of ground herbs and exotic spices.

The vaulted dining room with its magnificent long table could have seated dozens of diners. In the paintings were a fighting stag and a dancing bear.

In a master bedroom upstairs, a sprawling eiderdown neatly covered a massive bed and pillows. "The sheets will all be clean," said Laura, "with matching pillowcases." Near a mahogany valet stand was a polished dressing table.

Smaller bedrooms were no less neatly set with single or double beds and bedspreads. Thin dust slightly dulled the top of a wooden chest of drawers, which Brandon opened to find empty. The rooms could've been for children, if the lord and lady of the house had born them. More likely, they'd been kept for guests.

In the bathroom cabinets were medicines Brandon and Laura might need as they grew older. They might already be so old.

A door on a second floor of bedrooms was locked. "Do you know what's beyond this door?" asked Brandon.

"I've never been up here," replied Laura, "before today." She wandered elsewhere.

Brandon looked around him for a key. There wasn't space for one above the door and no furniture close to him on the landing. If he were to hide a key, he would hide it by his bed, and he returned downstairs to the master bedroom. To each side of the bed were small tables with drawers. In one were small possessions as a woman night keep. In the other was a single key.

Taking the key with him back upstairs to the locked door, Brandon opened it. The room could once have been a bedroom, but resting on hooks high on a wall were several rifles with polished wooden handles and scopes along the barrels. On a small table were several boxes of rifle cartridges and brass gunpowder flasks. So much as touching anything hidden in that hole seemed dangerous, risking accidental discharge.

People who had vowed never to fire a gun had done so in emergency. People who had armed themselves had died unwilling to pull a trigger. Brandon didn't know which people Laura and he were. Knowledge of those rifles might've been too onerous to impose upon her, or been too important not to share with her: to let her contemplate their choices.

Brandon closed and locked Pandora's door. He nobly slipped the key into his pocket.

Laura was in the games room, where on a table lay a folded flag. "Today was the first time I've seen the castle house without the English flag flying," she said.

Brandon unfurled the white and red. Before him was Saint George's Cross.

"We don't want to attract attention from people who despise it," said Laura. "If England is again England, we will fly it."

Near them, thirty-two chess pieces stood on a black and white chessboard table ready for battle. Playing games with Laura, Brandon could win or lose and so win again. Gently lifting the white king, Brandon saw the dust around it.

Laura following, Brandon found and climbed steep stairs leading upwards through the tower. Sunlight shone from the sky as they entered a terrace behind the highest parapet, with its empty flagpole. The sun became warm across his face, while distant clouds drifted slowly across the blue.

Themselves alone, they surveyed their rural scape: the Vale of York. Trees thick with leaves might have marked roads, running rivers, or the boundaries between properties, which like other ownership weren't important anymore. Whether it was one estate or separate farms of green, the castle oversaw an imaginary fiefdom, an empty world.

Green fields hosted other roofs, from which perhaps people could see Brandon and Laura. Sprawling countryside had often obscured people, but they didn't need to be visible to till the fields.

"Do you worry who might appear on the near horizon?" asked Laura.

If Brandon had heard such fear from his time at school then he would have dismissed it. That time had passed. They would share their home with a friend, but mightn't have any friends. The home was theirs more than the home of anyone who tried to take it from them.

"They laughed at us behind our backs," lamented Laura, "but

we felt too good about ourselves to hear them laughing. They mocked us, but we couldn't see the joke."

"I care more what people do than anything they think."

"They don't have to be bad people, they might even be good people by their cultures, but they might brush us aside, even kill us, because they think it's right. They might want us to do what we don't want to do, or be what we don't want to be. They might not leave us alone because we leave them alone."

Guns hadn't been part of their society, but their society had died. He and Laura would be secure inside their castle house if nobody knew that they were there, unless someone chanced upon them. Knowing that he was starting something that they might someday wish he hadn't started, Brandon removed the key from his pocket. "You might want to look inside that room."

She led them back downstairs, unlocked that door, and entered their small armoury. "Are the rifles loaded?" she asked.

"I haven't touched them."

Laura picked up a flask and then another from the table. "These are collectibles," she said.

Brandon picked up a box of bullets. "These aren't."

She took a rifle from the wall and examined it, always pointing the barrel downwards. "I never learnt how to use it," she said.

"It will recoil if ever fired, I know that," said Brandon, unable to imagine her firing it any more than he imagined him doing so. They would again flee anyone who threatened them and hide before they courted danger, but if a bad man or his army came to the castle house, then they had nowhere left to hide. His plans for peace seemed cowardly, cowering in a cupboard until the bad men left.

Laura offered the rifle to him. "How do we fight without anyone to fight?"

Timidly, Brandon took the temperamental weapon, slipping down with the weight of it heavier in his hands than he'd expected it to be. He firmed his shoulders, elbows, and wrists, holding it away from him as if it would poison him if he let it close.

"I wish we could bury all the bullets never seeing any of them again and reduce the guns to being collectibles," said Laura, "but it's too late for that. It's been too late for a long time now."

Clumsily, always pointing the barrel to the floor, Brandon examined the rifle for clues of what to do. He managed to release the lock, fold the handle, and open the rear of the barrel. He took a bullet from the box and slipped it into the barrel; there was space for two bullets but he inserted only one. He pushed the handle upright and forced the gun locked again. The gun was, he presumed, ready for firing. "Are we arrogant to place our lives above other people's lives?" Brandon worried. "Are we arrogant to presume the world is a better place with you and me in it?"

"Let our enemies call us arrogant," said Laura. "We need only be ourselves. I'm not proud of much my generation did, but I'm proud of what we are. I want to live."

If they were each other's guardian, then Brandon liked to be her guardian. "I'd kill someone to save you," he said, "but will the choices always be easy? I don't want to kill anyone we don't need to kill." He returned the rifle to the wall.

They left the room. Laura locked the door, keeping the key with her. Brandon could pretend the guns weren't there.

The lowest of the four storeys was a basement, secreted in the shadows. The basement garage was empty.

If the steel gas cylinders stored there were a plan for a contingency, then the contingency long ago arose. If they were precautions against emergencies, then the emergencies had come.

The walls of the wine cellar were filled floor to ceiling with racks of wine bottles maturing every year, waiting to be drunk. "I don't like wine," said Brandon.

"You will."

Other cellar stores were filled with light bulbs, soap, and other household consumables, along with preserved meat, fruit, and vegetables in tin cans, packets, bottles, and boxes. Marked on most of them were expiration dates before which their contents ought to be eaten. The dates Brandon checked were imminent or not long passed, but he would at least sample foods long out of date.

In one store were several boxes of Whitakers sweet chocolates. Brandon took a small rose-print gift box and offered it to Laura. "This is for you," he grinned. "I know the owner."

He started to walk away when she interrupted. "I better get you something," she said quickly. She took a box and gave it to him.

"My favourite," said Brandon.

"I also know the owner," she smiled. They might've been courting, in their two-people world, or she might've been ensuring they weren't.

He opened his box, in which were a white and brown chocolate. Laura did the same. She bit a piece of her white chocolate, as he bit a piece of his. "What is this?" he asked, of the unfamiliar filling.

"It's a truffle."

Brandon continued chewing, feeling and tasting, before finally swallowing. "My parents and I only ever ate normal chocolates."

Behind the castle house was a smaller servants' house, two storeys high and crafted from the same stone as the house. "Without servants anymore, not for a hundred years or more, this building was tenanted," said Laura. "I never saw who lived there."

That door was also unlocked. Again Brandon drew open the curtains, lighting their way through a hall into a sitting room.

Lying on a card table were five hundred jigsaw puzzle pieces: the Knaresborough Viaduct and River Nidd in autumn, according to the lid of the box near them. The perimeter and other pieces were in place, but most pieces lay in little compilations of colours or small images waiting for someone to insert them.

Jigsaw puzzles were the most fruitless of activities, working hard to produce an image less clear than it could've been in an ordinary picture, before being broken up and returned to a box as if it had never been arranged. Brandon left the pieces there.

Laura stood before a wall from which hung dozens of small square frames behind clear glass. Brandon stood with her, seeing in each frame a single butterfly through which a steel pin mounted it. The butterfly wings were beautiful, ornate colours in magical patterns. "Did somebody kill them to pin them under glass?" asked Brandon.

"They'd died from their short lives to remain beautiful to the person who pinned them there, but their deaths make them ugly," said Laura. "Is any creature living more beautiful than any creature dead?"

Brandon took a frame from the wall and dropped it to the floor. The glass remained intact, until he pounded his foot against the frame.

"We can't bring the pretty dead back to life," said Laura.

"What's dead should be clearly dead. How else can we face death?"

They explored the rest of the servants' house. A woodpile stood near the fireplace in the dining room. Beside the kitchen was a water closet, where Brandon pressed the cistern button and water flushed the lavatory bowl, but the pipes to the cistern were then silent, without the sounds of water coming. He pressed the button again, and only a small amount of water trickled into the bowl.

They proceeded through the conservatory and another hall, clean as was every room but the sitting room since Brandon made that mess. Upstairs were three bedrooms, where again the beds were neatly dressed with sheets and eiderdowns for guests that hadn't come. Turning the first shower tap released only a few drops of water from the spout. Turning the second tap produced even less. Laura led them back downstairs and outside again.

A wood store kept several short logs of wood for fires in interlocking rows, with bundles of twigs for kindling. The stables were empty of horses, but they stored more gas cylinders and other provisions, including several fifty-pound bags of chicken pellets.

Down sunlit steps was a square, tiled pond and dormant fountain. Brandon checked as he always did, but there weren't any fish in the water. "I don't know what this means," he said.

"It doesn't mean anything."

Long grass folded under their feet as they walked towards

a populated chicken coop. Sealing the coop was a wire mesh fence six feet high, with a mesh and timber roof on which was a solar panel. On the ground around the fence was more mesh, preventing foxes from digging underneath it. Outside the fence was a wooden barrel with pipes from the roof, offering water through the fence the chickens didn't seem to need.

Inside the enclosure were several feeders open from above, offering the chickens water. Other feeders were empty, closed from above, any feed once left in them exhausted, although the chickens seemed healthy without it. A wooden henhouse offered a long run from the grass.

Hungry birds pecked at the grass. Returned to the stable, Laura filled a metal cup with pellets she poured into the feeder.

"They'll be relieved to have seen you again," said Brandon, hoping to elicit an explanation from her.

"They won't remember." Laura drew open a tray from the henhouse, but it was filthy. The hutch was filled with eggs of indeterminate age, she started to remove. "We can't leave them here."

"Why can't we?" asked Brandon.

When they'd collected all the eggs in a bucket, he followed her to the long driveway from Whinmoor Hill. She led them part way down the hill far from the house, until the trees gave way to a hedge beside a pasture on which cows grazed. There, Brandon dropped them over the hedge.

After returning the buckets to the stable, Brandon and Laura removed the tray from the henhouse. After dropping the loose materials over the hedge where they'd left the eggs, she led Brandon to a creek amidst the trees. "How did you know this was here?" asked Brandon.

"Couldn't you hear the water?"

There, careful not to slip, Brandon washed the tray, before returning it to the henhouse. They thus cleaned all the trays.

"I should bring some things from home," said Laura, walking back to the courtyard.

"I can come with you. I can help."

"You look around here. Prepare us some food." Laura removed her bag from her car and placed it in the entrance hall inside the castle house. "There's a pond by Upsall Castle. You should find fishing rods and reels in the basement garage here."

"How do you know this area so well?"

"We're only seven miles from Northallerton," she smiled, stepping into her car and closing the door.

Brandon knocked on her closed car window, which she opened. "I still want to go to Cornwall," he told her.

"Not today," she replied, before closing her window.

Laura started to drive around the courtyard, around the statue above the plants. Brandon rushed the other way around them, until he stood in front of her car, obstructing her journey.

She stopped her car. She switched off the engine, and stepped outside.

"Will you please tell me how you know this house so well?" Brandon insisted.

She could have tried to drive around him, whereby he would again stand in her way. Instead, she walked a short way towards him, to where she could speak without shouting. "The last owners of this house had a son, Ogden," she told him, her eyes turning away. "I met him through mutual friends in York. We became close, particularly close, but weren't formally engaged so I didn't accompany them to Milan for the last Milanese opera. It happened to be when the Lombardy uprising broke out, when the insurgents didn't distinguish one European from another. Ogden and his parents couldn't escape. The International Red Cross arranged their burial in Italy, while Ogden's aunt, in Middlesbrough, made the necessary arrangements for the house. I don't think Auntie Eustice ever recovered."

Brandon continued staring at her, suddenly so much older than she'd been. He'd insisted upon an explanation and she'd not spared him. "If Ogden hadn't travelled with his parents to Milan," asked Brandon, "would you have married him and be living here now?"

Laura smiled a distant smile Brandon only saw in profile. "I'll never know," she said, "not for certain."

5

FISHING

Balancing a rod and reel across the basket on his handlebars, Brandon's bicycle glided down the driveway from the castle house to Whinmoor Hill. Riding from habit more than caution along the left side of the road, he rode back to Upsall Lane. Riding around an obscured corner, he rang his bicycle bell as he might once have rung it to warn a coming car or truck that he was there. Uncertain of all he thought and felt, Laura relieved him from missing the past too much.

If Upsall didn't take its name from the castle, then the castle took its name from the hamlet. Another manor castle as much a mansion, it might have also hosted a private generator and stores. It must once have boasted fine gardens, but neglected plants had matured to become fodder for animals. Fallen seeds had died without germinating, rotting back into the soil. Only grass and weeds were prospering.

Beyond it, an older castle, conceived by human minds and crafted by human hands and tools in ancient times, had fallen or been battered down since then. Brandon didn't know what the castle once had been, but only the remains they had become. Most things that people through past days took for granted had come in time to nought.

By the castle ruins, Brandon left his bicycle. He couldn't give life to anyone who once stood where he stood.

Beyond the long grasses and amidst a water-bank forest with flowers preparing to bloom, lay the pond. Tall trees starting to green grew twice: once into the sky and once in reflection in the water. Ducks and swans swam restfully with their reflections.

Careful not to slip, Brandon stepped to the water's edge. Delicately kneeling on the cool ground, his right arm reached downwards until his hand entered the cold pond. His white fingers shone through the clean water.

Fish in ponds, lakes, and rivers were endless resources for Laura and him to take and use; fresh fish to cook by wrapping it in foil and placing it in a fire. Closely studying the waters did not reveal to him any fish.

Brandon had never before fished. He fiddled with the handle on the reel until he released the rolled line. Soon, he released the hook. Anxiously holding the rod, he dropped the hook, lure, sinker, and line into the water, where only the sparkling lure remained visible.

There he stood, looking and feeling for any tension in the line with his index finger, replicating an image he'd seen somewhere. After a time, Brandon felt something tugging at it.

He turned the handle of the reel and pulled the line back to him, looking for a fish jumping from the water as it struggled to escape the hook through its mouth. He reeled in the line until the sinker and empty hook rose from the water.

The second time, he drew back the rod with line hanging from it and swing it overhead, so the hook, lure, and sinker dropped further from him in the water. Again he stood, more circumspect a second time as to what tension in the line might be a fish. Brandon sat on the ground.

Birds in slowly moving flocks flew in the sky, unaffected by what affected people on the ground. More birds sat near the tops of trees. Only they and the waters made a sound, but not because of him. The swans and ducks drifted, sometimes dipping their heads below the water surface.

The only person there in quiet time, the waters became hypnotic, drawing Brandon into their gradual reality. They hid from human view a world that rarely knew and more rarely cared that humankind wandered on dry ground. Much like the distant depths of massive oceans, it remained unchanged by the changing human story, unaware of what had happened to humanity. Aquatic life, like avian life, prospered through the aeons with no more interest in Europe's demise than in her past triumphs: eternity on earth.

Birds in the trees conversed between themselves. Brandon tried to understand their utterances, but didn't know what birds discussed.

More sensible than Europeans had been, too rarely watching them, birds and fish were happy and content, in their respective sanctuaries. Without the purposes with which English people had filled their passed-away short lives, birds ate, sheltered, and tended to their young. They would survive, peacefully unaware of what Europeans had called important.

Whether a falling tree made a sound if no one heard it fall was the riddle of the forest. Was a human life lived if nobody else sensed it?

Brandon drew the line back to him several times but never saw a fish, each time throwing the line back into a different patch of water. He wondered whether to wade into the water to catch the fish evading him, or if he was using the wrong lure, before drawing the line back for the last time and returning to his bicycle.

Riding back along Whinmoor Hill, a loud car horn behind Brandon startled him. In the mirror on his handlebars, he saw Laura's car close behind him. She again sounded her horn, pressing him to ride quicker until he rode as fast as he could pedal without dropping his fishing rod, but she drove so that her car was always the same few yards behind him. In the game she played, telling him she could outrun him, she chased him back to the castle house.

Her car was filled with luggage. Stepped from her car, Laura checked the empty basket on Brandon's bicycle. "Didn't you catch any fish?" she asked him.

"I have some cans of tuna in my car."

"I like tuna." She opened the passenger door to her car. "You'll learn to fish. We both will."

"I can help you with your bags," said Brandon.

"You have your things to bring inside."

Some clothes fell into his arms as Brandon opened a rear door of his car. He carried into the house his pair of warmest pyjamas, in his bundle of clean clothes and underclothes for one night and day. He placed them on the clean bed in a smaller bedroom, knowing he was just a guest. He pressed his hands on the mattress as he might feel the softness of an unfamiliar hotel bed.

Laura took a smaller bedroom much like his. On a chest of drawers lay a pen and diary, which Laura must have realised Brandon saw. "You don't have a diary?" she asked him.

"I don't have many engagements."

Laura laughed. "I guess not," she said.

Perhaps uniquely in the house, a battery-powered ceiling light lit the basement boiler room. Instructions for starting the boiler were affixed near it, with words and diagrams. Brandon familiarised himself with the knobs and buttons. Without electricity to start it, he pressed two small buttons releasing gas and igniting the pilot light: a small blue flame. Gas rushed through open ducts and kicked alight a brighter fan of flames, pushing pistons back to life.

Brandon stood up and reached for the wall, where he flicked a switch for a second light. Nothing happened.

Several conduits led to a panel affixed to the wall, from which a small coloured electric sheath had fallen loose. Brandon carefully slipped the loose cable back into its hole. The ceiling light flickered to life above him, as power flowed again throughout the house. He flicked it on and off and on again. Using a screwdriver, he fastened it into place.

Brandon rushed from room to room, switching on lights. "Not the lights," Laura chided him. "We don't know who might be out there." Brandon switched off most lights again.

Flicking the switch beside the kitchen oven made the digital light on the oven flash. Kneeling down beside the refrigerator and flicking that switch set the refrigerator cooling. The kitchen was a bit like all English kitchens once had been.

Laura stood rubbing her hands before a radiator in the adjoining cosy snug, where Brandon joined her. Unlike the rampant chaos of fires in fireplaces, the warmth from radiators around the house was steady and controlled. It soothed Brandon's hands he had forgotten needed soothing.

In the en-suite bathroom adjoining his bedroom, the water from the hot water tap slowly became hot. Brandon took a can of shaving cream he'd brought from his car and sprayed a small dollop of white foam on his hand, where it rose to something soft. Brandon spread the foam with one hand over the short whiskers from his cheeks and chin. Careful to be clean, his razor captured every hair. He then washed away every sense of doing so, spilling most of the warm water.

Laura closed and locked her bedroom door. Her bedroom also enjoyed an en-suite bathroom, although their showers mightn't be as long as they once were and baths might not be as full. Brandon hadn't yet found the rainwater tank.

The kettle on the kitchen bench was dry. Brandon poured into it enough water from the tap for several cups of tea. He plugged the cord into the socket on the kettle, flicked the switch, and heard the kettle start to heat.

After removing a can of Brussels sprouts from a larder and leaving it on the kitchen island, Brandon stood by the kettle becoming warm. Beside the kettle, he placed two cups, in which he'd dropped two teabags. The cups connoted him in company, as if for the first time in his life. Laura was his first night out with a beautiful woman about whom he knew too little, back at the home at which he lived. She was a long lost friend back in his life again. He might've become the man he could have been, just for a time.

The kettle whistle blew, when the kettle became too hot and automatically switched off. The whistle quickly faded. Steam rose from the water as Brandon poured it from the kettle into the cups.

Washed and cleaned, wearing a warmer dress than she'd worn earlier that day, Laura was in the drawing room. Sitting in the armchair she'd uncovered earlier that day, her wet hair was wrapped in a towel, until she saw Brandon entering the room. She whisked off the towel, frisked her hair a little drier, and brushed it down with her hand. "I haven't felt like this for a long time," she beamed, leaving the towel on the edge of the coffee table in front of her.

"I'm afraid we're out of milk and sugar," smiled Brandon, offering her cup on a saucer.

Laura took the cup and saucer from him. "How much do I owe you?" she asked, in a joke mocking the time people paid for anything that anybody did for them.

"I'll charge it to your room."

Brandon sat in the armchair he'd uncovered, facing her. The aroma of his twirling tea rose through his head, before gently he sipped it. What once had been a staple of their lives had become something special.

She slipped her shoes from her feet, exposing her stockings, and rested her right leg under her. If it seemed to Brandon that he studied her more than she studied him, then he did. "I always liked this room," she said, looking around.

He, not she, was the visitor. The house was not his home unless she let him. "Tell me more about you," he said.

"You tell me about you."

Her eyes leading him through his recollections, Brandon told her the story of his life, such as it was: of Darlington and school in the last class getting older. Enunciating his thoughts clarified them, as they'd not been inside his head. He'd not done the things his parents did. He'd not done much at all.

"How did your parents die?"

"Isn't that morbid?"

"Death is morbid. Talking about morbidity is just talking."

Collecting his concentration, Brandon talked of Tarpin Hobbs. Her face focussed on him, with a stern restraint that didn't respond to anything he said or the way he said it. Sometimes his voice wavered, and memories of tears watered the sides of his clean eyes, but he continued. His story intruded upon his experience of her, while she quelled his thirst for conversation until it wearied him. When he finished, he fell silent.

Laura continued to stare at him. "Death is always sad," she said, more sensitive than she'd been. "The more we love the people who die, the sadder death is."

"People who want to kill themselves shouldn't kill other people when they do."

Brandon wanted to hear anything about somebody other than himself. "What did you do?"

She smiled. "My mother and I talked about how funny it was that the first thing that anybody ever asked was 'What do you do?' and everybody always answered about a job. Maybe then they'd talk about where they lived, or where they'd been. Relatives asked about relationships because they hoped you had one and acquaintances asked if they hoped you didn't."

Brandon didn't like being a model, a statistical norm. Perhaps that was all people ever were.

"I was born thirty-two years ago in Northallerton," she started. "My parents raised me there until I finished school and moved to York for university; varsity, Ogden called it." Brandon watched her face, eyes, and motions of her hands, and listened. "I studied anthropology, before becoming a marketing manager for Natural Valley Dental Products."

Without trying to conceal what he was doing, Brandon leant forward and, across the coffee table, scrutinised her mouth. She smiled, deliberately pulling back her lips, revealing her shimmering white teeth.

"Why did you and not somebody else come upon Northallerton?" she asked him. "Why shouldn't you have entered another woman's town? What do you and I have in common?"

Her stare compelled him to say something. "I'm ordinary," he said.

"I never wanted to be ordinary, but I think now I was. I worked most evenings and some weekends. I went to the gym every Monday, Wednesday and Friday night, cafeterias and nightclubs other nights, and ate brunch every Sunday. I was busy all the time, although nowadays knowing what I did is hard. Working was something safe about which to talk."

Brandon considered what she said, as he considered

everything she said. Their conversations were more profound than any he'd previously experienced, about lives no longer theirs.

"I thought my parents had genetic conditions or other hereditary traits that made them different to other people."

"Maybe parents live a little longer than other people," said Brandon. "Parents should never outlive their children."

"I guess I had too much else I wanted to do, until Ogden."

Her words might've been a warning to him. Men more handsome and mature than Brandon had shared the life she used to know. She might've liked them, enjoyed them, and never thought too much about them when they went, until Ogden. Those men were no longer hers to have and not to have. There was only Brandon. For Brandon, there was only Laura. He was as much her only chance for company in that house as she was his. He didn't know how to construe the things she said.

"Married women complained about their husbands," laughed Laura. "It was a fashionable thing to do."

"You make it sound like all men are the same and all women are the same."

"Not all men and women on planet earth, but studying anthropology and working in marketing taught me to categorise customers and other strangers. With our demographic definitions, differences never mattered as much as commonalities. We – my friends and I, you and your friends – in most respects we were the same smart ignorant young Englishmen and women: the best educated and most intelligent fools alive."

"So what am I?"

"Someone who never spent much money on his teeth," she smiled.

"If I'd been born the day you were born, what would I have become before I was thirty-two years old?"

Laura fell silent, studying him at last, before finally responding. "You'd have become someone who spent too much money on your car, clothes, and girlfriends. One or two of those girlfriends might've loved you, but you, you would've been in love once or not at all."

He thought of phrases he'd freely utter wooing women, but they were lies and he wouldn't lie to her. "People can love twice in their lives," he said.

"How does someone love twice?"

"No one is suited to just one person," he explained. "Any man can love any one of scores of women, and any woman can love any one of scores of men. If they're very lucky, then twice in their lives they find people they could love and those people love them."

"So they move from one love to another?"

"They learn to live without someone they stop loving quite so much." If he was her final chance to love again, he didn't know she would.

"Whom did you love?" she asked him.

"I never had the chance." Brandon didn't know if his answers were good ones, but they were truthful.

Laura nodded. Brandon had passed a small test that she'd set him. "Some people have a propensity if not a disposition for loving."

Brandon might never love, but hoped he would. "What makes you unusual?" he asked her. "Where didn't you fit into your categories?"

"I didn't need to spend so much money on teeth care," she smiled.

Brandon smiled with her, but wouldn't let her evade him so easily. "What else?"

She might have been cautious with him as he no longer was with her, before replying. "I loved my parents," she said. "That had become very unfashionable, for English people."

"Being parents was more unfashionable."

Leaving her cup and saucer on the coffee table, Laura stood up. Stretching her arms, she ambled towards a bookshelf. As if she were at home, she pulled out a large book and flicked through its pages, stopping to examine something more closely.

"You do what I do," noticed Brandon. "You browse through books from back to front."

"Do you like wood badgers?"

"I don't know much about them."

"Do you like to learn?"

"Yes."

She returned to the coffee table, where she placed the book, about European animals, close to Brandon. "Being clever, like most things that people did, was never as important as people thought it was."

"What do you think is important?"

"Family, friends, that's all, once we can live and eat."

"You sound like you've spent some time asking yourself that question."

Laura smiled. "We considered ourselves intellectual," she said. "A lot of people died very clever, but what was the purpose of it all?"

"Everything you learnt never saved your mother's life?"

"I'd rather read novels now, because they're unreal. They help me think of anything but me, and I don't have to pretend I'm doing anything important."

The long day having become late, the room would soon darken. Brandon stood up and moved towards a light switch on the wall, which would have lit the chandelier hanging from the ceiling. "May I?" he asked her.

She shook her head. Instead, she went to a table where she switched on a small lamp. "I'm tired now," she said. "I think I'll go to bed."

He imagined her right hand reaching out to shake his, but it didn't. "Do you have everything you need?" he inquired.

She started to leave, before turning back towards him. "Do you want everything to be like it used to be?" she asked him.

"Do you think it will be?"

"I keep wondering where the people our age have gone," she said, as if Brandon's age were hers.

Brandon had become less conscious that no one else was there. "I don't think about those people as much as you do," he replied, wondering less what had happened to the world than what was happening to them.

"Please switch off the lights when you're finished," she told him.

Laura left the drawing room. Brandon sat back down in the sofa, with the company of that single table lamp.

She hurried back into the room. "We have to clean up now," she said, picking up her towel and empty cup and saucer from the coffee table.

She again left the room. To the stairs, up them, and to her room, the wooden floorboards creaked as they previously had not.

Brandon's empty cup and saucer remained on the coffee table. He would later return them to the kitchen.

His legs stretched out across the floor. His arms reached across the cushion back behind him. He felt strangely important, as if he deserved to be in that pretty place. No longer were they cavemen eking out hard lives. They had become the landed gentry.

The farms, fields, and paddocks were theirs to use: their neighbourhood. Refrigeration let him think of killing animals that he didn't need to eat immediately. He would cut a lamb or calf into portions to freeze in the large freezer until he thawed them. Equipped with light, warmth, and everything else they needed, Brandon would take up the life he'd previously been denied, learning things about which he'd only wondered.

His joy collapsed with him. Two solitary people with everything they needed, if only for a time, their lives replicated England's recent past.

6

CHICKENS

Sunrise lit the southern and eastern faces of the castle house. The country morning air was cool, before the rising sun warmed the day.

Brandon dressed into clothes better than those he'd worn of late, without seeming too much to have done so. He brushed his hair.

Dressed much as she'd dressed yesterday, Laura was already in the kitchen when Brandon went downstairs. She stood with a long spatula at the stove burning blue and a frying pan emitting steam. "Do you like omelettes?" she asked him. Lying waiting on the kitchen table were two plates with forks, to which she soon carried the frying pan and served equal portions of their breakfast.

"How much do I owe you?" asked Brandon, as Laura laid the pan in the sink.

She sat down at their breakfasts before he did. "Everything."

Brandon rushed into his hot food as if he might never again eat another, before realising he would. He slowed his chewing, becoming courteous enough to wait.

He remembered another maxim from the dead Western society: that friends and colleagues shouldn't become romantically involved together, because they couldn't readily part. Were England a society, then Brandon could rejoice in being with Laura knowing they were aspirants to relationship who could always leave each other be, but two were not society. She was everyone he knew, as he was everyone for her.

What Laura and he were doing remained unclear to him, in their extraordinary situation becoming ordinary. His only friend was his best friend, which implied too many things but not enough about their time together. They might've been the best of friends, except they'd met each other yesterday. If mere fear first drove her to him, he didn't know if it still did.

People had kissed strangers more readily than he dared think of touching her, but their situation made him cautious. He didn't know how they could kiss, or if they ever would.

Love could no longer be what it had been, whatever that was, but Brandon didn't understand what love could be when only two of them remained. They were already living together, involved with each other's lives. Unless somebody new chanced upon them, they had nowhere else to go. If they became too close, then they might lose other choices for love if other people came, or lose their only opportunity for friendship if other people didn't. He'd become accustomed to being with her, whatever being with her could mean. Without anyone else from whom to choose, they were conferred and condemned upon each other.

"Our next meal is your responsibility," said Laura, slower to eat than Brandon.

Perhaps he needn't fret whether sole companions could ever become lovers. Brandon needed most of all a friend to speak some words for him to hear that hadn't been his own and to hear his fresh response. "I could try to catch us a chicken."

"We need the eggs."

Brandon missed the texture, body, and taste of meat. Red meat was most inviting, but the fresh meat he could obtain most easily was white. "There are a lot of chickens," he told her, "here and I expect on all the farms."

She studied him without reply. At the end of their meal, she placed her plate in the sink. She removed a sharp knife from a cutlery drawer and laid it on the table in front of him. "You'll want this," she told him.

In their coop, several chickens wandered towards him as Brandon approached. He lifted the latch and pushed the gate open just wide enough for him to walk inside. Laura remained outside while he closed the gate behind him.

Leaving the knife on the ground, he took some pellets in his hand. Trying to seem gentle and friendly, he stepped slowly towards a chicken, offering it feed from his open palm. It scarpered away.

Brandon turned to another chicken, whistling to it as he might summon a dog. It moved away, into a corner in which Brandon tried to trap it. His knees bent ready to spring in any direction after it, while other chickens remained away. Sprinkling the last of the feed on the ground freed both his hands. In Brandon's hungry concentration, the ground seemed to absorb the chicken he wanted.

He lunged forward, grabbing its flapping body with both his hands. The chicken squawked, spraying feathers in the air. Other panicked chickens screamed and tried to fly away, fleeing for their small lives. His desperate chicken's head and legs jumped in his struggling hands, its beak trying to bite and claws trying to scratch as it fought to live, spraying more feathers around them.

"What do I do now?" he called out to Laura.

"Ogden's family never killed their chickens."

Holding the chicken tightly to him, but not too close to its beak and claws, Brandon forced his hands along its neck to try to twist and break that neck. He tried to bash its head against the ground.

"Take it away from the other chickens," said Laura, opening the gate ever so slightly.

Careful not to let other chickens escape while carrying his chicken, Brandon stepped out of the enclosure. With the gate again closed and Laura carrying the knife she'd given him, they moved out of sight of the chicken yard.

"Slit its throat," she said, offering him the knife.

"It's alive."

"You wanted chicken."

The knife seemed much too small. "There's an axe in the wood store."

Leaving the knife on the grass, Laura went to the wood store. Brandon continued holding the chicken, squirming a little less virulently the longer its life continued. She returned carrying unconvincingly with both her hands an axe, with a polished wooden handle and shining iron blade.

"I need a chopping block," said Brandon.

"I can't carry that."

Carrying the axe, she led them back to the wood store. Brandon, still holding his chicken and balancing on his left leg, used his right leg to push over and roll outside the chopping block previously used for cutting wood. On the grass, he stood the block upright.

Pressing the chicken's neck down against the wood, it sparked to fierce life again. Laura leant the axe against the wood block and, standing to the far side of the chicken from Brandon, took hold of the chicken's body. Leaving only his left hand on the chicken, Brandon's right hand held the axe midway down the handle, a short way above the chicken's neck. Gathering all the strength he could in his hand and wrist, he struck the axe through the chicken's neck.

Blood sprayed out, as the chicken with its head loose and bobbing broke away, crashing into a wall. It was insane, running amok; alive when it ought to have been dead.

Brandon watched, almost scared of it still moving. It might run about forever and never die, but Brandon still holding the axe crawled towards it and grabbed it again. His left hand holding its body down, Brandon's right hand through the axe cleanly cut off its neck.

The chicken's head fell to the grass but the body still shook, trying to jump, while Brandon held it down. Its legs moved frantically, wanting to run, but still he held the chicken down. After briefly squirming amidst a final spark of life, the body finally fell loose beneath his hand.

His right hand let go of the axe but, fearing the chicken would leap up again, Brandon's left hand continued holding it down, as he lay back exhausted on the grass. His clothes and shoes were scratched and soiled with the blood, dirt, and feathers of the struggle, but the chicken was surely dead.

Brandon's grip holding the chicken down did not relax, as he looked up at Laura in her clean dress, watching him. Aside from his panting, the castle grounds were strangely quiet again. The turmoil of the past few minutes had concluded. "I'm glad," said Brandon, "I didn't suggest beef."

"We should clean and pluck it away from the house," said Laura, picking up from the grass the knife and, more delicately, the axe.

Carrying the chicken's flopping feathered body by its legs in one hand and its head in the other, blood dripping to the ground, they returned to where they'd left the chicken eggs the previous day. There, Brandon threw the chicken's head over the hedge. "That," said Brandon, "might keep the chicken parts from coming back to life."

Laying the rest of the chicken on the ground, Brandon knelt beside it. He picked a feather from its bloodied, absent neck and pulled it, but only dragged the dead bird with him. Sitting on the grassy verge, holding the chicken body with one hand, he tugged the feather loose. The skin flapped back in place.

The feather was light to hold and Brandon tried to drop it, but the blood on his stained fingers attached it to him. He rubbed his fingertips on the grass until they were clean enough.

Laura sat with him, careful to keep any slivers of the mess from her clean skin and clothes. Cautiously, with Brandon's hand holding the chicken back, she plucked a bloodless feather.

With one or other of Brandon's hands always holding the chicken's body down, they plucked feathers from the chicken flesh in turn, leaving them on the grass. "Is this the career you wanted?" asked Brandon.

"I want to eat."

Laura moved a loose feather too near her dress away from her. Brandon's clothes were far too soiled for him to care about them.

"I used to think what I was doing, helping people keep their teeth clean, was special," she said, plucking another feather.

"We said that most things we did were special and believed it, but they don't mean anything and never did. I mean, my job was nice, fun even, and I would happily do it again more than I would do most other jobs, but it was never special. It was a job, like any other, maybe better for me than others, but just a job I could live every time I went out, and then amuse myself at home not to brush my teeth."

"You didn't aspire to being a great marketer?" asked Brandon, plucking another feather.

Laura looked at him. "I suppose I did," she admitted. "No, I did, for what it was worth." She tugged at another feather. "All I know much about is selling dental care products. I don't know anything worthwhile."

"We are in a natural valley, or vale, now," said Brandon, as they plucked.

"You know," said Laura, "there was never anything natural about Natural Valley Dental Products. It was a name, but consumers liked to think things they bought were natural. Our toothpaste, dental floss, teeth whiteners, and everything else we sold included the same chemicals as all the others. We called them natural chemicals among ourselves, knowing that chemicals are natural. Everything artificial is ultimately a mix of natural atoms."

The remnant of the bird became gaunt. It became less and less recognisable as a chicken.

"We weren't selling dental care," continued Laura, "but senses of a grass-filled valley to people who'd never seen one. We improved people's lives by them believing us. We gave each other good feelings with words almost untrue. We lied to everyone else and soon believed our lies."

"Does that make plucking a chicken," asked Brandon, "without brand names and slogans, more honest work?"

"We have no business plan, no budgets and accounts, but we know what we're doing," she said, again in a form of her career. "I'm hoping to forget most things I no longer need to know. This might be the most efficient work I've done. It's certainly the most useful."

With all the feathers on the ground or blown away, Laura

stood up and stepped back, brushing anything loose from her dress. The chicken wasn't yet recognisable as anything that once lay on butchers' shelves or graced restaurant plates.

Taking the axe, Brandon chopped off the chicken's tail and feet. With the knife, he cut open its chest from its neck to its breastbone. He pulled away the neck bone and poked his reddened index finger inside the carcass, where his hands ripped out the warm, wet, and bloody innards buried inside the bird, throwing them over the hedge. The bird's lightening body closed around his hands each time he dragged something out: the gruesome gizzard and other gut, lungs, and heart.

Having removed everything he could from the creature in his hand, Brandon turned to Laura. "Are you ready to order?"

"You should wash outside."

In the creek, Brandon washed the blood, muck, and feathers from his hands. Some had dried on his skin, but he scratched and rubbed until none remained.

Brandon washed the chicken, washing away its last entrails. The naked chicken was a tender pink, but much smaller than he remembered uncooked chicken being. He shook the dead bird, and laid it by the water.

Blood, feathers, and chicken body soiled his clothes and shoes. The water was cold but his clothes were already damp. He removed his shoes and socks, and waded fully clothed into the water flow, chilling him. Shivering but unbowed, Brandon tossed water on his clothes. He rubbed away more mess.

Laura's attention was on him. "How is it?" she asked.

"I'm becoming used to it." Satisfied that his two open hands were clean, Brandon clasped them to form a cup that he trailed in the river. His cup of hands collected water that he brought up to his mouth. The water was fresh and crisp to taste. He splashed it on his face.

"Do you want some washing powder?" asked Laura.

She was probably joking, but Brandon looked down at his clothes. "Good idea," he said.

Laura left him. She took with her the knife and axe.

Brandon remained in the water, picking more bits of waste

from the fabrics of his clothes. He washed more cold water into them and rubbed his hands on them, but the stains remained.

Laura returned with a box of washing powder, which she passed to him from the bank. "A present," she said.

Brandon poured a small portion of powder on a large blemish in his trousers, before resting the box on the bank. He rubbed water into the cloth, while white bubbles appeared in the water. Unable to tell if he'd cleaned his clothes much, he stepped from the water.

Laura carried the box of washing powder out of the trees to the driveway towards the castle house. Brandon, barefooted and dripping wet, carried the emaciated chicken and his shoes and socks across the pebbled courtyard, past their cars. They walked apart so not to let his damp and stained old clothes brush against her long clean dress.

"You wait here," Laura told him, when they reached the front door.

Brandon placed his shoes and socks on the doorstep. He remained outside, holding the raw plucked chicken.

Laura returned to the open door with a towel and a large cooking pot. Brandon took the towel and placed the chicken in the pot. She left him there.

In the open air, Brandon removed his blighted shirt and trousers and dropped them to the ground. Wrapping the towel around his waist, he brushed clean the soles of his feet, before walking through the house and upstairs to his room and bathroom.

After showering, he dressed into yesterday's clean clothes long enough to return to his car and bring more clothes and another pair of shoes into the house. After dressing again, he stowed his wet and worn clothes in the washing machine by the clothes dryer in the laundry. He left his wet shoes on the laundry floor.

Looking around the big house for Laura, Brandon found her sitting at the end of her bed. She sat hunched over, her head in her hands, looking forward not obviously at anything.

"We never knew anyone, did we," she sighed, without looking

at him. "Nobody asked about people's lives away from work. If anybody said anything, then nobody else listened."

"Tell me about your parents," said Brandon, sitting in the only chair in the room.

She smiled, sitting upright, but still not looking at him, as if she were thinking aloud and he happened to be there. "My parents wanted to change the world and keep it, as people did," she said. "They met when they began being old."

Laura spoke fondly of their attributes and failings beyond the specifics of their biography: their work, short hobbies, and trite interests. Sometimes, Brandon forgot Laura's mother had only been dead for one short week.

"My parents talked more of their joys than their disappointments that might unsettle me, but I wish they respected me enough to tell me everything they felt. I don't think my father finished loving the first woman he loved, but she died when they thought they were both too young to marry. My mother wished she'd learnt to dance the waltzes her great-grandparents danced, but her career consumed her time. They each regretted arguments between them and told the other not to regret. I never doubted we'd help each other when we required it. My parents' loves were also their duties."

"I wish I met them," said Brandon.

"Most of what I know I learned in the last years of their lives," admitted Laura. "My mother and I were lucky to have each other, after my father died. We were good together then; talking as we never before talked, imparting our feelings as we felt them, reciting our thoughts as we composed them. The realisation we soon would part gave us freedom and obligation to speak without compunction. The talk inside my head flowed out, more often spontaneous responses to the moment than anything profound.

"We lit candles at night when the electricity stopped, and sometimes talked until the last of the melting wax trickled down the candle sides. I think my mother stayed alive longer than she would've lived if I hadn't been there with her. She didn't want me to be alone."

"Are you and I like that?"

Laura looked at him. Brandon wanted to ask her about her feelings for him, but didn't know the words to broach them. They were the things about which they didn't talk, when they talked about so much. She seemed so uninhibited in most respects that he assumed she would say anything she felt, so she must not have felt anything about him. She might also have been bold in every other aspect but then been shy with him. Did she think as he thought?

His thoughts were more of her and him than anything else. Her mind had become his company, but Brandon didn't know what more of her was with him. They should speak without mores, for two people were too few to be society: they had no social sanction.

They might have both been cautious not to embarrass themselves, because they couldn't walk too far or hide away. He had no one with whom to be but her, and she had no one with whom to be but him. Without the luxury of others, they couldn't afford to hurt or be hurt so much as to need to be apart until they healed, and then be civil when next they met.

That gave him fear they shouldn't part and confidence they never could. Love and liking weren't critiques of either one of them.

"What can you tell me about your parents?" she asked him.

Brandon feared that he'd presumed too much of her and him. "My parents loved me," he answered, "and I loved them. How could I not, after they ignored England's rules to bear me. Their jobs were never as important to them as their only child, but they never taught me why we let England age and die."

Her eyes left him, before she slowly stood up and went to the small table beside her bed. She opened a drawer, from which she removed two photographs she carried towards him. One pictured a man and a woman not much older than she was, standing together and smiling to the photographer. "They're my parents," she told him.

Brandon took the photograph in his hand. The slowness of her fingers releasing it assured him that she hadn't expected him to take it. "They seem nice people," he said.

"They were."

He realised his words had been glib. The man and woman who had been young grew old, finally leaving only Laura at her dying mother's side.

"When I knew my mother was dead," said Laura, "I sat in the chair beside her bed and watched her. I felt as if I had lost a battle I should've won, and stared at her lifeless body hoping that a spirit might rise from her and either condemn me or forgive me. I'm grateful to my parents for the best of their intentions, and if remembering them saddens me, then it's only because it also makes me happy, feeling my good fortune to have been my parents' daughter."

Brandon offered the photograph back to her. She tendered the second photograph to him. "That is me with my parents at my graduation from the University of York," she told him.

Without resistance from Laura this time, Brandon took the photograph in his hand. The images affirmed her past fractured and unclear, but a past nevertheless: a place among people, love, and relationship. "You look very serious and professional," he said, reading the faces more closely.

"I was."

Laura returned the photographs to her drawer. Brandon probably felt more special that she'd shown him the photographs than he deserved to feel.

7

KIRBY KNOWLE

The chicken that Brandon caught that morning lay softening in the castle house kitchen, while he and Laura walked slowly down the driveway to Whinmoor Hill and then east towards the Moors. Beyond the hedges, interrupted only for the entranceways to gentle homes, were cows, sheep, and occasionally horses in meadows. The castle house sometimes seemed obvious beyond them, but only Brandon and Laura were there to see.

He thought of taking her hand as they walked. He would only do so if he knew she let him.

Coming into Kirby Knowle, the hedges by Whinmoor Hill became incomplete, revealing weathered wooden fences. Ahead of them to the right, a few cottages clustered with a wooden barn, much as they did in any other English village. Ahead of them to the left, perhaps a little higher and certainly taller than any house or barn, was a square-towered old stone church.

"Saint Wilfrid's Church," remembered Laura. "I had an uncle named Wilfrid, but he was hardly a saint."

Around the church grounds was a rock wall, about a yard high, among the similar rock walls by the road through the village. The church gates were closed.

However long a time had passed since the villagers died or

otherwise left Kirby Knowle, and for all the long grass and unkempt gardens, only one building was becoming derelict, with broken windows and slipping roof shingles. It might have once been a post office, for villages used to enjoy post offices, because embedded in the mossed and grassy rock wall around it was a red metal postbox.

The building had certainly been a public building of some form, for on the wall was a noticeboard. Behind a wire mesh, sheltered under a warping slice of wood, the notices were of a long finished dance, club meeting, and talk about homeopathy. They were shadows of a people no longer there, small excerpts of lives and times then gone.

Brandon and Laura proceeded past stone cottages large and not so large, more comfortable than merely shelter from the weather or place to keep a trade. What had been a nest of people's homes had become another empty village, never far from the dark, foreboding woods and Moors. If the men they'd seen in York ever came near Kirby Knowle, the woods and Moors would be a place to hide for Brandon and Laura.

The road north to Cowesby and Kepwick soon returned to countryside, the last village buildings being corrugated iron barns. Steel fuel tanks stood above the ground. An idle tractor stood under cover. Laura and Brandon turned back, remaining in Kirby Knowle.

"Are you like your mother?" asked Brandon. "Do you want to waltz like your great-grandparents waltzed?"

"With whom could I waltz?"

"You could teach me."

At the eastern end of Whinmoor Hill, before a gate to what had been private property, Laura stopped and faced him. "Do you know the Blue Danube waltz?"

Brandon shook his head. Laura stepped close to him.

She took his right hand as she'd not previously touched him, and placed his hand behind her back. She rested her left hand on his right shoulder, took his left hand in her right hand, and stretched it up and away from them. "La-la-la-la-la-la," she began to sing, her right hand leading them away, "da-da, da-da."

Brandon followed the motions of her feet across the ground. The flowing tail of her long dress could make her feet hard to see.

"La-la-la-la-la-la," she continued, "da-da, da-da." Laura led them veering from the road onto a great circle of driveway. "La-la-la-la-la-la, da-da, da-da."

He tried as best he could to copy her movements. It was his poor impression of a waltz.

"La-la-la-la-la-la," she went on, "da-da, da-da." They moved together, frivolously, as Brandon hadn't played for too long a time. "La-la-la-la, la-la-la, da-da, da-da, da-da-dada." Nobody remained to tell them they were silly.

Laura ceased trying to replicate the music, but they continued their imperfect waltz. His left hand holding her right hand and his right hand holding her waist, they proceeded around a patch of grass home to a weeping willow tree. She sometimes led them stepping and sometimes he led them, moving through the cooling afternoon. Her left hand rested carelessly on his shoulder, where he could feel it close to his mind.

Revelling in every sense of being with her, Brandon could forget the times in which they lived. They could've been the two of them together in any era of a place, dancing to music that all Europe once envied. They and the trees were guests at a Viennese late-season waltz in the precinct of the palace, where nature's hands applauded everything they did.

Brandon tired, but didn't let her go. Their pace slowed, around the willow tree. Looking past her to the houses, concentrating upon their steps and on each other, her hand on his right shoulder slipped down to hold his back much like his hand held hers. He lowered his right hand to her waist, letting her left hand fall away and finally settle around his waist, in a soft embrace between small equals.

Their dancing became swaying back and forth through little steps, holding each other. Drifting closer together, their chests softly rested against each other. Gazing beyond her into nowhere, every breath of her beating heart stirred through him. Her body warm against him, keeping out some cold around them while the air against his cheeks was cold.

Brandon became nervous of what he should be doing. She might've expected him to kiss her. He might've expected him to do so.

"I used to know things," Laura said softly. "I used even to recognise what I didn't know. Now, I'm not sure of anything."

Brandon pulled his chest away from her to see her face. Their slow waltz finished, she stepped back from him, too far from his lips to reach her.

Standing near them, watching them as nothing else did, was a deer. Whether Laura or Brandon first noticed it, the other soon did, as their faces turned simultaneously towards it. Laura dropped her arms and hands from Brandon and stepped further backwards from him, as if embarrassed to have been observed. The deer's head twitched a little, still watching them. The road was surely hard against its hoofs and the bits of grass there for it to eat less filling than in the forest.

"From the Moors, do you think?" asked Brandon.

Laura was busily looking back along Whinmoor Hill. "We should check something," she said, leading Brandon back past the church and around the corner to the road south to Felixkirk. She led them past more stone cottages, other buildings, and a timber store to the hedges and the fields. At the first farm they reached still stood a weathered sign offering organic free range eggs for sale.

"Everything we farm will be organic," said Brandon. Even if he knew where to find the hormones, fertilisers, pesticides, and anything else that organic food reputedly excluded from its preparation and learnt how to administer them, Laura and he didn't need to increase production with only them to feed.

While Laura proceeded up the driveway, Brandon paused at a timber cubicle near the road. Hanging there was a sign to say that it was closed. He nevertheless unlatched the door and pulled it open.

Inside, all eggs had gone. A notice declared the eggs that had been there had come from hens free from hunger and thirst, pain and injury, fear and distress, and discomfort. The hens also, said the notice, had been free to express themselves.

Brandon didn't understand what chickens did when they

expressed themselves; no chicken he'd ever eaten said anything to him. Brandon left and closed the door.

At the end of the driveway along which Brandon trod were two large hopper silos and a huge semicircular-roofed barn. Between them he found Laura, staring downward. Where rain and snow hadn't cleaned them, were scattered feathers sealed with streaks of blood.

"Foxes," she said.

She led them past more blood and feathers rotting on the ground, between the barn and other buildings, to the edge of a green field. Ahead of them stood a long chicken house, its shutters closed. At one end, a small silo and its downward-pointed cone supplied feed. Horses and cows fed on the grass around them. No chickens were in sight.

Brandon led Laura across the grass to the chicken house, where he dragged open a door. Inside, for all the light and ventilation, were the frailest chickens he'd seen, pecking at the last hints of grass, grains, and seeds in the dirt. Almost lost among the broken eggshells, drying remnants of baby near-born chicks, and scattered strands of soiled straw, shelves of nests and perches lined the walls. Water dripped from taps into a drinking trough, but the troughs for feed were empty.

The chickens were slow to creep outside. Brandon returned to the barns and other buildings, where opening a barn door revealed a wealth of hay, tools, and several hundred-pound sacks of chicken pellets. Taking one sack, he dragged it along the ground back to the chicken house, where he dropped it on the ground inside. Laura brought a long metal fork, which Brandon thrust into the sack.

Seeds of grain poured from the punctured hole onto the ground, to which chickens raced past Brandon's legs to eat. Chickens fought among themselves, climbing and falling over each other, trying to reach the unleashed feed.

Laura and Brandon stepped away from them, to a corner of the dirt. There, he noticed an egg lay tucked. Any hen that guarded it was among those crowded at the feed. Like a thief taking her children, Brandon picked up the warm white egg. "Do you know if a baby chicken is in it?" he asked Laura.

Inside the shell, the yolk and liquid white might've partially formed into a grotesque hybrid creature. Brandon imagined chicken eyes looking back at him if he broke open a living egg, with tiny claws and feathers screaming in the fluid. Knowing the baby chicken would die without its mother's warmth, he returned the egg to where he'd found it.

"We can return often enough to know when to bring another bag," said Brandon, "until the chickens exhaust the feed and all they'll have is open ground, but aside from closing the chicken house each evening, we can't protect them from foxes."

He closed the chicken house door. Again among the barns and buildings, Brandon noticed a metal cone hanging from a wooden stand, like gallows. The cone was open at both ends, with enough space at the thin lower end to expose a chicken's head.

They walked back into the village, where again in front of them stood Saint Wilfrid's quiet church. This time, having seen everything else in Kirby Knowle, Brandon climbed the two steps from the pavement and pushed upon one side of the gate. It creaked, not quite resisting him.

A pebbly footpath to the church door led through the graveyard: a higgledy-piggledy congregation of lopsided gravestones leaning over as if ready to fall in their exhaustion, denoting more people dead and gone. Beside the path, the first of the spring daffodils began to glow. Brandon knelt down and picked a yellow flower, he offered to Laura.

She hesitated. If she was uncertain what to do with it, she was uncertain what to do with him. If she felt embarrassed, she had no reason to be. She took the flower.

Rather than proceeding towards the church, she stepped onto the consecrated grass. Headstones not carved with crosses had crosses carved in them. People buried there were antecedents of other people buried there, olden lives long ago much alike more recent lives. Brandon and Laura had no reason to be different from them. Human history wasn't the story of a world, but of each little place and people.

The daffodil in Laura's hand, they proceeded to more recent gravestones, which stood more orderly than older stones still stood. Every epitaph not of parenthood damned all of them. Being a loving Dad and Grandpa, a long Mum and Grandma, should've been enough, even if those children and grandchildren were also dead somewhere.

"What happens when you and I are dead and buried?" asked Laura, of their old, collective deaths. "Imagine that, none of us left, not existing."

She inspired Brandon to picture their gravestones, except that nobody might remain to carve them. "Why did your parents call you Laura Trimm?" he asked her.

"They didn't."

Brandon faced her. "Aren't you Laura Trimm?"

"Laura is my middle name, but basically I made up Laura Trimm."

"What is your name?"

"Jane Laura Erian."

"What's wrong with being Jane Erian?"

"I thought Laura Trimm sounded better. It was more interesting, and I created it."

"What did your parents think?"

"When I was growing up, women were told not to take our husbands' names, because we would lose our identities as individuals if we did. I thought that choosing my name would guarantee me an identity, but I was wrong. It's just a name."

"What do I call you?"

"Even my parents eventually called me Laura."

"Did you tell your friends your real name?"

"No." The truth had made him special. "Did you tell your other girlfriends the things that you told me?"

The premise of her question surprised him. She, the only other woman in the world, must've been his girlfriend, if she presumed she was. "No, Jane."

"My father wanted my middle name to be Leela, for one of the travelling companions to a doctor travelling through space and time in an old English television series, but my mother didn't want people confusing me with the lady next door, whose name sounded the same, so my middle name became Laura. I saw some archived episodes to understand something of my father and what he imagined his daughter to be: a primitive warrior, cunning and resourceful. I was nothing like her, except that I knew how to be independent. I studied too hard not to be intellectual; we all did."

They wandered around the church. The perimeter rock wall confined them to church grounds.

"Leela was also the descendant of human colonists on another planet whose civilisation had ended," continued Laura. "What matters to us now are the same things that meant something to her: growing the food we need to eat, maintaining our shelter with heat and cool. Survival wasn't something I needed to know when I was young, but really I always did. That's all anyone ever needs to know."

They came back upon the pebbly path at the front of the church. Outside the church front double doors were three stones more like museum pieces than markers for the dead. In an old stone font, more daffodils grew. Brandon checked that Laura still carried hers.

Another old church door latch turned with an iron ring, as had the church in Northallerton. Brandon pushed it open.

In the church porch, affixed to a stone wall, was a tall but tarnished sheet of brass, which Brandon needed to examine closely to read. It listed men from Kirby Knowle who'd served in the Great War: nineteen in all. Several surnames were repeated, including three named Cornish. "Would you have bothered saving us and England," asked Brandon, "had you known we'd then erase ourselves and her?"

He asked without expecting any answer, before again entering and standing at the rear of an old church, where stone dust, not human dust, permeated the air. This time, he stood with company.

As much as sunlight through tall windows, white walls within the church brightened it, as whiteness could. Whoever were the figures in stained glass above them, they'd been worthy of golden halos around their heads. The radiator against the wall behind them was cold, but churches cool on warm days could be warm when days were cool.

"After my mother died," said Laura, stepping forward, "I prayed I would find somebody."

Brandon followed her. "You pray?"

"Death compels us to pray. I didn't pray when I was busy, but I prayed with my mother after my father died. When she died, God was my last friend left."

Brandon remembered the only time he'd prayed. He didn't know his prayers inside that Northallerton church brought Laura to him any more than he knew they hadn't. By chance or a design, she was with him. "English people stopped believing in God," he said.

"Studying peoples in the world who didn't stop, and peoples of other religions, taught me about faith, even if I wasn't paying attention at the time."

The pews were empty, but for a single book in the rearmost pew. Laura stopped, reached down, and picked it up.

"Do you know the story of the Garden of Eden?" she asked Brandon.

"I've never read a Bible."

"Neither had I, a week ago." She opened it and found a page. Keeping it open there, she gave the book to him. "We have the time."

If congregations could seem comfortable in routine, mind games of school and social lives had been no less routine. Brandon took the Bible, sat down in the pew, and read the open page: from the Book of Genesis. The first man Adam and first woman Eve were in paradise, perfectly content, comfortably nude, until their knowledge of original sin shamed them for being naked. They survived their strengths and failings to make men and women who overcame the earth. If he and Laura were Adam and Eve, they were England starting over, with a chance to utilise their knowledge of human history.

Laura sat beside him, slightly apart from him. The more Brandon read, the longer he knew she would sit there. He daren't move away when she might move, or he would need to choose where he sat returning to her: closer or not closer to her.

As he did with books, Brandon turned to the final chapters. He could then turn back to earlier pages.

"If divine rapture carried God's people away," said Laura, "it hasn't taken you or me. If this is not the end time, it might be when we die."

Brandon thought carefully for something to say, but he didn't mean to challenge or contradict her. When he finished reading, he closed the Bible and placed it beside him, away from her.

She was the first to stand, still carrying her golden daffodil. The pews at either side reached the walls, so the only place for them to walk towards the altar was along the centre aisle. Stepping from the pew, Laura moved slowly past the pews to the pulpit, choir stalls, and organ pipes. Before the altar, she stopped, gazing upwards. In the middle of three stained-glass windows above the altar, illuminated just enough by the sun outside, was Christ crucified.

Brandon rose and followed her. When he reached her, he stood close beside her, staring where she stared. The Christ he'd seen alive in Northallerton stained glass was dying in Kirby Knowle, but if He rose from the dead, then so could England.

"I don't want us to die," said Laura, in a muted confessional voice. "I want England to endure."

Without turning, without knowing whether he had anything to lose, Brandon carefully took her hand free, her daffodil in the other. She didn't try to move away. She might've been indifferent to what he did, but let him do it anyway.

Together, they walked slowly along the altar rail. Marble plaques remembered a dead rector, reverend, and their relatives who'd tended to that place and passed away: people known only within those walls and village, but known nevertheless. When he'd held her hand long enough to know she wouldn't rebuff him, Brandon locked their fingers together as lovers did.

They continued admiring together every artwork and memorial, every carved stone and woodwork, around their private church. When they finished, Brandon and Laura stood again at the rear of the church, looking along the aisle to the altar. Brandon released Laura's hand to put his arm around her waist beside him, pulling her a little closer to him. She put her arm around him.

He turned towards her, starting to put his other arm around

her, when she pulled away, leaving Brandon's hands and arms behind. "We are in a church," she said, a small horror in her face.

Brandon withdrew from her, but she offered her arm and hand to him. Again, she let him touch her, their hands sharing a long alluring moment, before she took his hand and led them along the aisle to the altar. There, she let go of his hand and stopped. Facing each other, they stood in long still life, under God inside the glass. "Whatever we do," she said, "we do before God."

Trying to see through her eyes into her mind, Brandon saw only the gentle waters of a tear. He raised his hand prepared to wipe away that tear with the soft side of his finger before it fell, but she turned her face from him. Believing people should only become romantically involved with their friends, Brandon wondered how to kiss a friend.

He placed his hands against her waist, when her face turned back to him. She rested her hands against his arms, dropping her daffodil to the floor. His hands firmed around her, holding her close to him. Erasing any barrier between their timid thoughts unspoken, her arms proceeded around him, embracing him as he embraced her, binding them together.

Moving his face towards her, his eyes closed, never needing to yearn again. With Laura, Brandon felt more fortunate than any other man alive. In their lives without careers and conversations with passing strangers, he'd come to love her very quickly. As gently as he could, more gently than he'd ever before done anything, his lips kissed hers.

8

CANDLELIGHT

Late that afternoon, with the boiler in the basement generating heat and electricity through the castle house, Laura and Brandon's chicken lay roasting on a metal grilling grid beyond a glass oven door in kitchen. Laura used the longest cooking fork she found to prod the bubbling flesh, spitting steam into the air. The drumsticks of the bird bound with string, Brandon used that fork to roll it over. Droplets of fat and moisture fell from the carcass into the tray below it. Laura roasted with it some carrots from a can.

She noticed Brandon watching her. She smiled, and he smiled for her.

Ahead of them was the fullest meal in their new lives and Brandon's fullest meal since before his parents died. It warranted them eating not in the kitchen but in the vaulted dining room.

"I don't want you worrying about electric lights," smiled Brandon, as he set a silver candlestick and candle in the centre of the polished dining table.

Laura set cork place mats with imprinted images of English country villages. They'd found them in a box in a sideboard.

In the house was tableware the like of which Brandon had never before seen. He set silver cutlery and two shining crystal glasses to make it the most formal of settings. "I need you to choose the wine," he told Laura.

With a bottle of white wine, she brought up from the basement a box of fifteen round Whitakers Mint Crème chocolates. "They're for afterwards," she told him, resting the box at one end of the table.

Its skin dark brown with smatterings of black, Brandon carefully drew the roasted bird from the oven and set it on a steel serving plate. With due fanfare, he carried the serving plate from the kitchen to the dining table, where the candle was burning and Laura sat waiting. After holding aloft a large bone-handled carving knife and fork, Brandon stabbed them into their feast, releasing fragrance from the flesh. He served them the thickest meat from the chicken breast and sides.

Sitting across the table from each other, they ate their banquet. "It is tough," said Laura, chewing slower than Brandon did. "I think we should have waited another day before cooking it, to soften it."

The warmth in food, the once familiar full but not overbearing flavour, supplanted the mere sustenance of Brandon's recent meals. Savouring each sensation, picking every morsel, his stomach filled as it hadn't filled for a long time, but after he'd proceeded beyond his first enthusiasm for the meal, his pace of eating slowed. As the sun set outside, the burning candle became their best and soon their only light.

Paused from eating, Laura looked at Brandon squarely in his eyes. The candlelight flickered in her eyes. "If we knew that people," she said, "young people, English people, were coming our way tomorrow, or the day after that, even weeks or months from now, would we have kissed today?"

"We can't live like that: dreaming about people we might never meet, or meet again."

She nodded. "If other women find us, will you still be with me, if I need you to be?"

"We'll still need each other. We'll all still need each other."

"Can I rely upon you, Brandon? Can I trust you?"

"I trust you."

She looked back at her meal, slowly cutting a piece of chicken.

"In another time," she said, "when you would have been settling into your first job or your continuing studies, you could kiss a woman, you could even make love with her, and both of you leave it at that. We're not in such a time. There's only you and me, and we have no middle path." She looked back up at him. "We can be friends or we can be lovers. If we're lovers, we must be willing to be parents, if that's the way things go. Even if we wanted to separate the nexus, we don't have the means to do so, not now."

Brandon took a reluctant sip of wine; he'd not particularly liked it. "I'm only eighteen."

"You were only eighteen this afternoon too, when we kissed. If you're old enough to make love, then you're old enough to be a parent, but we can't be parents if I don't know you'll help our child when he or she needs both of us, that you'll protect your child at least as much as you'll protect yourself. You can do whatever else you like, with whomever else you like if we find other women, but still I need to know that any child you father with me can count upon you. I need to know that, whatever other people might require of us or we require of them, or even we desire of them, you will support me if I need you."

Their conversation was without precedent in Brandon's life, when women made decisions about their lives and men never thought to ask. She led him to a place he'd never before been, but she'd been doing that since first they met.

"That's a lot to ask of you when you're only eighteen years old," continued Laura, "but England getting old means the last of us must grow up very quickly. We have no clergy to marry us, no registry to record us, but I need to know that you'll think of any child we make as Master or Miss Frewer and so me as Mrs Frewer, at least in his or her regard."

Brandon ate silently, begging for that chance at loving her, kissing her, with time to wait and see what they both wanted. If he could have been a robin in the rafters watching another man in his position, he would have hidden there, instead of sitting in her sight. He'd thought they might confide everything in each other, but he couldn't confide his separation from her.

"We both know what England needs of us," she resumed,

"and, I think now, what we personally need. I think we always did. Do England and we need it of us, together, with each other?"

Brandon finished eating. The bones and other inedible bits of chicken to the side, he placed his knife and fork together in the centre of his plate, as his mother taught him to do at the end of every meal. When he looked back up at Laura, she was again staring at him, past the candle. Only that slow wick burning, that single flame of fire, lit her face.

Laura finished eating. She picked up her plate and empty glass, walked around the table, and succinctly kissed his cheek, as if he'd done something good. She left the room.

Brandon collected his plate and glass and followed her to the kitchen, where she'd already switched on a small electric light. He pushed her fewer scraps of dinner onto his plate.

"Without anything else to do," Laura said to him, "people can wonder and merely wonder, or they can also start to think. I commissioned advertising programmes to encourage people to wonder, without wanting them to think; that was strictly for new entrants challenging the market leaders and Natural Valley stopped being a new entrant a long time ago. Wondering was another fad we followed without progressing. Wondering alone is travelling without reaching anywhere."

"I don't know how to be a parent," confessed Brandon.

"Neither do I."

"I don't know anything about babies and little children. I can't even recall being one."

With his torch in hand to guide him, Brandon carried the plate out of the house, across the courtyard and down the driveway. The exercise helped settle his stomach, and his brief time away from the house might've been good for both of them. He tipped the scraps of food over the familiar hedge.

His torch lit his way back towards the castle house, which was ominous in the night as it hadn't been by day. In the courtyard, he paused to point his torch upwards. The round beam fractured in the random crevices of the roughly cut rock wall and breached the parapets. He couldn't know if ghosts were hiding there.

Brandon returned to the kitchen, where Laura had rinsed the

cutlery and plates and left them by the sink. She or he would wash them in the morning. The chicken they hadn't eaten was on a plate on a shelf in the refrigerator, to be a later meal.

Laura wasn't in the dining room, but she'd taken her box of chocolates. Brandon sealed the cork back in the neck of the bottle of wine. He extinguished the weak candlelight.

The only light shining downstairs was the kitchen little light, until Brandon extinguished it. Lights upstairs guided him up to the galleried landing, past the master bedroom, towards his bedroom. The door to Laura's room was closed, with a strip of light shining beneath it.

Brandon stood there alone, imagining her removing her clothes beyond the door, wondering if she wanted him to knock. He was ignorant of everything.

The time elapsed enough for her to change into her nightdress and prepare for bed. The sound of an electric switch could have been the small light beside her bed. The light below the door vanished into night, as she extinguished the main light in her room. She was climbing into her bed.

She must've been established in that bed when Brandon retired to his bedroom. He switched on the small light beside his bed, removed his clothes, and dressed into his pyjamas. He climbed into his cold bed and extinguished the small light.

Brandon stared upwards into the night, wondering if she was thinking about him as much as he thought of nothing except her. He could still feel their last embrace, hours earlier in the church: the touch of her skin against his.

Away from the peace of villages, England's melancholy glory lay under deathly grey, while people from other lands were alive with their small children. Reasons not to be parents had always been pathetic in his and Laura's former population and could not pertain to their society of two, but the reasons lingered in Brandon's brain. Without Laura's knowledge of nature prevailing over postmodern lunacy, he couldn't lose the facile fears that swelled inside his modern mind.

Dim light appeared across his room. Brandon turned his head to see the door a little open, the light coming from somewhere beyond it.

"Are you awake?" whispered Laura.

If he'd closed the door, then he hadn't noticed her opening it. He might've left it open. "Yes," said Brandon.

She closed the door. She might not have heard him.

Brandon rose from his bed, following the strip of lesser light under the door until he opened it. The light illuminating the landing came from the master bedroom, but wasn't the bright light of the middle of a room. The light shining was the table lamp at the near side of the bed.

Reaching the open door, Brandon saw Laura sitting at the end of the massive bed, looking away from him towards the big bay windows. She was still dressed as she'd been dressed earlier that evening, leaving Brandon a little embarrassed to be in his pyjamas: pyjamas he'd brought with him from home. Beside her was the box of mint crème chocolates she'd brought up from the basement earlier that evening.

"Do you mind if I sit with you?" he asked her.

She took the box of chocolates in her hand, making room for him on the eiderdown but also offering the box to him. He shook his head. His feet relaxed by the warm, soft carpet in that room, he stepped towards her and sat beside her, almost slipping from the soft mattress.

"Nobody taught me about relationships," said Brandon, "and I never thought to ask."

"I don't know much," she said, almost philosophically. "There was only Ogden, and not as much to that relationship, not physically, as you probably presume."

Brandon laughed, a little nervously. "The boys and girls at school who talked about relationships never said anything helpful."

"My friends were too determined not to be like our mothers. Even I wanted to be different to my mother, and I at least liked her. I think we ended up becoming too much like our fathers."

"I don't think that the boys and girls with whom I sat in school wanted to be like anyone we knew," said Brandon, "even if we were."

"It's different for men. Most men don't know their fathers, so they don't have to try not to be like them."

"May I?" asked Brandon, reaching his hand to the box of chocolates. He took one; the mint crème was much nicer than the truffle had been.

Laura laid back on the eiderdown, her feet still on the floor and the box of chocolates still in her hand. "We can just lie here," she said.

Having swallowed his small chocolate, Brandon also lent back, looking up at the plaster ceiling. "I feel self-conscious in my pyjamas," he said.

She giggled, and sat up again. "I'm sorry." Brandon sat up again with her. "You'll probably find a dressing gown in the dressing room," she said, motioning her head towards the open door to the right of the bay windows. "I never saw him in anything but a suit, or something close to it, but Ogden's father was the regal sort of man who'd wear a dressing gown before he let anyone see him in his pyjamas."

Brandon stood up from the bed. He walked to and through the dressing room door.

Switching on the light, he saw the dressing room contained cupboards, closets, and wardrobes. Opening a door to the larger wardrobe, he saw only women's clothes: Ogden's mother's clothes. Opening the door to the smaller wardrobe, he saw hanging several men's day and dinner suits, along with a deep green silk dressing gown. He removed the dressing gown and put it on him. The gown was loose, as such gowns might have been meant to be; Brandon had never before worn one.

Posed before a full-length mirror, the gown looked rather good on him and he in it, as if he were meant to wear it. It was almost aristocratic, and so he was almost aristocratic. It also made him seem much older.

Returning to the open door back into the master bedroom, having switched off the dressing room light, Laura watched him from the end of that massive bed. "Very suave," she smiled.

To the right of him, coming through the big bay windows in the dead of night, shone the moon. It was fuller and brighter than when last he saw it, the night his parents died.

Laura must have noticed him looking out, for she stood up and moved towards the glass. Soon, they stood together, staring across the land at night. The only lights were the moon and stars of night, along with the reflection of the table lamp behind them.

Perhaps it was the moon and lights of stars in the eternal universe they connoted. Perhaps it was them standing so close together at such a bulging window from the master bedroom of such a castle house, overseeing the night. Perhaps it was the silken dressing gown, in which he already felt so comfortable. He was at home in that gown, room, and house, as was the woman at his side. "Waiting for a better time won't change anything, will it?" said Brandon. "There won't be better times."

He turned to her, collecting his thoughts into words he could say aloud. She looked back at him.

"I am old enough to love," he told her, "with all that love entails."

She continued staring at him, as if expecting him to qualify his words. He did not. "Is this our home, then?" she asked him, pensively perhaps. "Is this our room?"

Laura gave him time to think and to finish thinking, in the silence of that solemnity between them. He nodded.

She stepped away from him into the middle of the room, where she looked around the walls and furniture: the polished dressing table and the king-sized bed. Taking away her box of chocolates, she left the room.

Hearing her walk along the landing back to her room, seeing the furthest reach of light cast from it, Brandon wondered whether he should still think of that other room being her room. Her room had become his, the master bedroom, in which he stood alone for the first time. In spite of the only light shining within the room being a table lamp by the bed, that room seemed much bigger than it had previously seemed. The house seemed bigger than it had previously seemed, since first he saw it: room for two, or more.

She took so long a time to return to that room, Brandon wondered whether she would, that night. He might have misunderstood her. She might have misunderstood him.

The mahogany valet stand stood empty, until Brandon removed his silk dressing gown and hung it there. Dressed again in only his pyjamas, Brandon switched off the table lamp, leaving only the light from her bedroom shining along the landing towards that open door and him. He walked around the bed to the far side from the door, away from where she'd come. He raised the eiderdown and sheets and climbed into the cool bed: his bed, knowing his body would soon warm it.

The sheets had been presumably untouched for however many months or years had passed since the last nobleman and woman to sleep there had travelled to Milan, or perhaps since Auntie Eustice set them there. Brandon couldn't recall the Lombardy uprising, among all the uprisings around the West. If he sat upright with a pillow behind his back, waiting for Laura, that might be presumptuous. Instead, he lay flat, as he had already lain in a bed that evening, looking upwards.

Her quiet voice again intervened. "Are you awake?" she whispered.

Brandon sat upright, away from the wall behind him, and turned towards her. In the open doorway she stood in silhouette against the light beyond her: a long nightdress giving form to her figure he'd not previously seen. "I'm not sleeping well tonight," he replied.

She turned away and left again. The light around her illuminated the silver silk she wore.

The light down the landing extinguished, the house was darkened. The room was dark, as Brandon hadn't previously seen it.

Her footsteps were just enough for Brandon to hear Laura returning to their room, closing the door behind her. She lifted up the eiderdown and sheets and climbed under them into the bed, their bed, the mattress dipping slightly as she lay upon it, drawing him a little towards her. She nestled close to him, peacefully among the pillows, in the middle of their world.

Waiting for her to say or do anything more, Brandon thought of stretching his arm along the pillow to place his arm around her, but didn't. Through the darkness, he guessed where her face lay.

She lay there quietly, close to him. Less confident than she'd been, Brandon wondered whether he should touch her. She might've wanted him to say something, but he couldn't choose the words to say. She might've been falling to sleep, but he couldn't sleep with her beside him.

Laura leant across to him and kissed him briefly on the cheek, again as if in gratitude or recognition for what he'd done or hadn't done. She cuddled close beside him, warming him, her head rested against his chest. Unfamiliar with experience like the one he made with Laura, Brandon looked upwards into nothing.

He had never before shared a bed. Neither might Laura.

The time since they had met was very short, but that time together was the shared time of weeks and months in the lives England once led. English society had died, those lives lost, and England fallen. Certainty for life had vanished in the twinkling of old eyes, but had set Brandon on a path of paths that brought him by chance and trust to lie with Laura in that bed: two souls he'd come to know.

If Laura loved him as they lay together, he didn't know if she loved him as he loved her. She hadn't talked to him of love, as he hadn't talked to her. He thought of waking her to tell her that he loved her, but would not disturb her from her sleep, if she was sleeping. When only fools would try to think, he hoped that she was happy.

Too many people had died or gone away for Brandon not to fear that he would wake alone in the new morning without his love and life. He might have been lying alone beside her even then, if in fact he'd failed to woo her. With nothing left to think, but still too much time for thinking, his mind was running far away.

Foolishness might have fed his imagination, for Laura was unlike the people who had died, but still he feared that he would lose much more on top of all he had already lost. He wanted to remain awake with her all night and never let her go. Sometime through it all, before or after she fell asleep, when what might have been forever might've merely been a minute, Brandon finally fell to sleep.

9

THE GAMES ROOM

Brandon woke in the morning, collecting his mind and eyes, with the bed beside him empty. He retrieved his dressing gown from the valet stand, before seeing Laura in the dressing room. Wearing her long silk nightdress, she'd placed a hat on her head. The hat was too large.

"Good morning," said Laura, as she returned the hat to a wardrobe. She took another hat, but it was also too large.

"Good morning." The men's hats were too large for Brandon's head.

They inspected the many men's and women's clothes in the wardrobes in that room, with the care they would treat new clothes in a store rather than the collective hand-me-downs they were. "I remember Ogden's mother wearing this to a reception in the Golden Lion Hotel," said Laura, of a sparkling black dress. "My family wasn't like his. I feared I could never emulate her."

Laura stood before a full-length mirror holding a bright blue frock in front of her. She arched her back, posing with it. She then took a paler blue strapless long dress, holding it before her reflection. She took it into what had been her bedroom, as if that remained her private space, closed the door behind her, and locked it.

Brandon picked out samples of Ogden's father's clothes. He didn't need to dress into them to know he was too tall and thin to wear them.

Her door reopened, Laura reappeared wearing the paler blue dress exposing her pale shoulders and hugging her wide breasts, curved into her waist, and hanging over her hips and legs. A silken scarf draped from her neck. She returned to the dressing room where she faced the mirror.

Her fresh white face and figure, blue eyes, and flowing brown hair modelled clothes for an aged continent. "You look beautiful," said Brandon.

She turned and twisted to see her dress from every side in the reflection, until her motion slowed. Her smile slowly subsided from her face, merely looking at what she saw, until she stood motionless before her mirror image. "It's of no consequence, is it?" she said. "The clothes we wear?"

Brandon couldn't answer her. He didn't think he should.

Laura wandered back into her bedroom and closed the door. Brandon wearing his pyjamas and dressing gown placed his bare feet in his shoes to walk outside into the courtyard, as any owner of that home could. The sun that day was warm, the sky above him blue. He retrieved from his car his best clothes and shoes.

Having showered, Laura reappeared wearing a simple white blouse atop a long dark skirt. Her full hair was neatly curled, flowing sprightly around her face and to her shoulders. "I needed to look good in my job; we all did," she said. "Only people who were brilliant could pretend they didn't care about their appearance, but they still spent hours and money to pretend they didn't. We made fashions our best friends, losing ourselves in labels like they were real."

Using what had been his bedroom much as Laura used what had been hers, Brandon showered. He dressed for the day, wearing his best clothes.

Laura was in the master bedroom, their new, shared bedroom. She placed her two photographs of her parents on the dressing table.

"Which bedroom was Ogden's room?" asked Brandon.

"Upstairs was for the family. I only ever saw the ground floor."

The wardrobe and chest of drawers in what been Brandon's room were empty. With Laura following, he checked other bedrooms, apart from the master bedroom and room that been hers. At the far end of the floor was another bedroom with a dressed bed and en-suite bathroom, but with several men's jumpers in different colours and patterns folded in the drawers.

Laura stood before the jackets and trousers hanging in the wardrobe. "Ogden was a snappy dresser," she said.

"Was he about my height and build?"

"To a point."

Brandon didn't try to dress into Ogden's clothes. They weren't his to do so.

He and Laura emptied most of their possessions from their cars into their castle home. They brought their toiletries to the master bedroom en-suite bathroom, mixing some of them with bars of soap and shampoo bottles already there. They'd brought so many with them, they left most in what had been their bedrooms. All that remained in Brandon's car, parked beside Laura's car in the basement garage, were his stock of torches and unused batteries, tools, and consumables for his car in the boot.

Anything Aunt Eustice left in the house wasn't Laura's or Brandon's to discard. There was space enough in the cupboards and closets of their new dressing room for them to push aside Ogden's parents' clothes and accommodate theirs. They removed enough undergarments from the chests of drawers to accommodate theirs, consigning those cast-off underclothes to dark corners in out-of-the-way second-floor bedrooms.

The last room on the second floor, at the far end of the house, was the lengthy games room: the second biggest room in the house after the drawing room downstairs. The polished block parquetry floor reflected the bright lights outside through long opposing walls of windows, one looking back towards the courtyard and grass, the other overlooking the servants' cottage and woods. A lounge suite at one end of the room and chaise lounges beneath the windows lay under white linen covers.

Their tasks for the day complete and with nothing obvious for them to do, Laura retired there with her unfinished box of mint crème chocolates. She stood at the billiard table, hidden until Brandon pulled away its satin cover. Its green velvet cloth remained pristine and sturdy dark timber frame impeccable. The white and coloured balls, presumably however many of them were supposed to be there, lay in a tray at the side, stowed where the last game played there left them.

Against the wall was the rack of half a dozen cues and a small shelf with cubes of blue chalk. Above that were the scoring rollers returned to zero for both players, above which rested a wooden triangle.

"Ogden tried to teach me how to play snooker," said Laura, "at the home of some friends of his in Easingwold. This table might be the reason he played so well."

"Am I supposed to be like him?" asked Brandon, taking the white cue ball from the side of the table and setting it on the velvet. He took a billiard cue from the rack, leant against the table, rested his hand on the velvet and the cue on his hand, and prepared to strike the ball towards a pocket.

Laura reached across the velvet and rolled the ball into the pocket, down which it dropped. "You're supposed to stay alive," she told him.

Brandon returned the cue to the rack, before walking around the room, the heels and soles of his shoes squeaking on the parquetry floor. The chess set remained untouched. The flag of England lying on a table almost made him think he should be there, as nothing else did. "What are we doing here?" he asked her, turning back to her.

Laura had remained beside the billiard table. She looked around the room, as she'd done when she entered the room and as she'd done two days earlier when first they entered it, before looking back at him. If her long gaze at him was time for her to think, she needed a lot of thought, before finally replying, "Eating chocolate."

Whatever she meant by those words, Brandon wasn't going to learn from the end of the room. He walked slowly towards her, over a rug and the parquetry floor, until he stood beside her. Without taking any chocolates, he took the box from her, removed the lid, and placed the lid underneath the box. A dozen or so round chocolates remained there, laid out orderly in rows. He offered Laura the open box.

She continued looking at him, more thoughtfully than inquisitively. He looked further into her eyes, offering her the same soul of him he sought in her.

After a time, she leant a little closer to him. As if the chocolates weren't all the same, her pinched fingers playfully searched them and picked one. Instead of bringing the round mint chocolate towards her mouth, she brought it to his. He started to withdraw, but her hand followed him until she pressed the chocolate against his lips. Only then realising what she was doing, he opened his lips and bit the chocolate.

Her seducing eyes never leaving his, she brought the chocolate that Brandon hadn't eaten back to her mouth. Slowly, she bit it, taking another part of it in her mouth.

The last portion of chocolate, she returned to his mouth. He stopped chewing what he'd already taken and opened his lips. Her fingers rolled the last chocolate piece between his lips towards his tongue. His lips feeling her fingers, she slowly pulled them away.

Laura took the box of chocolates from his hand. Before she could offer him any, Brandon put his back to the side of the billiard table, pressed his hands at each side of him on its wooden frame, and pushed himself up so he sat on it. Laura moved closer to him, offering him the box.

Brandon took a chocolate from the box and slowly moved it around the air close to her face, teasing her. Her welcome eyes watched it encircling her mouth, gradually moving closer to her. She snapped forward and quickly bit it.

She pulled away, leisurely chewing the chocolate, but Brandon's fingers remained there, holding the uneaten portion. Her first portion of that chocolate eaten, her mouth returned to his fingers. Taking the rest of the chocolate in her mouth, her soft lips touched his fingers, remaining with them. She watched his eyes, her massaging lips remaining at his fingers, as she chewed. Laura had fast become the most sensual woman he'd ever known.

That chocolate finished, she walked across the room to a

cocktail cabinet, atop of which she left the box of chocolates. She opened the cabinet door, inspected the selection, and removed a bottle and glass. After pouring herself a portion, she dragged the white linen cover from the sofa and sat at one end of it, crossing her legs, holding her glass. "If you're too young for wine," she told Brandon, licking her lips, "you're much too young for Cointreau."

Brandon stepped down from the billiard table, walked towards her, and sat beside her on the comfortable cotton sofa. Before she'd drunk from it, he took the glass from her hand. Taking a mouthful, keeping the liqueur in his mouth, he rested the glass on the floor. He held her head in his hands, pressing his hands through her hair, massaging her mind. Putting his lips to hers, opening her mouth with his, Brandon's tongue helped the liqueur to her mouth.

Touch brought them closer than words could ever make them. They continued kissing together, her face softer than he'd known a face could be. His roving hands rubbed her sides and stomach through the fabric of her blouse, circling closer to her breasts. She became tense, but didn't move.

His eyes fell from her face to her cotton blouse, with white buttons fastened in their buttonholes. Brandon brought both his hands to the uppermost button, drawing her attention. Her hands pressed down upon it, but he slowly pulled them away, kissing her lips as he did. Laura let him carefully pull the button free.

Her blouse like a small bed sheet might have opened a little, without revealing anything of her. Another button and another unfastened, her blouse separated just enough to reveal hints of her pale chest.

Some buttons of her blouse came away more easily than others, forced through their buttonholes, exposing the white lace trimmings of her bra. Finally dragging her blouse from her skirt, her legs no longer crossed, Brandon released the last buttons.

Her open blouse hung loosely from her shoulders. Brandon drew apart her lapels, unwrapping her chest and cleavage. Her bra enveloped her ample breasts.

Brandon dipped his head and, his cheeks pushing her blouse aside, he kissed her rising flesh. Her skin climbing into gorgeous mountains, he ran his tongue along her bra lace and cups, sometimes slipping between them and her every curve and feeling. Laura rested her hand on the back of his head, keeping him at her bra and breasts, while he tasted the senses of her skin, so lovely to his lips.

When he could do no more for her there, Brandon sat upright again. She pulled her hand from his head, as he started to pull at one side of her blouse. She drew back her arm for him to pull her blouse from her shoulder and arm. She dropped her other arm. With his other arm around her back pulling at her blouse, the rest of her blouse fell easily from her shoulder and arm.

Slowly, Brandon reached his arms around her to the back of her bra. His hands and struggling fingers couldn't release the clasp, so she reached her hands behind her, briefly touching his, and released it.

Her bra fell a little loose. Her breasts fell a little forward. His hands pulled the straps of her bra from her shoulders, so they fell short ways down her arms. Her bra rested on her breasts, before he pulled the straps a little more and the whole bra fell away.

Her audacious white-pink breasts hung naked before him. He picked up her glass from the floor and, holding it above her heart, delicately poured the liqueur onto her skin. She giggled at his indiscretion, as the liqueur slipped over her breast, falling around her nipple. He placed his face against her flesh and softly licked the trickling liquid.

He kissed her breasts, tasting the liqueur as he rolled her nipple between his lips and tongue. He poured more liqueur onto her other breast, dripping towards her waist. Reaching down, his tongue collected liqueur that he guided into her navel, before licking it away. He returned her glass to the floor.

"I was wrong," she said, half naked. "You are old enough for Cointreau."

While he kissed her again, he loosened the soft belt around her waist and unfastened a button and a zipper from her skirt.

He ran one hand across the firm skin and spine of her bare back and body and the other under her legs, lifting her onto his lap.

Her feet above the floor, Brandon pulled away her shoes. Again kissing her but struggling a little with her sitting on his lap, he removed her stockings from her waist. The palms of his hands and fingers rolled her stockings down her long smooth legs, until they fell finally to the floor. Kissing her when he could, his hands dragged her white pants from her hips, until her legs became thin enough for him to flick them away.

Thus Laura lay completely naked across his lap, while Brandon sat concealed in all his clothes. He kissed her sweet skin while his hands and fingers worked to stimulate her, feeling her as she felt herself. Her head fell back over his right arm and mouth hung open, slipping beyond her mind's control. Pampered womanhood, she writhed in pleasure for both their benefit, her eyes closed in ecstasy for her. He aroused her in her glamour, sighing with him for both of them to feel. The seductress had become the seduced.

Priming his muscles, she became light in his embrace. Her pure white body seemed to float, as Brandon lofted her high in his arms. Laura might've laughed, before he carried her exalted across the room to the billiard table. Past the rim and pockets, he laid her onto the green velvet.

Opening her unfolding self to the air, Laura reclined art-like in her magic nakedness and sovereignty stretched before him. Resplendent in her resting royalty, he tenderly kissed her forehead, and edges of her eyes. He kissed her ears, the little lobes, rolling them with his tongue; her cheeks caressed his cheeks as his caressed hers. He kissed her strong nose, gently mellow skin around her mouth, tender lips again, and supple chin. She arched her neck back inviting him to press his mouth against her long arced throat.

He kissed her naked shoulder, savouring her. He kissed her arm and hand, intoxicated with her. His lips gliding over her, he kissed her tender thigh, knees, and calves of her shapely curving legs. Completing his grand journey, he kissed her firm ankle and soft feet, his love complete.

Brandon stepped back to see her better. All his senses were of loving fervently the woman nude before him: her heart, mind, and precious soul. He would surrender every battle or wage every war for her. The world might have expired but he could forgive all of it for going, if he could wrap himself in her and never leave her.

The clothes that kept him from naked love burdened him, unsettling him that all the love was his for her. If she were to leave him, then she should leave him then, but she should tell him she was going before he cried too much. If everything he did he did for her then she should tell him so, and he would gladly do it all again.

Laura slowly sat up, dragging her legs over the side of the billiard table. She held out her arms towards him.

Brandon returned to her. He lifted her from the table to the polished parquetry floor.

She took a button midway up his shirt, embarrassing him not to be as beautiful as she was. She grappled with the button, but he believed everything her fingers said of her. He expressed nothing to disturb her concentration, while she became more certain of what she did. Finally, she released the button.

Every accidental touch of her fingers as she found and unfastened another button excited him, until she reached the last button above his trouser belt, pulled up the last reaches of his shirt sliding against his skin, and unfastened it. She knelt down to the floor and untied the laces of his shoes, whereby he raised his foot for her to remove that shoe. She slowly pulled away his sock, leaving it on the floor. He raised his other foot, and she took away that shoe and pulled away that sock.

Laura slowly reached up and unfastened the buckle on his belt. She tried to pull the long leather belt through the loops around his trousers, but couldn't do so. The ends of the belt hanging from his waist, Brandon drew in his stomach to help her loosen the button on his trousers. She slowly pulled down the zipper, whereby his trousers fell to the floor.

She stood up before him, when he held out his open hands and arms for her to unfasten the buttons at the end of his shirt sleeves. He helped her pull his shirt from his shoulders and arms, as she'd helped him pull her blouse from her. Only his underclothes remained, until she pulled them down his legs as he'd pulled her pants from hers, until they reached the floor. Brandon stepped away from them and the rest of his clothes there.

They thus stood naked before each other, wholly exposed and vulnerable, without secrets or shame. Softly she kissed his chest, empowering him before her. She knelt down and kissed his masculinity.

Again she stood before him. Looking into her eyes, her hanging breasts were too big for his open hands to hold. He held them upright, soothed them down. His hands in unison moved around her malleable flesh, working her breasts, manipulating them.

Brandon bent his knees, lowering himself. Her great breasts were as beautiful every time they confronted him as they were the first time he unveiled them. His moving mouth massaging her, he kissed each of her breasts in turn, tasting her, adoring her. Feeling her nipples through his mouth and face, almost chewing them, he would've eaten them if he could.

Gracefully kneeling to the floor, Brandon's hands rested on her thighs. Amidst her gentle curves, his tongue slipped into her navel, played there, and slipped onto her skin around it. Her dry warm skin squeaked against his cheeks. Reciprocating what she'd done, his face brushed her femininity.

He stood again. Laura took his hand, and led him to a window and chaise lounge, still under a white cloth.

She might have lost her balance and so fallen onto the long lounge, dragging him down with her. Poised above her, held up by his strong arm, Brandon looked upon her his wife lying below him. Looking up at him, her husband, from among her long curls of luscious hair, Laura's arms lay loose beside her. He stared into the light and darkness of her eyes and knew the woman there, never more glorious than she was glorious then.

Laura was strong enough to get away from him but she remained, surely knowing what he was about to do. He lowered his face towards her.

His tongue sliding into her mouth, their swelled tongues wrestled like playing lion cubs in a warm water den, trying to suck her soul from her mind to bring it into his, while his free hand caressed her heaving breasts and fingers held her tightening nipples. They made unyielding love, without compromise or conjecture, vibrant and poetic amidst each other. Amidst the mania bursting back, Brandon pressed their flesh together, feeling her through him in their euphoria.

Silently he lay upon her, feeling her from every end of their long bodies. Content within their unity, he lay satisfied with everything they ever did. They were the universe.

10

FARMING

Laura and Brandon collected chicken eggs from their coop most days. They cooked them in their kitchen in every style of meal of eggs they knew, without the skills that had been the providence of chefs and other experts. With a frying pan, they poached and scrambled them, treating them with herbs and savouries. They boiled them in a saucepan of water on the stove and, after breaking them and tapping onto them some salt, ate them from eggcups at the table.

Brandon became careful to finish his meals when Laura did, although he wanted her to finish hers more quickly. When they did, they carried their plates of broken shells and other remnants of their food outside the house and dropped them over hedges to adjoining farms.

They cleaned their home after themselves and kept it clean together: washing soiled crockery and cutlery. Returning empty bottles to their places in the wine racks was as good a means as any of dealing with them. They had become the domestic help that most people in lives gone past had rarely noticed, but the people they were helping were each other. They performed less work than people once performed to earn the money to pay for them.

Brandon and Laura talked. When they had nothing more to

say, they sat together. They walked where they had already walked, holding each other's hands. They kissed each other the few times they parted and when they saw each other afterwards.

Like the hollows of trees in which squirrels hoarded nuts, the basement remained a subsistence storehouse of all they needed to eat and drink. They picked from the cellar stores the chocolates the other liked and placed them on the other's lips, in a game of love they played between themselves.

Brandon learnt to hold the buttons of her clothes between the thumb and forefinger of his right hand and deftly pull them through their buttonholes, loosening her clothes, undressing her, at the end of many days. They shared their bed and made their love most nights and sometimes days. The sense of her with him became innate.

Exploring the homes and farms around the castle house, they were careful not to knock anything. There were more hats, clothes, shoes, and slippers than they could ever wear.

They browsed through books, borrowing a few about farming and about preparing food, which they would later return. (None of the books in the castle house were concerned with agriculture. Ogden's family might have already held those skills or, more probably, they employed people who did.) They perused the spines of entertainment disc cases for any films or music they might like.

They closed the doors to seal those homes when they left them, keeping them secure from inclement weather and from birds and wandering animals. The village was as much their home as was the castle house: their myriad estate.

They checked the chickens on the farm at the southern edge of Kirby Knowle, leaving the chicken house door and shutters open for short spells while they were close at hand, replenishing the chickens' feed when required. Wearing the clothes he dedicated for that exercise or other rural labour, Brandon sometimes raced after a chicken, caught it, and starved it for half a day before killing it, without bloodying himself. He and Laura sat by the creek near their castle home and plucked the feathers from the bird, before letting it soften for a day or two and cooking it in their kitchen oven.

Calves had replaced the farmers extracting milk from the udders of grazing dairy cows. Grimacing at first, in spite of the thick gloves he wore, Brandon learnt to draw their milk into steel buckets. He carried two at a time back to the house.

Brandon thought of closing barn doors before storms, but the animals of the farms had survived the winter with them open. The farmers who'd known they'd not return when the weather was tolerable had left them open. The animals wandered back into the barns and outside again at will, remaining healthy without disease or misadventure. Perhaps as good the judges of coming weather as human beings had been, they knew enough what threatened them.

He and Laura had lived their lives distinguishing the animals mulling in the fields from those they ate, but Brandon would learn in time to kill livestock for meat. Each day, he deferred deciding how to slay calves and lambs.

Fruit trees survived around some farms and country houses, providing apples and pears to pick when they matured. Brandon picked one apple from a tree and ate it. He discarded the core in a garden.

Hanging from high hooks in abandoned farmyard sheds, he and Laura found farming tools. Among the pairs of dirty gloves and wellingtons they tried to wear, they kept those that fitted them.

Careful not to stumble on the uneven ground or slip on sodden refuse, they entered the fields that wasted since farmers last tilled them. Among the withered crops that had matured and died, they pulled from the ground enough fresh and nearly fresh vegetables to feed them.

In the stables and other shelters around their castle home were tools for amateur gardeners. Brandon shovelled through a lawn of long, green grass to clear a patch of dark, dank soil. He speared the soil with a gardening fork and dragged a hoe to break and turn it. Removing the dirty glove from his right hand, the moist earth seethed through his pale fingers. The rich material and fertile nutrients would nourish what would become dirty vegetables they ate.

Laura also removed a glove, crouched down, and picked some

tiny hints of soil between her thumb and index finger. "I remember people saying they found touching fertile soil, and green leaves for that matter, fulfilling," she said. "It isn't, but that's all right."

Not needing sprawling fields for future stocks of excess food, they created vegetable gardens for human sustenance. Using a trowel, they planted rows of seeds of vegetables they'd found in barns: broccoli, cabbage, carrots, and cauliflower. Bags of fertiliser fed the soil. Their only irrigation was the rain and rivers, although they sprinkled water on the ground around the seeds whenever a few days without rain let it become a little dry. They would watch and nurture their small crops, until their new food became strong.

Brandon and Laura weren't gardeners, for they didn't tend to plants they couldn't eat or trees not offering them fresh fruit. Brandon cut grass only when he needed to walk on it. He trimmed plants only when he needed space to walk past them.

They weren't farmers, for they weren't producing anything to sell, feeding people they didn't know. Their chores on the farms and in the castle house weren't careers, as work had been for Englishmen and women; they had no grounds for ambition. They had nothing left for which to work except themselves, and did no more than they needed to do to grow the food to eat. If Brandon and Laura could live without that work then they would take that chance. No work alone fulfilled them. They didn't pretend it could.

Tin cans of preserved food from the slowly declining stocks in the cellar stores gave them a small variety of meals, beyond the food they garnered. Beyond the turning of a can opener were exotic seafood from distant oceans, processed meats not recognisable from the calves and lambs in paddocks, and casseroles. The processed meals in sealed packages tasted better than they once did, since their memories of more lavish meals had faded. Living without luxuries no longer theirs, their food remaining was still extravagant aside that in other places.

Those people in other places might never taste wine as Laura and Brandon could taste it every day. That their packaged food would eventually expire made it worth savouring.

Among the bicycles in the stables was a woman's bicycle. Laura adjusted the height of the seat from the frame and the rear vision mirror on the handlebars to make the bicycle hers. Leisurely, she and Brandon rode their bicycles over country roads and paths.

They rode through hamlets and villages in gentle exploration. Churches were the village's biggest buildings, taller than the trees. There weren't any retail shops.

A road slightly uphill was work again. A road slightly downhill was a chance to rest. The air was a freshening breeze into Brandon's face and through his hair that could exhilarate him.

A river flowed well enough to stir a gently whirling flutter into the air. Several ducks swam against the flow to stay where they were.

A lamb looked at them, curious at the distraction. A group of cows below a tree did not.

A hound barked and ran along its side of a fence following them on their bicycles, until it reached another fence and couldn't run any further. It continued barking, calling out to them, while they rode away along the road.

Where animals weren't grazing, long grass could be like waves. Amidst those waves, they saw a mound of grass several feet too high. Laura stopped her bicycle on the road. Brandon stopped his.

At one side of the mound, a space led down into a landing area and a steel door in a concrete frame. After pressing his path over the long grass, Brandon trod down the steps and turned the handle on the door. The door was thick and heavy, but Brandon pulled it open easily.

Affixed to the interior of the door was a large bolt drawn back, for sealing the door from the inside. Stepping forward, daylight shone around him into a dark, windowless room.

Beside Brandon dangled a cord from the ceiling he presumed was ineffective, but he pulled it anyway. A light flickered on, brightening the room.

The room was very large and much too small. Between a concrete roof, walls, and floor, two bunks stood by the wall furthest way from him. A transistor radio, like that from a museum, sat on a desk, with a large battery connected to it. Brandon turned back to see the cord to the light above the door and saw another battery connected to it.

Several cylinders of liquid oxygen stood upright against a wall. Hanging there were several face masks.

Laura stood beside him. "Do you know what Europeans worried about instead of worrying about demographics?" she asked him. "We worried about things that maybe we should once have worried about, but still worried long after we should have stopped worrying. We worried about things we should have never worried about."

The bunker was a refuge from wars that never happened: refuge from the outside air. The concrete, steel, and ground above would've protected people inside it from radiation, gas, or other poisons until the air was again safe to breathe.

Brandon stepped forward to the desk and turned the switch on the transistor radio. Only the sounds of static emanated from the speaker. Rotating a plastic knob through changing frequencies of reception didn't change the noise. Nobody sat at another concrete bunker radio to answer him. Nothing was broadcast to which anyone could listen.

Their fear of war might've consumed the people who'd built the bunker, curtailing their lives. Even if their fear was fairly founded, it was a crass distraction from the perils people hadn't seen were coming. The calamity that caused their world to die wasn't one from which a bunker could protect them. If they'd drawn comfort that the bunker would protect them, it hadn't. They died as England died.

The underground bunker had become a tomb without entombed, but with possessions for the pharaohs in their afterlives. Unlike the pharaoh tombs apparently secure, nobody had bothered to loot the bunker.

Brandon pulled closed the door, without fastening the bolt or turning a small wheel that would have sealed it. He pulled the cord to switch off the light, subjecting them to abject blackness as night would be without stars or the moon. "I was curious," he said.

Laura took his hand, keeping them from losing each other.

His other hand pushed the door open, bring back the sunshine. She led them out, after which he closed the bunker door behind them. They rode back on their way.

South of Kirby Knowle, they rode upon the biggish village of Felixkirk. Laura stopped her bicycle outside the Carpenter's Arms, a pretty white two-storey inn where a sealed courtyard spared the front from the long grass of other places, but not from rotting leaves. If the flowers in the flower boxes under the bay windows and pots hanging from the walls weren't quite as dainty as they once were, they were nevertheless daintier than time had made most other flora. Between the inn and the road stood a few tables and chairs, set up as if guests were coming any minute. Brandon stopped his bicycle beside her.

"I often sat here with Ogden," said Laura.

"We don't have to stop here."

"We were headed to his parents' home and this place, the last place to drink before we got there, helped me to prepare, or we'd been there and it helped me to recover."

Two large wooden barrels marked the way to the front doors, to which Laura led them. Inside the inn, timber beams along the ceilings and the tiled floor exuded old England. The coffee pots on a sideboard did not.

"I wish you could have eaten their Yorkshire pudding for a main course and then their sticky toffee pudding afterwards," said Laura. "I wish we could eat any of their meals; meats and vegetables were fresh and no meals were stored afterwards."

The blackboards still denoted menu items. Brandon didn't believe them.

"They were a bit naughty," continued Laura, "but they could be, near the Moors. Only customers and local people, and I think all the local people were customers, knew they were here. They kept serving pork, ham, and bacon after the government banned them from restaurants all over Britain. They even kept a children's menu long after there stopped being any children, at least children who would eat in a restaurant serving pork, ham, or bacon."

Behind the bar, Brandon pulled the beer handles. The kegs were empty.

From the shelves, Laura took a bottle of Pimm's with lemonade. "Ogden's mother drank Pimm's," she said, "without the lemonade." Laura poured herself a glass. "There's more Pimm's than anything else in the cocktail cabinets in the castle house; you wouldn't have noticed."

"Why then did you drink Cointreau?"

She smiled. "I wasn't ready to be so much like her."

Brandon examined the label on Laura's bottle, with the signature of one James Pimm who'd developed the drink in 1840. Laura should have served it over ice.

"The Cointreau I opened with you had been unopened," continued Laura. "It was probably a gift to Ogden's parents they didn't know where else to keep. The games room was the place Ogden and his father took guests playing billiards or snooker, so it was a place for them to offer it. If they'd ever invited me, I could have drunk it for them."

Brandon poured himself a glass of Pimm's. Holding the glass near his nose, he smelt it, not for anything in particular.

"Rich people drank Pimm's," said Laura. "I guess we're all rich and poor now."

Brandon tasted it a little, as he'd never really tasted the Cointreau. If the lemonade was sweet, then the Pimm's had body.

"We should drink it with fruit," said Laura.

"Next time, we'll have fruit."

Laura led them into the kitchen area, left very clean and orderly. "This wasn't on any menu I read here," she said, standing at an open cupboard door. Inside were several tin cans of baked beans in tomato sauce. "This might have been for guests after the restaurant closed."

"It might be for guests like you and me." Brandon opened a tin.

"My friends and I used to quote the names of chefs, like the names of travel destinations, with such deep esteem," said Laura, serving the beans into two bowls. "I know this is simple food, but I don't mind."

Brandon slipped forks into the bowls. He carried the bottle of Pimm's and lemonade and their two glasses while Laura carried the bowls of baked beans outside, to one of the tables and chairs. The village was their outdoor cafeteria.

"I used to think my life was nice," said Laura, sitting down, "and it was nice – I know it was – but it could've been so much better."

From his chair, Brandon looked around their village of population two. Had England not grown old, he and Laura could still have sat there. People talking with each other might also have talked with them. A stranger in his old town hat might've served them apple cakes. "Do you ever wonder what we're doing?" he asked her. Laura made him think too much of time.

"I like what we're doing, more than I ever thought I would. I've learned to enjoy things I don't buy."

"What do you want now that you didn't think of wanting then," asked Brandon, "now that nothing distracts us?"

She ate a mouthful of beans. "I want to look good because I am good, healthy, not because I'm losing my life to think I look good. I don't want to work so hard."

He sipped some drink. "If you had your time over, what would you have done?"

"I'd have spent more time with people I wanted to know. I'd have done something really important, really worthwhile."

"Like what?"

Laura fell silent, confessing her failure to know. "Maybe I don't like the way things were quite as much as I once did."

"You like Pimm's," said Brandon, leaning forward and tapping his glass against hers.

"I'm glad we can eat and drink what we do," acknowledged Laura, "but I can't help but think there's nothing great about us because of it."

"What about the original Mister Pimm?" asked Brandon, holding his glass close to his face. "What about all the makers of English lemonade. Weren't they great?"

Laura smiled, before taking a mouthful of her drink much fuller than had been her prior sips. "I want to enjoy my drinks without thinking about them."

After refilling Laura's glass and then his, Brandon drank his longest, slowest mouthful. "Food and drink are still sustenance and survival, aren't they," he pondered, "however pleasurable."

"As are our chores at home and on the farms," replied Laura, with the authority of her work beforehand, "perpetuating one day into the next until we die."

"If our sustenance, aren't ends unto themselves, they're means to important things I don't understand. Basking in the journey won't reveal our destination."

"Is it purpose we lack?" asked Laura. "You should only rue what you lack if you're willing to try to get it."

Long after they finished eating their beans and the bottle of Pimm's was empty, Laura and Brandon cleaned their cutlery and crockery as best they could on the grass. They returned them to the inn. Brandon returned the empty bottle to its place on the shelf behind the bar. "Next time," he suggested, "we might drink Cointreau."

"We don't need it," replied Laura, reaching up and kissing him. She took some tinned artichokes from the kitchen.

The farms and houses that had been interesting became less so, again riding around the Vales of York and Mowbray. Every rolling vision past Brandon was like another he had seen, until it became like every other he had seen. However pretty they had been through English eyes, without Englishmen and women, theirs were very hollow homes, subsumed by overgrown grasses and flourishing weeds. Every English village had become a quiet place to sit.

If they continued riding because they were again looking for people, they remained disappointed. With the sun reclining for the day, their journey chasing nobody gained them nothing but the knowledge that nobody was there.

Having taken too long to follow the signs back to Upsall and Kirby Knowle, the moon between the leaves of trees lit their way from Whinmoor Hill, pushing their bicycles up the driveway back towards the castle house. The trees stood high in shadows from the sky, behind which the veil of stars could briefly hide and soon appear again.

Birds of the night, not only owls, made unfamiliar sounds. Outside, Brandon had reason to think of them and roaming animals as he'd not thought of them inside. They shared the darkness, but Brandon was less familiar than they were with the wilderness. Their immediacy made the doors and windows of most homes fickle, barely adequate to avert the encroaching natural world, but not the castle house so resolute.

"This house is all that remains of Ogden's family," said Laura, as they stepped inside, out of the night, switching on a light and quickly closing the door behind them to keep the house warm. "Wouldn't that be awful: to die, and leave nothing behind you but someone else's home? It isn't very much."

The house retained a purpose only because she and Brandon retreated there, but the boiler in the basement depended on gas. Brandon probably couldn't repair it if it stopped working. Everything in time might finally fail, whereby their chance for light and certain heat might lapse. They might need to live again without them, huddled in their home with wood and kindling, keeping close to burning fireplaces, warming each other.

"The stone walls wrapped around us are neat, clean, and pale today," said Laura, "but they will weather and darken." The castle house would again be drab and empty in a soulless country scape, before someday decaying into ruins like Upsall Castle.

11

KEEPSAKES

From the big bay window of their master bedroom, Brandon gazed across the Vale of York. By night, the moon full and bright lit much of the country ground. By day, he imagined lying with Laura among those peaceful meadows, where only birds and animals would know.

One morning, Laura took Brandon's hand and led him to her car. "I've got somewhere I want to show you," she told him.

The castle house had become their home and Brandon rarely thought back to their time before arriving there, but she drove them through Upsall, north again. "We're returning to Northallerton, aren't we?" he said.

Laura parked her car on Crosby Road, outside an aging semi-detached house much like any other. Her childhood home seemed to Brandon very small and plain after the castle house, but it wasn't much smaller and was certainly no plainer than his childhood home had been.

The hinges didn't squeak when she pushed the front door open. She led them through the lounge room, with its walls long ago painted in a cream beige tone of time. Under shelter behind the house were several pieces of wood and kindling. "Did you chop that?" asked Brandon.

"After my father died, I did."

In the garden was a mound of upturned soil, through which rose shoots of grass. A wooden cross had begun to lean, until Laura straightened it. "There's no inscription on the Cross," said Brandon.

"God knows who's there," said Laura, standing up and facing the dirt. "I want to introduce you to Brandon Frewer," she said, addressing the mound of dirt as if her mother might hear. "I'm now Mrs Frewer."

Brandon supposed Laura was right. He'd never heard the term in relation to his mother.

"He's Mister Erian," continued Laura, as she would in introduction.

Brandon didn't know if saying anything aloud to the old lady in the earth would console or offend her daughter. He remained silent.

Laura smiled at his discretion. He smiled with her.

She turned back to face her mother's grave, standing there silently for a time, before reaching down to the ground to pull out a little weed Brandon hadn't previously seen. She went to a side fence and threw the weed over it.

"What else can I do with it?" she asked Brandon. "If you saw next door's garden, you'd know the weed probably originated there."

"Can you see your room?"

Laura led him upstairs to a smallish bedroom. If he'd thought pictures on a wall might have revealed something of her, there were none. She opened the wardrobe door as Brandon wouldn't, revealing several dresses hanging there in space for many more.

"I thought you brought all your clothes with you," said Brandon.

"I left more than this in York," she said.

Among the shelves in that wardrobe with and without clothes on them, was one on which stood five ornaments. Brandon moved closer to them, pushing open the wardrobe door a little more to shed more light.

"They're keepsakes from the longest holiday I ever took," she told him, "after my studies." They implied as much about the little girl as they did about the adult she'd become. "The polar bear is from Norway, the moose from Finland."

The polar bear was a shining crystal glass effigy. The moose was a clay figure, standing awkwardly. Its body much too short for its height and legs so close together might have made it easier to mould and easier to stand. "You don't do pets?" asked Brandon.

"The polar bear is a stranger," she told him. "The moose is a show-off."

"They're both beautiful."

"They're both dangerous."

Brandon turned to three clay pottery structures. Two were like castle towers from ancient fairy tales, with patches of white enamel snow and whimsical decorations.

"The castle without turrets is from Lithuania," said Laura. "The one with them is from Latvia. It broke when I brought it back here, but my father glued it back together and people couldn't see where it was broken, unless they looked very closely."

"I won't look closely," said Brandon, staring at the castle in its entirety. "So you didn't always hide them in a cupboard?"

"I stood them in my living room in my flat in York. A lot of my clothes, furniture, and other stuff I left there when I returned home, but these I brought with me."

"Why hide them?"

"I wanted to keep them, where they couldn't be accidentally broken. I didn't want to be reminded every day of Europe, my time in York, Ogden, being young."

One castle had round towers. The other had openings to the roof. Their differences were trite by comparison with their similarities, as they were with the castle house.

The third structure was a simple square tower. "The smaller one is from Estonia," she said.

In all three clay ornaments stood small unlit candles, waiting to burn. "Have you ever burnt candles in them?" asked Brandon.

She looked long at him, as she hadn't for some time. "Will you think I'm silly?" she asked him.

"When have I thought you were silly?"

She looked down to the floor. "In the last moments of her life, I promised my mother I would light those candles in one circumstance, but only that circumstance." She raised her right leg a little and rubbed the front tip of her shoe on the floor. "I promised her I would light a candle when I knew I was pregnant." She then looked back at Brandon. Her expression had become more serious than it had been, looking at his eyes. "Do you want us to have children?"

He studied her eyes for truths her words might not express. "Do you?"

"It mightn't be my decision anymore," she said, reserving most of her thoughts to herself.

Brandon didn't know if the issues were hers alone or also his. He hadn't found a paternal sense in him.

"What would we do if I became pregnant?"

Any pregnancy would be far more onerous upon her than it needed to be upon him. "What should we do?"

She sat at the end of her bed. "Sometimes, being just two of us leaves me feeling we haven't any chance. The people in York and other places will eventually come for us. I won't prevent myself from becoming pregnant and won't end a pregnancy if I do, but sometimes I start not to care whether I fall pregnant."

No woman Brandon once knew had done so much. "We should take the clay towers with their candles with us," he said to her, "back to the castle house."

She nodded, standing up. "There are three clay towers," she said. "There are three candles."

"We have the space."

The larger towers separated into two parts each, along with their candles. They were lighter and more fragile than Brandon imagined clay replicas to be. Laura wrapped them in spare clothes and set them in a box.

She then took the sturdier moose and polar bear and slipped them into the sides of the box. Looking up at her and Brandon, the moose might've smiled.

He carried the box to her car more carefully than he'd carried anything else in his life, even Laura. She pointed him to a place in the boot in which he set the box, before closing the boot.

"In the kitchen," she grinned at him, "we have a whole box of candles."

Brandon hesitated, looking back at the house and then at her again, before leaning forward and briefly kissing her. "We can come back again, later."

She drove them slowly around her childhood town, telling him stories of where she'd been to school, places her parents shopped and worked, and people she had known. Brandon listened to the voice of a younger woman and the girl still in her head, telling him her reminiscences of many lives and one. If she thought most about her parents, he thought most of her. The small girl had become a woman, and every memory reflected in her heart made her more complete to him. Her parents began a continuum in her life, and Brandon wondered what time would make of the continuum through him.

Around the grassy, flowered roundabout where East Road met Thirsk Road, the homes and shops on three corners and most of the fourth corner were the comfortable old premises one or two storeys high common around Northallerton. Brandon had stopped thinking of their prettiness, until he saw a darkly building without it.

Built in the late twentieth century, when beauty was old fashioned and the future foreboding (although not for the reasons England then thought), was a grey-black building block. Too few windows along East Road suggested death would be relief. Too many windows in the pedestrian façade facing the roundabout meant nothing left to say.

"Is that the morgue," asked Brandon, "with viewing space for spectators?"

"It's the public library," Laura told him, stopping her car. "I know it's ugly, the ugliest building in Northallerton, maybe all of Yorkshire. I sometimes think the architect declared he didn't want to be an architect or a council bureaucrat decided he did. The only people who came here for the architecture were the only ones who shouldn't have: architecture students."

Brandon and Laura stepped outside. Thankfully set below and back from road level, the library appeared a little shorter than its two or something storeys.

Laura led them down the path to the library forecourt, much as she'd led them throughout the day and through most of the weeks (or was it longer) since Brandon met her. Leaves that had fallen or blown into that confined space had never been blown away, making the rotten rug underfoot thicker than rotten rugs of leaves had been along the pavements. Plants covered most of the fading sign that the building was the Northallerton Library and Information Centre, although Brandon wasn't expecting information. With cover overhead, the premises beyond the glass-panelled double doors were unduly dark.

"My mother used to come here," said Laura. "When she fell sick, I did: I brought her books. She said she'd rather sit with a good book from a bad library than a bad book from a good one. I think she meant the library building being good or bad. It's actually a very good library in a very bad building."

Public libraries were their best repositories of books: wisdom to peruse, parting amusement. The works of fiction and less often of fact, of science and history, were their leisure and education. Brandon and Laura could read them without cost to a future they would never see. "I don't have a library card," said Brandon.

"My mother did."

The library doors were locked. Brandon pushed the right-side door, which moved a short way along its hinges until a metal locking bolt pressed against a hole in the left-side door. The left-side door was bolted fast to the ground and door frame above it.

With his hands on both doors, Brandon pushed them both. The bolts didn't break from their holes. He let the doors slip back again.

Without the threat of determined thieves and vandals, public libraries had been less secure from theft than other buildings. People purloined books by subterfuge rather than force.

Brandon kicked the centre of the doors. The thud of wood and glass vibrating resounded through the air. In case the doors and lock were weakening, Brandon pushed the doors again, forcing the bolts against their sockets and straining the edges of the lock. He pushed the doors repeatedly for several minutes and thought he felt the lock weakening further each time he did so, but the doors still didn't open.

Sighing in his impatience, although nothing else imposed upon his time, Brandon stood before the doors. Leaning backwards to balance himself, he raised his right leg and kicked a glass panel in a door, ready quickly to pull back his leg before the glass fell on his trousers, but only hurt his foot.

"We could look for a key," said Laura.

"Who hides a key to a library?" asked Brandon. "It's not a home."

"Have you met any librarians?"

Brandon inspected the leafed-in corners between the paving stones and windows to see if a key was hidden there. He checked the crevices around the bicycle rack. His fingers explored the dirt along the edges of the gardens until, close to the surface, they found a little clear-plastic sachet. Inside it was a key. "Blow me down," he said.

If the key didn't open the library door, Brandon couldn't imagine what else it opened. It did. The library lock turned, bolt moved, and door opened when Brandon pushed it.

Laura and then Brandon entered the shaded library. Ahead of them were a café area and cushioned chairs around timber tables.

By a reading lounge, racks on which the last editions of newspapers and magazines might once have lain were empty, taken away by people who might have finally grown tired of seeing the dates on which they had been published. Older newspapers reduced to microfilm might have survived in university libraries Brandon's parents had described to him, but reading them through magnifying glasses would be cumbersome without power to scroll through text and illuminate the words and pictures.

Laura led Brandon further into the shadows, to the empty bookshelves. If people hadn't taken those books to read, they'd still taken them away.

Tucked into one low shelf, at the darkest end of a row of shelves where only the most dedicated of library patrons ventured, were a few dusty books. Laura brought one with her towards the windows, where she and Brandon could better see it. The cover pictured a boy and girl in a small boat bearing inclement weather in the sea. Tentatively, she opened it. The pages stuck together.

The books for children might've survived there because the librarians were too tired to condemn them into pulp that would become something else. If the books were there for adults who wanted to remain within their childhoods, then those adults never matured enough to bear the children to read them. Laura kept the book.

Lit by daylight from upstairs were the steps up to the reference library and sections for local studies and family history. There, the long glass window lit the empty chairs and tables better than they'd been lit downstairs. Computer terminals stood dark and stupid.

The bookshelves were again empty – people uninterested in their region and families presumably took interest late in life – until Brandon and Laura reached the farthest corner. There, where they had to stand to the side to let the little light reaching them illuminate the titles, were shelves of the oldest books imaginable. Perhaps they'd been kept purely for reference, when anything old was unimportant. Perhaps they'd been hidden where people taking everything else wouldn't take them, where people who struggled walking up the stairs since the lift ceased functioning wouldn't pilfer them.

In all events, there were the classics in such a number as Brandon had only once previously seen. Hans Andersen idealised a childhood; idealism supplanted inadequate reality.

Laura drew from a shelf *The Canterbury Tales*. "This book is the reason I was headed to Kent," she said, "but if York isn't a place for English people, then neither is Canterbury."

Brandon picked up *A Tale of Two Cities*. The pages seemed to breathe as he opened them. "*It was the best of times, it was the worst of times.*"

Those words might've said too much. He slipped the book back into its place upon the shelf.

Laura pulled out a copy of *Nineteen Eighty-Four*. "Orwell

thought of calling it *The Last Man in Europe*," she said. "That might be you."

There were Dumas, Dostoyevsky, and Defoe. Robinson Crusoe, shipwrecked on an uncharted, deserted island far from England was more of a portent for a life than a small boy reading it could've imagined. The footprints in the sand he'd followed every time he saw them might've brought him to the woman who would save him. Brandon began to believe she would.

"I wandered lonely as a cloud," he muttered, "with all that words were worth."

The books proffered a plethora of ideas and ideals, values and principles, imagination and construction: sentinels of Western thought. Like paintings for the artists, written words could've been immortality for people who composed them. There survived the words of scholars and storytellers who'd died centuries ago, neglected by the people who passed away alone. Brandon wished the books could teach him something of anything they knew.

What might've been immortal had become mortal. Books reflected and rebuked philosophies, but deep thoughts and the crusades didn't survive without people to comprehend them. Books were fodder for the dust without people to read and revive them. Ideas only just alive would die if nobody believed them or thought enough about them to reject them. They were parasites needing people to sustain them.

Lying on a shelf near the books was a colourful page torn from a magazine. Brandon picked it up, dominated by an advertisement for Patek Philippe watches, from Geneva. Ornate clocks with hands that could no longer turn with time remained ornate, when artless clocks meant nothing. "*You never actually own a Patek Philippe. You merely take care of it for the next generation.*"

He showed it to Laura. "I wonder...," he said, looking around the floor.

Near them was a movable short round step he'd only ever seen in his school library. With his feet, Brandon pushed it along the floor to the books.

Standing on the step, he could almost see the tops of shelves.

Running his hand there, where he couldn't see, he found a small box he retrieved. Stepping back down beside Laura, he opened it. Inside, was a watch: a Patek Philippe.

The small, strong golden hands flowed smoothly along the time, the correct time Brandon felt certain, in ornate Roman numerals. Three smaller dials denoted the weekday, date, and month.

"Maybe the library was locked and the watch and best books hidden upstairs in a corner to protect them," said Laura. "The last librarian might have been protecting them from us, if we don't look after them." Perhaps those books and watch weren't so lost, after all.

Laura and Brandon collected several books each to take away with them. In spite of any security gates common in public venues, without electricity, the sensors that once detected books and discs not properly borrowed were less than docile.

They packed as many books as they could into Laura's car. Many more books remained behind.

After closing and locking the doors, protecting the books remaining from animal and bird life, Brandon returned the key to the plastic sachet from which he'd taken it. He slipped the sachet back in the soil where he'd found it.

Their responsibility wasn't to defend the books from other people reading them. If other people entered the library, Brandon hoped they would return their books to the shelves without leaving any marks of having read them and close the doors when they departed.

Laura and Brandon brought all the books they'd brought from the library into the castle house. Books filled shelves that had previously been more decorative than functional.

Finally, they stood before the thin glass display cabinet in the drawing room, as they rarely had. (Ogden's family keepsakes meant less to them than did their own.) The few items of ornamental luxury that Ogden's family kept there were sparsely set among the shelves, so that Laura needed only move one from the shelf at her eye level to another shelf to make that first shelf empty. Carefully as always with them, she and Brandon carefully set each of her five treasures from Continental Europe through York and Northallerton to their castle home, one at a time.

Sometimes, Brandon glanced towards her face. She smiled too briefly to disturb what she was doing.

When she finished, Brandon laid the watch he'd brought from the library on another shelf, with its box to one side. If the watch ever no longer turned, it would still be beautiful. Laura closed the cabinet door, leaving the key in the lock and the door unlocked.

On chairs in their drawing room, snug, and other rooms or lying beside each other in their bed, Laura and Brandon read books. They recommended the best of them, if they hadn't already said too much.

Hidden within cabinets, so it wouldn't spoil the mood, was technology for leisure and entertainment. They listened to the old recorded music that either one of them wanted to hear, sitting together when they sat, waltzing around the room when they waltzed. The notes of dead musicians and voices of dead singers recorded into disc recalled them with young lives, playing and singing unconcerned for the time that would elapse. Two people weren't a symphony or chorus.

Brandon and Laura didn't disturb each other by talking through old recorded films. They talked about them afterwards.

Many books they read, music to which they listened, and films they watched were glimpses of England, America, and other places passed: stories of the greatness and failings of Europe's past they might never understand. The adventures, love, and mysteries solved in however many pages or however many minutes were reflections of imagination, but maybe not always of truth. They often were, at best, impressions of a world their authors, composers, and directors wanted to be. Some perhaps never were. Experiencing impressionable abstractions and foolish fantasies, Brandon and Laura could enjoy entertainment they knew was false, but Europe's people passed should never have believed that matters false were real.

12

HERITAGE

"I've never been in this situation," said Laura, lying with Brandon in their bed one morning, "and I don't know how to tell. Some days, I think I'm pregnant if only because I don't feel I'm not. I'm not sure I understand what might be happening deep within me. Is uncertainty reason to believe I'm carrying a miniscule child or reason to believe I'm not?"

Brandon knew less than the little Laura knew. If she was anxious for what they might be doing, he should be too.

"People only ever talked about the problems pregnancy created," she continued. "Pregnant women couldn't smoke cigarettes, drink too much alcohol, or eat everything they liked because it might harm their children. Was caffeine another pleasure pregnant women had to forgo? I can't recall."

"We can live without them."

"Pregnant women could suffer morning sickness any time of day. Could you live with that? As the baby grew inside them, they couldn't freely move around. They became ugly."

"You would never be ugly."

"Have you seen a pregnant woman?"

"Have you?"

"Not an Englishwoman." Laura turned away from him. "My

mother never talked to me about how she felt being pregnant, beyond what her sister had to say."

Brandon dragged her face back to him and embraced her. He knew less what he should think.

"If I am pregnant," said Laura, "then we might've conceived the child the first time we were together. I don't know if that augurs anything us."

She alone recalled the date on which they first made love, as if the date of every day was still important. With pen on paper, she'd maintained a calendar since before they met, to see the date that day.

Laura, more than Brandon, tended to the grandfather clock in the drawing room. Whenever the three pendulum weights fell low, she opened the door, inserted the crank into each of the crank holes in the dial face, and turned it, raising the weights again. Between them, the pendulum had swung back and forth uninterrupted since they arrived. They thus maintained its ticking. Laura had silenced the chime.

Occasionally, she reconciled the turning minute hand with the watch in the display cabinet. She kept her smaller watch in her dressing table without ever wearing it.

Brandon often contemplated the chance of a child growing within her, without lesser matters to distract him. He wanted lesser matters.

"Doesn't York have a famous art gallery?" asked Brandon, another morning. Paintings didn't need power to be seen, wherever skylights and windows admitted daylight.

"York isn't safe."

"The people we saw aren't visiting galleries, except to loot them." Without any sense that artworks were their heritage, thieves had long stolen them for sale to private collectors, who hid them in their homes until they died with them.

"I always liked the Joe Cornish Gallery in Northallerton," said Laura, "if you like landscape photography."

"Don't we need to see paintings of people, right now?"

"I've heard it said the best art gallery is the Mercer. We won't have to worry about the people in Harrogate, I hope."

Harrogate was almost as far south as York, but comfortably

far westward, towards the Yorkshire Dales. A town much bigger than Northallerton, Harrogate had been famous as a spa town through the seventeenth, eighteenth, and nineteenth centuries, when English people holidayed at home rather than abroad.

As the grandeur in stone up to four or five storeys tall still evidenced, Harrogate had also been much richer than Northallerton, but English towns endured better than English people had. Rich Englishwomen ceased bearing babies before poor Englishwomen had.

Few cars were scattered about kerbs and fewer old people plodded along pavements, when Brandon drove him and Laura by. The parks were rife with thick long grass again becoming rural fare, like country paddocks for grazing animals. Their only interruptions were the paths and moulting wooden benches that had become perches for the birds, unconcerned by what might've been.

Watching Brandon slow his car to park was a tall gaunt dog with too little hair and its ribs visible along its body. Without master or mistress, the dog passed no judgment on him. Animals knew little of the people England was. Brandon too knew little.

Apart from the pervasive rotting leaves, both the kerb and pavement were empty outside the Mercer Art Gallery. It was an impressive columned building, as town halls once were, with its ornamental stone façade and intervening windows. At the top of the stone steps to the entrance were two tall solid doors.

With Laura beside him, Brandon tried to turn the low-set brass knob on the right-side door and then the left, but couldn't open the doors. For good measure, he knocked as loudly as the bones in his fingers allowed, without response. He pushed at each of the doors in turn and then both of them, but couldn't move them. The security against thieves remained, for whatever art might still be worth. "Opening hours aren't what they used to be," he said.

They walked along a path through the park around the building, to where the stone walls had few decorations. At the top of a short ramp and railing, presumably for people who couldn't manage the steps at the front of the building, was another pair of solid doors. They too were locked. Brandon tried to turn the knob and shook the doors has hard as he could, without result.

"Is there a key?" asked Laura.

Brandon examined the edges of the door and building, but couldn't see a spot for a key to hide. In the long grasses were too many spots.

Returning to the imposing gallery front, Brandon couldn't even see a spot to look. Preparing to apologise to Laura, he thought again about his car parked close to them. From the boot, he removed his heavy iron axe that had lain there since he left his childhood home.

"This is the only key we need," Brandon told her, closing his car boot as habit had him do. Brandon carried his axe up to the gallery entrance.

"Are you sure about this?" asked Laura. "What if we can't reseal it when we leave?"

"What's the purpose of art that nobody sees? Arts are meaningless configurations of light and long dead texture without anyone to view them. Pointless without spectators, they have no consequence."

"People might see it. Did you think of that? Someone might have the keys to open the doors: someone who worked in the gallery might've carried them home without duress, or hidden them in a place we can't find."

"They might be hidden where nobody will find them," replied Brandon. "They might be lying neglected in somebody's dark drawer, among the unimportant last possessions of the dead."

Standing before the gallery door, Brandon's hands gripped his axe. The alarms installed inside the building didn't concern him, for any surviving sirens were a chance to hear a noise, until the sirens stopped. Nobody cared about a door breaking to dark and dying premises, although somebody might come to see what he or she could take. That person might be disappointed to find only works of art, but still take one or two away. Heavy duty batteries could make burglar alarms operational for years after anyone remained to steal or suffer theft.

His arms outstretched, Brandon drew back his axe behind

him. He sucked air into his lungs and swelling chest, as he stood ready to swing his axe.

"No," said Laura, stepping in front of him. "It isn't ours alone."

If Brandon knew they were the last of a fallen era, so that they would be the last English people wanting to walk through the gallery, then he would break those doors. He would perpetuate England's art for his and Laura's lives before it dissipated. He couldn't make that prophecy: that they would be the last English people left alive. None of them could afford the luxury of Brandon treating art as just a means for private meditation or other leisure until the future came. The axe becoming heavy made his hands begin to tremble.

Disappointed, perhaps, Brandon released the air from his lungs. He and Laura inherited their arts and other culture only to their custody. Their role was to protect and pass their latent heritage securely onto people coming after them, however short or long a time they might take to come. Resting the axe at his side, he took the right door knob and shook it. The door was securely locked.

Confined outside the gallery, the palms of Brandon's open hands rested against the doors. The last warmth from his fingers drained into them, while his head shook in his despondency at the insurmountable barrier before him. His eyes trained upon the hole, little for those doors but big for a keyhole. It seemed strangely inadequate, but he couldn't see what other bars and latches sealed the door inside. The lock was only inches away, but if Brandon learnt to be a locksmith then he could toil there for a hundred days without opening those doors.

The gallery of great works was only a few yards away, but Brandon wouldn't see them. The paintings would remain inviolate, untouched, and unwitnessed.

At the end of the road on which they stood, only a short walk away from them and commanding a complete street corner, was a nineteenth-century stone rotunda. Annexed to it was a much smaller glass-walled building, complementing it. With the axe hanging from his hand, Brandon led Laura walking towards it.

A brass plaque identified the rotunda as the Royal Pump

Room; a spa bath would have been fun. Low down near the paving stones was a fountain. Brandon pressed the button above it, but no water came; a sign warned him the sulphur water had been unfit for drinking anyway.

Since ceasing operation as a pump house, although while that fountain still functioned, the building had become the town museum. Like arts, scholarship had been the means by which civilisations achieved more than mere existence. Wisdom had encouraged and discouraged them with knowledge of their ignorance. People no longer working to survive had become more than simple scavengers.

A pair of doors was closed. Brandon knocked on the wood and then a narrow glass pane in a door, without reply. Without a doorknob or handle, he tried to push open the doors, but they were locked. Still, he could easily snap them open. "There must be hundreds of little museums like this in England," he said to Laura. "Can't we visit this one?"

"You'll find every one of them has unique exhibits: knowledge that electronic bits and even paper pages could only mimic. Do you want birds and animals getting through a broken door or window?"

Artists and scholars were among the Englishmen and women who'd lived great lives and deeds. Brandon's small knowledge about anything wouldn't contribute to the museum bank of knowledge. He would be educating only him if he explored it, and didn't know enough to learn much without a guide escorting him on tour. Brandon was just a fool who might learn but would soon forget the brief trinkets that clever people left behind. Neither an artist nor a scholar, he wouldn't dilute England's legacy by pretending that he was.

The axe slipped from Brandon's hand onto the ground. It fell onto its side.

Partial records of English wisdom weren't for little him in sustenance trying to understand the things important just to him. They were for populations who, by miracle or in a smart new world, might take them.

Brandon had long stopped believing in miracles, if he had ever been so foolish or clever to believe them. A future English era might learn much from the knowledge left behind, and save England's learning from being as pointless as her art had come to be, without anyone to know it. The future mightn't care about their little knowledge, but would have the chance to learn as much from her great wisdom as from her gross stupidity.

The relics and captions to them were too important for Brandon to jeopardise by breaking that door. The sanctity of science and history wouldn't be spoiled merely to interest him and expend his passing moments. He was clever enough only to leave buried as a treasure the arts and learning left to him, leaving his people's knowledge for people whom he might never meet.

"I feel like breaking something," sighed Brandon.

"Break something that doesn't mean anything anymore," replied Laura, looking around. "We'll find you something."

Brandon picked up his axe. He and Laura walked away.

They proceeded towards another roundabout with flower beds once prettier than they'd come to be, past the majestic Crown Hotel spread like a palace; great and grand old England had been filled with palaces. Every stately building a beacon to thieves no longer coming and rich people no longer there only reminded Brandon of all that England lost and all the world would lose without her. Buildings weren't architecture but were merely shapes of caves, without people appreciating them. The glories of their civility were tragic if they were past.

Offices in which people once worked each day and then too late at night stood empty. Restaurants with their cosmopolitan cuisines retained decorations serving the same mentalities.

The rooms above some shops might've been the homes in which shopkeepers once lived, and in which some of them died. Brandon paused to peer through pavement windows for anything to see. He and Laura could take anything their parents' generation wanted, but didn't want it. All the gold that anyone could hold could not elicit the living from the dead.

Nothing remained on display in the metal trays behind a butcher's window. A stopped clock read eight thirty.

In the oldest antique windows were round ripples in the glass.

They reflected not just light but the craftsmen long passed away who'd made them.

Their wisdom hadn't saved them, but more than mere stupidity let England age and die. "We stopped learning about important things, didn't we," said Brandon as they walked, "but we should always learn. We didn't check our arrogance and conceit long enough to think." Sometimes England reached too far.

Straddling a well-rounded corner was a three-storey tall branch of Barclays Bank. The building was stone, but the big door in the centre of the street front was a thick pane of glass set in a steel frame. There, Laura stopped. "Break something that needs breaking," she said. "We've given all our money away, so there's none left to keep."

Brandon smiled. Standing close before the glass, preparing to bludgeon the bank open, he drew back his axe. He swung it hard against the glass. The axe bounced backwards, jolting his arm, without so much as cracking the thick plate glass. No siren sounds exploded.

Holding the axe with both his hands, Brandon drew it still further back behind him and swung it still harder against the glass. The axe again bounced backwards, jarring his arms and hurting them. His finger rubbed on the glass where the axe struck it, and couldn't feel a scratch.

In one last mustering of his strength, with his fists gripping the axe and muscles clenched, Brandon drew the axe fully backwards behind him, as far as his arms could reach. With all the force his limbs and body could raise and drive through the head of an iron axe, he crashed it into the glass. The useless axe bounced back, flying from his hands into the air until it crashed onto the pavement and slid away. In spite of all he'd done, the glass remained intact.

Brandon would never break that glass. All other glass sealing the bank was surely just as tough.

She looked at him and laughed. He laughed with her.

For all his disappointment and the overgrowing trees and grasses, Harrogate was too pretty a part of England's heritage for Brandon to leave an axe behind; the person who picked it up might not care for England as he did. Brandon picked up the axe again. They resumed walking.

Inside a small grocery store were visible several tin cans of corned beef, all of them organic. Brandon and Laura hadn't seen organic foods among the cellar stores in the castle house; Auntie Eustice might have taken them.

The store door was closed and locked. After knocking on the door expecting no answer, Brandon carefully prodded the sharp end of his axe into the space between the door and frame, but couldn't lever them apart. Holding the axe a short way from the lock, with the blunt side of its head facing the door, he struck the door just hard enough to break open the lock, without breaking any glass or unduly damaging the door or frame.

The galleries of art and schools of science languished in their obscurity. What had been indulgences for people with too much food to eat were very lonely places: the world that they had lost. The arts were savouries to life for people who no longer fell too sick, cold, or hungry, but Brandon and Laura might suffer any or all those predicaments. Necessity condemned the arts and most sciences to insignificance, if they couldn't keep their people.

Entombed inside libraries, galleries, and museums, English arts and learning might survive the passing of her people. They would be like the paintings in the tombs of ancient pharaohs, unseen by mortal eyes for millennia before archaeologists and self-appointed scholars walked upon them. Before or after Brandon and Laura died of their old age, wise travellers might one day breach English doors to find artwork, exhibits, and books intact, resuscitating something from the lives England had lost.

Centuries would pass before soil buried England's streets, but all the splendid buildings would ultimately decay to rocks and other refuse without people to maintain them. The prism Brandon and Laura wanted to survive would do so only for a time, before the grass and trees pushed through the growing cracks between them, reclaiming the ground.

If their paints on canvas and jaded words on aged books endured among the rubble, then archaeologists and adventurers from future empires might walk upon England and find her arts and wisdom in the dirt, if vandals from afar hadn't looted them as they looted the pharaohs' tombs before the scholars came. They might copy words still left to read from fading pages and the books might begin their lives anew, if the mongrels of decay hadn't ruined them.

Later empires of the earth would know England by her wares and other records left behind, if they cared enough to look. Brandon's fear was that they wouldn't care what England made. They might as soon grind them all to dust as neglect them all to rot. He couldn't blame them if they did.

If nobody perused England's art or read her books, then her arts and other wisdom had come to nought. Great lives were no longer great without their people left behind.

Their knowledge of all England achieved saddened Brandon for all they'd lost. It was also reason to encourage them for what England might be again.

The books Brandon and Laura read were very thoughtful, but they were other people's thoughts. They'd become like the people who'd watched television programmes about gardening without ever touching soil, or people who'd read books to teach them the sort of person they should be without ever being that person. What mattered weren't just the stories they read and heard but, ideally, those worth telling. Brandon wouldn't read about a life without leading one, but could not lead a life alone.

Two people were inadequate. They couldn't think of everything.

Loving literature had inspired in some English people a yearning to write for all the languages of Europe. Listening to music led others to compose and perform. Admiring art moved some of them to paint or draw. Loving theatre compelled others to act or direct.

Artists and scholars should bestow upon the world a few works of utter brilliance, rather than burden future minds with masses of mediocrity. Brandon lacked the talent to enhance their heritage with art or other arts. He wasn't brilliant at anything, except for being alive. The only stories for him to tell were the stories of his life.

Their arts could only revive in galleries of people, their

wisdom in museums for the multitudes. Brandon would gladly forsake his chance to savour every building and other work of art if doing so brought them the children who would preserve the remnants of their dear heritage and craft. Only English people might strive to revive and keep alive their way of life and other culture, their civilisation, however little they had done as much in recent years.

An historian might one day determine what happened during Europe's almost final generations, when people hadn't paused to be parents. Amateur raconteurs might theorise about those years the people without people whittled themselves away, between their days of other expertise. They might make more sense of things than Brandon had.

Brandon asked only that they not judge too harshly the generations that nearly died, in their peculiar wave of ignorance and foolishness. He'd come to see the limitations of theory in his life.

The only wealth they'd ever needed, the only cause worth pursuing, the only leisure ever gratifying, had been their people. England would not rise again within the lifetimes of men and women aged so cold.

13

THE FRIARAGE

The moon shone in the sky most nights and sometimes days. Brandon followed the passage of its phases through the sparse and whispery heavens. With springtime warming a little more each day, the passing of the year was in the passing of the seasons.

After rain, the sun dried roads before it dried other ground. The treads of Brandon's boots and Laura's shoes couldn't always grip the grass and rotten leaves. Holding each other's hands as they walked, supporting one another, they would keep each other upright if one of them began to fall, or they would fall together.

Brandon drank bottles of Yorkshire Cider he finished without her. Laura drank glasses of lemonade (without Pimm's or anything else) from bottles only hers. Four crystal decanters that Laura found stowed in a cupboard, she stood empty equally placed along the mantelpiece beneath the mirror in the drawing room, collecting a little dust. They carefully made their love together.

He woke one morning to find their bed beside him empty. Brandon found Laura downstairs in the drawing room. She stood at the display cabinet, its door hung open. On top of the cabinet, she had placed one of her three clay towers. The top portion of it stood beside the lower portion, in which stood the unlit candle. In her hand was a box of matches.

"How do you know?" asked Brandon.

"I know." She removed a match from the box, struck and set it alight, and lit the candle.

"Woo," said Brandon, sitting in the sofa.

She followed him there, sitting sideways beside him, with her head turned to him and legs behind her on the cushion. With the side of her crimson face pressed against the cushioned backrest, Brandon saw a tear slipping from a corner of her red eyes.

Looking at her as something different to what she'd been, he didn't quite know what she was, or what she made him. He knew little of what they were doing.

"I won't break," she told him. "It's not contagious."

Brandon reached forward and kissed her forehead. He put his arms around her. "Let's try to find you a doctor."

They left the candle burning as Brandon drove Laura to Northallerton. A voice inside his head teased him, trying to persuade him that he would be a father. Conclusion to one doubt left him no more certain of his feelings about it.

Laura kept her thoughts inside herself. She might've concealed emotion too great and complicated for her to confide them in a man, much younger than she was.

The Friarage Hospital surrounds remained the busiest place Brandon had seen of late, although perhaps a little less busy than it had been when he rode past it on his bicycle during his first day in Northallerton. It was a massive modern complex of connected buildings, all of which must once have done something important. "The children's unit," said Laura, "like everything else, even the accommodation block for trainee doctors, was gradually turned over to geriatric care, of one form or another."

The hospital car park was the only car park Brandon had seen full of cars. Ahead of them, an ambulance stood at the hospital main entrance.

"We don't want to go to the waiting room," said Laura. "It's like day release from the morgue. We don't want to see the patients' rooms. They're like the morgue."

"A morgue with visitors," Brandon elaborated.

"There are no visitors. The patients who would have had visitors and the visitors would prefer to be at home, where those people who would have been their visitors care for them. Doctors and nurses want to make house calls to get away from the hospital, or want those visitors to see them in their rooms. I know: my mother was one of those patients and I was one of those visitors. We want to find the doctors' rooms, or nurses' quarters, or wherever the medical people are. We want to talk with them where no one else can see us and no one else can hear."

She directed him around the complex to a hospital road between brown-brick buildings. Outside a small tucked-away entrance, a middle-aged woman climbed into her car. Brandon parked his car behind hers.

"This is where I'd find a doctor or nurse for my mother," said Laura, as they entered the Wensleydale Suite. "I think it used to be for rich people, then became one for anyone willing to pay for healthcare, and finally became one for anyone not coming to the hospital to stay."

The nurse receptionist's desk was unoccupied. The reception area was comfortably but antiseptically furnished, as cleanliness on carpet could be. An empty coffee percolator stood on a sideboard, its glass sides stained brown. A rack of brochures on issues of geriatric health stood on a low oval-shaped table beside it. In the middle of the room, several single cushioned chairs stood around two coffee tables. Several frayed magazines lay on the tables and on the shelves under them.

"Do you want a magazine?" Brandon asked her.

"They bore me."

"I'll cancel the subscriptions."

In what had been a consultation and treatment room, a single electric light shone. Through the open door, Brandon saw not a tall hospital bed with white sheets lying across it, but a long woollen sofa. Lying on it was a man in a doctor's coat. From his grey hairs and the sinking in his cheeks, he was perhaps seventy years old. He lay with the back of his hand draped across his eyes.

"Are you sick?" asked Brandon, as Laura stood beside him.

"I'm tired," he replied, without looking up. Near him, a plastic model of a spinal column stood on what was a desk as much as a table. "I come here, away from out there, to rest a while, or I'd be falling over in the wards."

"We've met, Doctor Hendricks," said Laura. "I'm Laura Trimm."

"I've met a lot of people," he sighed, slowly sitting up. He pulled his hand from his eyes so his two arms could support him and looked at her. "You, I remember. You wanted medicines for your mother."

"She passed away."

The doctor nodded. "People do."

"I want to talk to you about me."

"That's more the introduction I'm used to."

"I'm pregnant."

"Worry not," he told her. "When we stopped investigating ways of creating babies, we kept developing means of preventing them." The doctor rose sluggishly from the sofa. "I'll get you a pill."

"No!" said Laura, taking Brandon's hand.

The doctor looked at Brandon. "I can diagnose what you've done. I am a doctor."

"What do I need to know?" asked Laura. "Who can help me giving birth when the time comes?"

The doctor shook his head. "There's so much medical knowledge," he told her. "No doctor could know it all. Now there's no more knowledge coming in, but still no doctor can remember everything. Whatever I used to be, and I can't always remember what that was, I'm a geriatrician now."

"You know more than I know about pregnancy."

The doctor sighed again, rubbing his hands across his face and eyes as if trying to wake up. "Women gave birth for thousands of years without doctors and still do in much of the world," he told her, "even much of England now."

"Some of them die."

"Your husband, or whatever, can hold your hand. You push.

He can help draw the baby out, cut the umbilical cord for you. You'll feel so glad it's over, you won't care who's there."

"What about nitrous oxide or something? Can you give me an epidural? I wouldn't have a filling in my teeth without anaesthetic. I don't want to have a baby without one.

"You can't have had a filling for a while," the doctor told her. "We became accustomed to living without pains or fear, but we became accustomed to many things." He dragged his hand through the air, ushering the rest of the hospital to her thinking. "If you can find anaesthetic, I can administer it, but if there was one thing everybody wanted getting old, it was something to numb the pain. I don't even have the morphine left for me anymore. At least I've got booze."

"A glass of Pimm's won't get me through labour."

"Have a bottle."

"What if I need sutures?"

"Teach your man to sew."

"Should I try the hospital in Harrogate?" asked Laura.

"Do you want a second opinion then, do you? You'll get the same response everywhere, although at Harrogate, you can probably get your Pimm's."

Laura sighed. "I thought you'd help me."

"You might think you're saving us," the doctor told her, "and maybe you are, but the rest of us are doing all we can to stumble through this merry old mess we're living in. I can't be waylaid by someone young and healthy wanting my attention. I've got hundreds of people like your mother was, who don't have daughters like you to help them. As each of them die, another comes in. It won't end for me until I'm one of them, and what good will I be then?" A baby and the elderly were equally whole human lives, in moments of their passage.

"Isn't that the same excuse we've been making for years?"

"Pregnancy and the processes of childbirth are much more difficult than they would've been before our world abated, but you remember the Friarage being one of the best hospitals in Britain? We're still one of the best, but best isn't what it used to be. We've got pneumonia-ridden patients more likely to infect an untouched baby than I am to help you in your process. I can't even vaccinate your baby; all the vaccinations went to places where the babies are."

"What if you came to our home, to help us with the birth?" asked Laura.

"There are no telephones for you to call me when you're in labour. Birth doesn't naturally happen by appointment."

"It happens unnaturally by appointment."

"I'm not cutting out your baby if you and your baby don't need it."

Laura turned to Brandon, her eyes trained upon his. Torrid fear threatened their rustic lives.

Suddenly, he was again too young to be a father. "I've no idea how to help a woman giving birth," he said, in a reason to be cautious.

She turned away from him. "I'll have my baby on my own." She walked away from them.

"Laura," said Brandon, following her into the reception area. He caught her shoulder.

She could have pulled away. Instead, she slumped into a chair.

Brandon sat in the chair beside her. The armrests between them made putting his arm around her difficult, but he did so anyway.

"I don't feel like a mother," she said, tears dripping from her eyes. "I never have."

Her crying made her vulnerable, as it also made him. "I'll look after you."

Laura smiled, but still the tears came. "Childbirth was another thing I never had to contemplate."

"Not even with Ogden?"

"Marriage was one thing, parenthood another. That might sound stupid now, but we were stupid."

The doctor appeared before them, sitting in a chair facing them. "You're lucky today," he told them. "We've got power. In the warren of lanes and corridors out there, you'll find signs to the hospital library. I don't know if anything there will help you, I've never had to look, not since I was your age, but the patients who wanted books to read didn't take medical books. They didn't want to know too much."

Laura slowly nodded, sniffling a little and drying her eyes. "Thank you."

"When you're finished, see Niamh in the pharmacy, then come back here and I'll have left you what I can. We were supposed to send our leftover medical equipment to London, but I kept a little back. We have vaccines; they didn't want them there."

Guiding Laura and Brandon, a smattering of electric lights shone throughout the hospital. Proceeding through successive double doors and along corridors of old linoleum, turning away from the moans and tears reaching them, they walked their uncertain way towards the library. The few people they passed were less surprised to see them than Brandon had expected, although few of them looked their way at all.

Opening the library door, the library was empty of people. Chairs like those they'd seen in the Wensleydale Suite formed a small reading lounge. A large table stood empty, as did five computer terminals and a printer set along the tables by the wall. In a place with electricity, Brandon switched on a computer. It remained dark.

Most importantly, several stacks of shelves kept hundreds of books, medical magazines, and journals, in specialised arrays of health and occupation. Psychology might've been the most important medicine or the most indulgent. Brandon had no reason to try so hard to understand him and Laura if nobody survived who cared to judge them.

The newest publications described the medicines and methods by which doctors treated aged adults when they were sick. Those publications were all old, others very old, as old as Doctor Hendricks. The librarian might've discarded them only when later editions replaced them, but no more editions would replace those remaining. Knowledge had stagnated.

Nevertheless, the library retained a rich erudition in the arts and sciences of medicine, covering most risks and procedures, except in one respect. "All the books on women's health are concerned with issues other than giving birth," said Laura. Businesses and people had become too proficient at dissuading

Englishwomen from falling pregnant for anyone to read about it.

One book instructed men and women raising adopted babies and keeping foster children from foreign cultures. None of the books was concerned with raising children born to the men and women reading them. Taking that first book nevertheless, Brandon would try to adopt some aspects of those foreign cultures for their child and them. They'd already left Europe's most recent ways behind them.

Brandon also took a book of human anatomy, for fear of ever needing it. Books of medicine might help them treat injuries they might sustain or illnesses they might suffer.

From another shelf, Brandon pulled a particularly old book. In his hands, the surface of the brown leather binding broke into dust. The gold impressed lettering was illegible to read. Opening the front cover revealed it to be *A Textbook of General Practice*. That book alone among the books Brandon or Laura found described the exotic and extraordinary processes of pregnancy, childbirth, and tending to a child. It might almost teach him enough.

"We will have to wait and see," said Laura. Brandon closed the library door after them.

They ambled back along corridors and through doors, checking the signs for anything to the pharmacy and anything else of interest. None of the few hospital staff in their hospital garb they passed paid them attention, however much Brandon lost all bearing of where in the maze of corridors they were, relative to the Wensleydale Suite.

On the second floor, they finally found the pharmacy. Sitting on a stool at a long table was an old woman, wearing a white hospital blouse and dark hospital cardigan. To all sides of her were shelves and trays, stretching from low near the floor to high near the ceiling. Scattered around them, far from filling them, were boxes, bottles, and other vials of medicines marked with names on labels that Brandon didn't understand: the last vestiges of modern medicine available to them.

"Have you a pregnancy test?" Laura asked the woman.

The woman laughed. "For you?" she asked.

Laura nodded.

"Patience."

"Doctor Hendricks sent me," said Laura, sitting on the stool facing her. "Have you anything you can give me?"

"I can give you tablets and tools for contraception and I can give you tablets and tools for termination. Hospitals in this country might run out of everything else, but we always have stocks of those." Women could take abortion tablets more easily than they could take a test to know if they were carrying anything to abort.

"I don't know much about medicine," persisted Laura, "but I know to take antibiotics for bacterial infections. Can you please give me some?"

"Would you know a bacterial from a viral infection? Are you sick now?"

Laura shook her head.

"We don't hand out medicines on speculation. When you're sick, if you're sick, you speak to someone in charge."

Brandon stepped forward, standing beside Laura on her stool. "How do you stop people stealing your supplies?" he asked.

"I'm not worried about you," the old woman scoffed, reaching her hand under the table, "but if you mean the people like those who came to Bedford, Hull, and Preston, I have a friend." She pulled out her hand and laid on the table, still in her grip, a handgun.

"Is that legal?" continued Brandon. "Would you use it?"

"You'd be surprised what seeing enough death can do to a person; I came here to knit tea cosies after my secretary's job finished. Besides, I know what the gangs did to the nurses at Great Ormond Street and Manchester, who'd helped them and their children." She returned the gun to its place under the table. "Nothing reminds us of our mortality more than other people's deaths, except, of course, our own."

"There's only you here, then?" persisted Brandon.

"All over this room and all over this hospital are little red buttons," the old woman replied. "If any button is pushed, sirens will sound like it's the coming of hell; it probably will be. It'll frighten the patients, but every person working here will grab his or her friend, like my friend. The first place they'll come is here; we all know what they want, what they demand. I might already be dead, but the people who killed me will be dead before they take anything out of here."

"What's left in the pharmacies around town?" asked Brandon. More secure than other stores, pharmacies safeguarded drugs from users they'd called addicts. Prescription and other drugs might have stalled and concealed the evidence people were aging, but hadn't saved them from dying of that old age.

"They sent their last stocks of medicines here when they closed," the old woman told them. "People took their skin creams and potions; I did. All that's left are the items that pharmacies learned to sell too late at night and the chairs for people to sit waiting."

Brandon, like Laura, fell silent. He looked around the room if only to know what was there should ever they return, without knowing for how long packets and bottles would be safe to use, beyond their cautious expiration dates. He couldn't know what medicines Laura could safely take; packaging didn't need to warn pregnant women not to use the contents when no women reading it were pregnant. They couldn't teach him anything about Laura's condition. Brandon wasn't certain about anything.

The old woman watched them, apparently not perturbed. "You can stay as long as you like," she told them, "but when I leave, I lock this room. Doctors and nurses have keys if you want to ask them anything."

"Have you vitamins and other comforts," Laura asked the old woman, "precautions and soft treatments for people becoming sick?"

"Why should I give them to you and not someone else?"

"Because," said Laura, "you came here to make tea cosies."

The woman stared at her for a time, before standing up and going to the shelves. She gave Laura some sachets of tablets and bottles of liquid to treat headaches, colds, and other ailments. "I wish," she said, "I could have made little woollen socks for babies."

The most innovative technology for saving and improving

human life was in the hospital, but Brandon didn't know how to use it. He and Laura needed a geriatric doctor or temperamental nurse for their medicine to help them.

Finding their way back through stairs, corridors, and walkways to the Wensleydale Suite took Brandon and Laura a while. When they reached it, Doctor Hendricks had gone, but he'd left beside the magazines on the coffee table in the reception area a metal tray. In the tray was a pair of white surgical gloves, along with the surgical scissors to cut the umbilical cord and a plastic clasp to seal it. With them were the unsettling sharp scalpel that Brandon might need to cut Laura's baby from her and the needle and soluble black threads he might need to treat her tearing. A can of anaesthetic spray would only partially numb the nerves below the skin. Small bottles of antibiotic ointment and peroxide, cloth bandages, and buds of cotton wool and gauze were more consoling.

"The way things are now makes everything feel so hard," said Laura, sitting back down in a chair. She rested her medicines in the metal tray. "Even if it isn't harder, it feels harder. I don't think that I'd be doing this if I didn't have to do it."

Brandon rested his medical books beside the tray. Again, he sat in the chair beside her, as he'd sat before they'd visited the library and pharmacy.

"My career gave me a confidence that was never really mine," she confided. "My work and friends were somewhere to hide."

"You haven't lost any of the strength you once had."

"Have you lost any of yours?"

"I suppose not," he smiled, "if I want you to believe the same thing of you."

Laura looked at him, before her eyes turned away. "Hope isn't enough," she said. "I wish my mother were here."

14

LEARNING

The candle having burnt out, Laura's clay tower was back in the display cabinet in the drawing room. She and Brandon tended to the chickens and current crops around their castle home, picking fresh food to eat and keep small reserves in the kitchen. They broke the ground and sowed the seeds that would become crops for three.

"I'm not sick," insisted Laura, when Brandon tried relieving her from a chore: creating, collecting, and cooking food to eat. "I am having a baby."

She made him feel inadequate. Perhaps he was: the spectator passing for the ride.

Laura was often sick through the ensuing weeks, especially but not only in the mornings. She burrowed alone within their bed or the bed in which she'd first slept in the house. She scampered into the bathroom and hid there before slipping back to bed again. Her sickness emphasised their deep ignorance of what they needed to do through her long labour.

Feeling helpless, Brandon let her be: her experience too personal for him to intrude without her asking him. Waiting patiently and not, he listened through the silence for any call from her. His first preoccupation was Laura being well again, but all he could do was surreptitiously take up more of the chores, while she grew their baby in their bed. Their child set their new routine in a family of three, divorced from clocks and hours of day.

Laura had been proficient in her career, but technology couldn't absolve them of the differences between them. Economies ought to be efficient but efficiency had changed. They became models of an ancient past that English people had despised.

Reading and rereading words and diagrams in the medical books, Brandon learnt some of the things Laura already knew about her woman's body. Pregnancies should last nine months, but some babies didn't survive the first three months inside a woman's womb. With no more reason for dying than for staying alive, some lives ended without a chance to start.

After about three months, the small bump of a baby should appear from Laura's belly. That bump would, after four or five months, become a bulge.

When the baby large inside her womb pressed against her smaller stomach, she might suffer a return of the gastric reflux burning her throat. Standing for too long a time and moving would become awkward with the weight around her waist, in the final weeks of pregnancy.

Babies born too soon didn't survive or survived with cruel handicaps. Without the modern medicine to which Laura had little access, her baby needed to go full term inside her womb for a best chance to be born well.

Life was a puzzle without clues through which Brandon could reason. A quirk of genes might save one life or condemn another with fate's crude injustices, when neither thought nor exertion justified it. Being born was an infinitesimally small chance among the millions of tiny bits for life that struggle to be fertilised, and who then survive to become a little person.

That would be to wintertime, Christmastime: the time to think of Christmases past and start to think of those ahead. When the outside air was cooling, immeasurably far from then, every day closer to the baby going full term that labour didn't start would be a good day. Each day was just a day until their child was born.

The medical textbook advised expectant mothers not to stray too far from a hospital. Brandon couldn't imagine cutting open Laura's skin and uterus to release the baby. "If you need a Caesarean section," he said to Laura, "we could return to the Friarage Hospital."

"Where's Doctor Hendricks going to open me, in the reception area?"

"You saw the consulting rooms."

"We might not have the time to get there. He might not be there when we do."

Nothing less than a formal education would be enough for Brandon to learn all he needed to know. One man could never learn so much.

If Brandon were in Laura's position, he would have contemplated baulking from what they'd started: taking the relief that would end what was happening within her. Every passing day made those tablets less assuring. She persevered, while he sometimes said to her the words of comfort he knew were meaningless.

Like everything else about her then, Laura's reasons for doing what she was doing, without doing what she could've done, were too private for Brandon to intervene. She might've wanted to save England or to save her parents' line. He wouldn't ask her to make so brave a choice for him and his family line. He didn't know she would've answered him if he did.

Willing to suffer childbirth without emotion to be a mother because she should, Laura might've been heroic as Brandon shamefully wasn't. Her fears made her nobler than any other person he had known. Brandon wasn't so good.

She didn't need to love him, loving any father of her child might have been love enough. For his mind to dwell upon the nature of her love would be a crass self-obsession, of the type that ruined England once already. Only his love for her would be his pleasure and concern. He boiled the tap water she drank because a book suggested people boil it to remove dangerous germs. They became wary making love.

When Brandon was alone, not otherwise engaged, he tried to comprehend her carrying a speck of person hidden deep inside her. She was special; a creator and carrier of a little life form unlike any other, and yet alike her and him. It placed her beyond extraordinary; strong for bearing a child and yet fragile in doing so.

Brandon imagined himself so tiny, inside his mother's womb, before everything he became. Laura was in the bathroom when he slipped into the basement garage and sat in his car. In the glovebox, along with maps his parents had procured, was a silver frame and photograph from his school graduation. Sitting there alone, Brandon gazed into the images of his parents' faces smiling back to him. His life had moved far away from them, but their photograph refreshed his imperfect memories: his fondest recollections. The time had passed since Brandon played in his delinquency, cried for what he lost, and found more than he had known.

His past so close, he knew again what he already knew. A child embodied his and Laura's time already spent together and new times coming: their always present union. The three would forever have the reference points of one another, no matter how wide apart their lives might be. Their child might love Laura and Brandon, sometimes grow to hate them, but even a thousand miles and years away will always know that they were there.

They might prove to be a little bit like unlosable close friends. Unseen for much too long a time, they wouldn't need to notice the other to maintain their care and interest, before sharing thoughts and feelings as each one came to mind. More likely than relationships that people born apart afford each other, theirs might endure when too few things around them would.

Brandon brought his photographs upstairs to his and Laura's bedroom, where he stood them on the mantelpiece. Laura moved them to her dressing table, beside her parents' photographs she saw every morning when she woke and every evening when she retired to bed, making a small gallery. Their child made her family his and his family hers.

Laura's and so his achievement would be something more significant than any other thing she or he had ever done, who should outlive them when nothing else they'd done could. Brandon wondered whether to feel proud of Laura and him, but he'd seen in recent years where pride could take a people. He'd never come so far from the life he had known, but would go further still.

"We've become something like our parents," he said. Brandon and Laura were returning crockery and cutlery they'd cleaned and allowed to dry to the shelves and drawers in the kitchen.

Laura stopped what she was doing, midway through returning some spoons to a drawer. After a moment, she resumed it. "If we don't have his baby," she said, "then we haven't learnt anything."

The nearest market town to their castle home was Thirsk, about four miles away. Being much smaller than Northallerton and without the demands of being a county town might have made it even quieter.

Brandon and Laura entered an abandoned pet shop, the first patrons of a new season. Through Europe's childless decline, companion animals had proliferated while the people they'd companioned hadn't. Cats and dogs enjoyed the conveniences that Europeans developed through prior eras to nurture human babies.

"There are no prams," complained Laura. "I so much wanted to push our child around town, around Northallerton and every other English town, in a pram chariot."

"My parents kept theirs," said Brandon.

"Mine didn't," said Laura. "Mrs Dougherty wanted it for her poodle and my mother was much too generous."

"Does a poodle remain in a pram?"

Laura laughed. "I hope not."

Among the last store stock left to take, they found a clear plastic bath, cradle, capsule for rear car seats, and small crib to mount on a bicycle. The last of the imported kits to make cots was in a large cardboard box, crafted from dark-stained timber. In spite of the material and colour being stamped on the ends of the box, Laura opened one end to reconcile the colour with its description. They collected every small sheet, blanket, towel, and clothing for a pet that might warm a human child.

Nappies for pet animals could also have served their baby, but those shelves were empty; old people might have taken them for themselves. Laura and Brandon would find cloths to use.

The sprawling Tesco supermarket car park was empty, until Brandon parked his car outside the store. Among the food all gone had been small tin cans of baby food. The oldest of people, their teeth and dentures failing them, would have taken the cans.

Also gone were the big cans of baby formula: powdered milk that became drink for babies when dissolved in boiled water. When fresh milk became scarce through England's decline, English people had used the formula in their tea.

"People protested against companies selling formula to poor countries," recalled Brandon. "They wanted poor mothers to feed their babies healthier breast milk, but didn't care whether the few English mothers used less nutritious formula." English parents mattered less than other parents, in their paternalism over people smarter than they were. England's decline had cured Brandon of pretend paternalism.

The truth was much simpler than Brandon's speculation. "European women needed to use formula," explained Laura, "because they weren't the mothers of the babies they fed. They were adopters, temporary care-givers, whose breasts weren't feeding babies."

Importing other people's youth hadn't stopped Europeans getting old, even if replacing them deluded some of them from seeing their age. If exotic skins were supposed to prevent white skins from wrinkling, they didn't. Laura's white breasts of beauty Brandon adored would become teats for a small person.

"I don't know if I can feed a baby," said Laura. "Nobody taught me. I'd be guessing a technique without knowing what ought to be innate, or if I'm doing anything right."

Brandon had no answer. Any provision, nourishment, and sustenance flowing from her would be better than anything from farms or cans.

Having stowed in Brandon's car all that they would take with them that day, they could wander around Thirsk. Near the supermarket, they'd already passed an entrance to a racecourse.

"I've never seen horse racing," said Brandon, "except on television."

"You won't see it today," said Laura, as they began walking towards that entrance. "Being so frenetic every race day, even if for only a few minutes every half hour, racecourses were oddly serene other days. Now, every day's another day."

The space in the sign informing passers-by of the date of the next racecourse meeting was empty. In the Hambleton Stand were restaurants apparently as good as any, but nobody still cooked the food that nobody still served and nobody came to eat. The betting shops were closed, their windows long shut. The bookmakers had gone, taking with them their boards of betting odds.

The racecourse itself could have been the flattest and greenest of fields, but for the fences confining the course and huge stands presiding over it. On close inspection, horses' hooves had left the ground rougher than it first appeared.

Without anybody restricting admission, Brandon led Laura up into the highest seating he could see, where they sat to watch over the green flat. Around the perimeter were trees in which birds might have also been spectating, but there really wasn't much to see.

Above them was a roof they didn't need. Around them were neat rows of empty seats, all the same. Birds had scratched some seats without etching words that human beings could read, leaving behind their moments of black, brown, and white.

From the ground near his seat, Brandon picked up a betting slip, a little damp and starting to rot. "Thirsk, three twenty-five p.m.," he read aloud. "Bob for Apples, twelve to one, ten pounds to win." He handed the slip to Laura. "It lost."

"The punter lost," said Laura. "Punters always lose, eventually." She rested the ticket on the empty seat beside her, away from Brandon. "The horses don't care."

Without racing, that horse the subject of the bet might never have been born. Having been born, but without saddles, stirrups, reins, and jockeys, thoroughbreds and other horses that might have galloped around the long wide course grazed leisurely before them. If Bob for Apples was among those horses, Brandon couldn't know; the horses were unlikely to tell him. The quirky names that quirky owners gave them, which were momentarily famous whenever Brandon heard them on the news, no longer applied.

Laura and Brandon didn't address each other by their names; they must've stopped doing so soon after they met. Names had become otiose without anyone else whom they could've been addressing, but names might again become important.

"What name will we call our baby?" asked Brandon.

"Shall we call a boy Cain?" asked Laura.

"He murdered his brother." Cain was a son of Adam and Eve.

"You remembered," she said, more surprised than impressed. "Should we call a boy Abel?" She tested and teased him.

"I don't want our child named after a victim."

"I don't want our child named after our parents, obfuscating them in our minds."

"I don't want our child taking our Christian names, suggesting he or she must be like us. Mindlessly choosing to be the same as us would be no better than mindlessly choosing to be different. It might even be worse."

They walked around the racecourse grounds, past more abandoned food stalls and other empty places once catering to crowds. As they did, Laura and Brandon suggested names not for horses but for their child: names already of human beings and not words they created for entertainment or quips of humour. Some names the other dismissed out of hand: a boss of that name had fired Laura's friends; a child of that name had been a pain at Brandon's school.

More than the creativity was the responsibility. The first important decision that Laura and Brandon would make for their coming child would be the name by which the child and then the adult would be known.

"The name my parents gave me remained the name by which I judged me," said Laura. "Jane never completely ceased being my name inside my head." Their lives should be more genuine than the life in which Laura feigned her name. Other names remained for them to think about again, until one of them dismissed them.

"I never liked the ambiguity of names that could be those of men or women," said Brandon, "even if that ambiguity can't arise among us. Men's names became names for men and women, but women's names never became names also for men."

"Brandon can be a girl's name," Laura pointed out.

"So I know what I'm saying."

Brandon slowly acceded to Laura the greater role in naming their unborn child; she was bearing him or her. "We could choose a middle name from our grandparents," she said.

Without other families, family names might be important. Brandon, Laura, and their child might be a family without a family name. "If she is a girl, then she can take your surname, Trimm or Erian," said Brandon, trying to be fair. "If he is a boy, can he take mine?"

"She too can have your name: the house of Frewer," Laura told him. "I want you to know your responsibilities." Christian names were less important than the family names they shared.

Leaving the racecourse, hands together, Brandon and Laura started walking back along Station Road, past their car in the supermarket car park. Brandon studied everything they passed as much for suggestions of baby names as for anything else to see.

Following the familiar style of old white-on-green sign towards the town centre, they proceeded along Westgate. They passed brick shops and homes, a stone court house.

"I wonder what our child will be like," said Brandon, outside the town hall. "I suppose there'll be no chances to choose vocations, but might he or she be an artist, a scientist, an engineer, or will he or she be content being a farmer, as I suppose you and I have become?"

"This is our child," said Laura, stopping them in their place, "not someone's worker."

They faced each other, still holding each other's hands. Brandon had been remiss. Europe's glorious careers and boundless designs to save the world had resolutely failed, but their child inside her would grow and come to think and feel. Arts and sciences were important, but the very fact of life was more profound than other glories. "So you and I are just parents-to-be," said Brandon.

"Not just parents," declared Laura, "but parents, in lieu of all the lesser things we are. Our child can't have been made except by you and me, in that one moment. We can't have bought him, taken her, or accepted our baby as a gift. Our parental roles make everything else about us trivial and everything else important. Our other acts won't matter as much as being a parent matters, not just to our child and us, but everyone. The Great Pyramids of Egypt will be like sandcastles on a beach aside what we make together."

Their child was their common purpose and success: a trait that only they in their indissoluble union shared. No working life, conversation over coffee, or charitable donation could affect anyone as they could affect their child. Their progeny was pure vocation in career, working and thinking, making everything worthwhile. "What about the acts we do as parents?" asked Brandon.

Laura might've been thinking of an answer, or she might've been judging him, before she started to smile. "You're learning," she told him.

She turned and started to run towards the town centre, dragging Brandon forward with her. "Should you be doing that?" he asked, holding her back.

Laura again looked at him. "Horses gallop," she said, before drawing a large breath into her lungs. She released Brandon's hand and raced defiantly ahead of him, moving freely without constriction.

Brandon watched her running away from him for several seconds, before he started after her. He ran as fast as she ran, following her around one corner. He might've been approaching her before she turned around the next corner, but his lungs and muscles became sore. Turning that next corner, Brandon slowed to merely jogging in some exercise. Far ahead of him, Laura slowed her pace to rhythmic running.

Laura continued running along the road and through the Market Place. She stopped at the Clock Tower, which Brandon didn't need to check no longer told the time. She turned to face him.

With his face red and lungs and muscles sore, Brandon finally reached her. He expected her to say something about his health and condition being inferior to hers, but Laura merely watched him panting more than she was panting. Laura and her child – their child – were starting to survive.

"Let me know if you change your mind about running," said Brandon, recovering his breath. Up the steps of the Clock Tower was another ancient drinking fountain, no longer dispensing water.

His hands on his hips, Brandon hunched forward, easing the strain from his lungs. There, his eyes idly faced near him Laura's tightly fitting dress and smooth stomach. He'd seen enough of it to recognise a soft and gentle arc he'd not previously seen, reaching forward.

"Is that the baby?" he asked.

She placed her hand on the arc. "I think it is," she said.

Brandon continued in his stance, although he'd recovered his breath and could have stood upright. The truth had become more credible and incredulous, the fascinating little person absorbing more of his thoughts with every sense of someone there. "He or she is real," he said.

"He or she is getting bigger," she replied. "You'll want to feel the first ripple of a kick."

Brandon looked up at her. He didn't otherwise move.

"Come on," she said again, reaching her arm and open hand towards him.

Merely being courteous, Brandon cautiously placed his fingers on her hand. She drew his hand towards the dress around her belly and gently pressed the palm of his hand against her. Brandon didn't push against her, for fear of harming that tiny life in nourished darkness. He let her control what he was doing. "I can't feel anything," he said.

"Neither can I," she said, "not yet."

15

SIMULATION

Laura chose the empty bedroom across the landing from her and Brandon's room to become the baby's bedroom. Brandon laid their new baby bath and cradle neatly on the floor and assembled their new cot. Laura packed the baby wear, sheets, and blankets in the drawers. Their baby capsule lay in the garage, to be affixed to a rear seat of Brandon's car after he or she was born. Without the assistance of anyone but each other, they moulded their lives around their coming child.

The castle house was becoming their family home, their child changing everything about it. "If we can find an old camera and the means to maintain ageless pictures from the dark and dating stores and homes," said Laura, "we'll photograph our child in every evolving phase of life." They were too many years for Brandon to comprehend so soon.

Still half a year before he'd need them, he set the medical textbook, anatomy book, and equipment on a table in his and Laura's bedroom. He set with them the watch he'd found in the Northallerton Public Library, uncertain why.

When the birth was pending, the baby's head would point downward. Brandon didn't know whether Laura would feel the child well enough inside her to know where his or her head pointed. He didn't know what he would feel through her skin, but he'd keep the textbook open where he could follow its guidance to reassure him in his ignorance and refer to it in an emergency. He'd also bring a pile of clean white towels.

If their bedroom looked too much like a hospital room, it still was not a hospital. The textbook referred to labour and delivery of a baby without anaesthetic and hallucinogens as natural childbirth. Any renunciation of technology had been a crusade for a natural world and effrontery to human progress, but Brandon found himself in the midst of being both. He, the hopeless patient, would feign being a novice gynaecologist and midwife.

Nothing Brandon used to know or do would be akin to Laura giving birth, when the life that grew from nothing would be large enough for him to meet: the greatest introduction that any man or woman made. Brandon longed to look back and know he had done what Laura needed him to do.

He carried the medical books and then that table to the end of their bed, where he would want them to be when time came for their baby's birth. Standing beside the table, he imagined Laura on her usual side of their bed in front of him, poised in childbirth: their baby's head starting to protrude from her. His twitching, anxious hands rehearsed a firm and gentle hold of a small head, edging it out of her towards him.

His hands rehearsed their chores until they could no longer find more ways to undertake them. He then rehearsed them all again.

Laura appeared at the door. Remaining fully dressed apart from her shoes she slipped from her feet, she stepped to their bed and climbed under the sheets and blanket, lying where she normally slept. "There'll come a night you're lying asleep," she told him, "undisturbed for so long a time, when my voice and motion will intrude upon your dreams. I'll break you from your sleep, when your brain slow to revive will recognise my hand tapping you from the darkness. 'I think it's starting,' I'll tell you."

She sat up in their bed, facing him. He watched from the end of their bed, as a student would stand before a teacher.

"You'll grapple for the light," she continued, "probably

knocking something to the floor. The small light will shine upon my anxious face in the midst of the small glow." Under the bedclothes, she placed her hand on her belly. "You'll have learned everything to do but forgotten all of it, begging the night for a nurse and medicine, but still leap from our bed, rush to the wall by the doorway, and switch on the room light. The room bright, I'll use my watch to measure the time between contractions.

"You'll ask me 'Are you breathing?' I'll answer, 'Of course, I'm breathing!'

"You'll reach for your book on the table trying to keep the pages open, but the book will slip from your hands and fall to the floor. You'll pick up the book, push the table away from the bed, and stand beside me in our bed."

Brandon took the textbook from the table. He stood beside Laura.

"'Give me your hand,' you'll tell me," she continued. "'Find your place in the book first!' I'll tell you. You'll flick through pages of your book for the familiar childbirth text and diagrams, you'll hold open with one hand and thumb while you take my hand in your other hand."

Brandon offered her his hand. She took it, before lying back down.

"I'll squeeze your hand when I feel a contraction. You'll check your watch. The contraction might last, say thirty seconds.

"We'll pause. I'll collect my breath and pace it. You'll study your book again, waiting for me to squeeze your hand again.

"I will. You'll calculate the contractions at, say eight minutes apart. You'll read from your book that I'm in the first stage of childbirth, which you'll tell me because you think I don't know."

She let go of his hand. He left it where she could take it again.

"I'll rest without sleeping," she continued, closing her eyes, "sometimes flinching. You might think of sleeping, but won't risk being unable to nurse me so you'll drag a chair near me."

Brandon looked around for the closest chair. He dragged it to her side of the bed.

"You'll sit reading pages of your book you've already studied a thousand times but barely recognise. One moment you'll crave more time to learn what to do. The next, you'll long for the night to finish. If a doctor or anaesthetist were with us, with the resources of our modern history, then you'd be free to be useless, observing the strain and wonder I'll perform, but you won't be free. I'll need you to do more than you've ever before done, if I'm going to survive.

"Trying to wake, you'll dress out of your pyjamas into clothes for the distant day. You'll then sit again in the chair beside me, sometimes muttering small words I won't hear."

Brandon sat in the chair. He was already dressed for day.

"In the last hours of your long anxiety," she continued, "you'll be relieved I'd have lasted full term, but still fear for my well-being and the life bound within me. The coming hours will be the most arduous of your life and mine. I'll stir now and again, sometimes looking at my watch on the bedside table without looking at you." She opened her eyes, before closing them again. "I'll be feeling forces inside me you can't feel, but you'll wait patiently for me to tell you what I want you to know.

"When the shining light of morning fills the room, your mouth, face, and throat will yawn to have been awake so long. You'll switch off the lights. I won't want anything to eat, but you eat if you want to."

She again opened her eyes. "The pain in me will increase and be excruciating," she said, squirming about in her bed. "I'll gasp, my pain becoming more intense, tightening my body in my bed." She threw the bedclothes from her and raised her knees, opening her skirted legs. "You'll rush from your chair to my open legs poised to do something, but will watch helplessly. If you offer me your hand to hold, I'll refuse you." She held her belly as if it were swollen, as if the moment of birth was imminent. "You put the pillows behind my head."

Brandon did just that. He gently lifted her arms and shoulders until she sat upright against the pillows and bedhead.

"I'll want you at the end of the bed watching for the baby, ready to guide our child from me."

Brandon returned to the end of their bed. He waited for her next instruction.

"I'll be immersed in my agony and then ecstasy each time

that agony abates," Laura grimaced. "My pain will intensify, my body trying to force our child away. The contractions becoming greater and more frequent are five minutes apart. I'll scream with every seizure and shove or do whatever I do." She arched her back. "I'll slow exhausted waiting for the next contraction. You'll make sure your table of medical utensils is nearby."

Brandon pulled the table a little closer to him. He set every implement a little neater in its place.

Drawing back her legs, Laura forced herself higher from the bed. She raised her knees further apart as if ready to expel their child. "You'll lift my nightdress to expose myself to you. You might see nothing coming from inside me yet, but you'll push some towels under me."

Brandon looked around; he'd not brought towels to the table. He rushed into the bathroom, grabbed both towels from the rail, and rushed back to Laura. He unfolded the towels and pushed them under her, still wearing her dress.

"I'll scream, I'm sure, and scream again," she said, clenching her fists. "You'll force your hands into your thin surgical gloves."

Brandon didn't think he should waste the gloves. He left his hands bare.

"You'll watch, waiting for anything to do, while I slump back into bed." Laura lay back against the pillows, before suddenly sitting up again, her knees up and legs open again. "The routine of my pain and your irrelevance might continue for most of an hour or more, without me saying anything and without you doing anything." Her body again convulsed. "Sometime, when you're thinking the baby will never come, a small lip of bloodied flesh will appear from within me. 'I can see it,' you'll tell me, excitedly and nervously." Laura tired for one improper moment and rested again. "The baby will slip back into my body."

Her body convulsed again. Laura gripped the side of the bed with her hands as she arched her back and screamed, as if trying to force the baby from her. "The reddened baby head, bald but wet with blood, will appear again. 'You're doing great,' you might tell me, but I won't be listening. You'll reach your open hands around the space to which the head is coming."

Brandon complied. He reached his hands towards her more confidently than he'd reached forward in his earlier rehearsals.

"No!" she screamed. Her body unfolded. "The baby's head will become large enough for you to touch. 'It's coming,' you'll tell me, as you place your hands on the malleable small head trying not to harm the tender skull. 'Keep going!' you might tell me, as the opening from my body becomes larger for the baby and the tiny hairless head too large for me peeps out. I'll scream, striving to eject the pain, before the head slips into your hands and my body closes around the neck. You'll hold held the head so it doesn't fall, while saying to me something like 'You're doing fine.'

"I'll scream and pant but you'll ignore me, because all you can see in this world is our baby trapped midway out of me and still inside me, in the eye of our great mayhem. 'It's nearly there,' you might say, as I scream and force the infant I desperately want out of me. You might see a bloodied shoulder, before that shoulder hides again. 'Come on,' you might say, but neither I nor our child will need to hear you. 'I am!' I'll tell you, as the bloodied shoulder appears again.

"The opening from me will become even larger, as the baby shoulder leads to a baby chest and other baby shoulder. The widest part of its body will be suddenly within your grasp, when leaving my body is easier than trying to remain behind. The baby should rush suddenly and smoothly into your waiting hands. As the last of the baby's legs and feet slip from me, I'll sigh exhausted, falling back onto the bed. If I cry, it's because I can."

Brandon held his hands as if holding a small child. It made everything much easier to see.

"You won't be concerned about me crying and smiling, laughing and weeping," continued Laura, "because you'll know you won't need to be. In your hand, above the towel, the growing lump inside me would have become a little life of battered crimson pink lain before you. Behind closed eyes, virgin arms and hands will feel the space of open air, seeking familiar warmth and fluid from inside a mother's womb: the single world they'd known, where those eyes had no reason to open and those ears heard no sounds beyond the beating of two hearts. Only the thick white and blood red umbilical cord will join our child and me together.

"You'll tell me it's a boy or girl, for something to say. You'll notice the time on your watch because you remember being told the time you were born. Our baby might be gasping, not crying, when you lay him or her on a clean space on the towels."

Brandon complied. The space he nursed a child would occupy someday.

"The umbilical cord will have become obsolete, a nuisance even," continued Laura. "You'll pick up a little plastic clasp from the table and fix it across the cord, sealing it, close to the baby's stomach." Brandon mimicked every instruction she gave him, without fastening the clasp he mightn't later be able to release. "You'll take those surgical scissors from the table with one hand, while your other hand tries to grasp the tough and tender cord.

"When first you try to hold it, the cord will slip from your clumsy fingers. On your second or third attempt, you'll hold it well enough to place the scissor blades around it. They'll push away the cord more easily than they cut it, but your other hand will grip the cord more tightly and force the scissor blades against it. The cord might seem to struggle to evade them, but soon enough the blades will cut clean through. The clasp will seal the bleeding from what will become a navel, when the small stub of the cord clots and eventually falls away."

Genetic factors rather than the cutting of the umbilical cord determined whether the centre of a baby's navel protruded inwards or outwards, Brandon had already read. His navel protruded inwards.

"Our baby will have been born," Laura told him, "a patch of near-death England come alive, but you're not finished yet. If our baby cries a virulent angry upset scream or if he or she doesn't, you make sure our baby's breathing. If not, gently suck his or her little nose and mouth to remove any secretions. Hold him or her up; you'll be anxious not to drop our baby and you won't.

"You'll have that baby bath in the bathroom – don't worry

about it now – to wash more blood from our fretting child. Discard your bloodied surgical gloves if you must; I wish we had more pairs. You'll be careful not to let water slip into our trembling baby's mouth or eyes closed fast, or to disturb the clasp on the last of the umbilical cord close to the navel. You might see white little heads you've not seen in adults dotting the baby's crimson face and skin, and blemishes in shades of pink across the baby's flesh, but they're normal traits of healthy English babies."

Laura sat up on her bed, her arms open, her knees still up and legs apart. "Our baby clean," she said, "you'll dry our newborn child with a towel. Needing to be warmer than we'll need to be, you'll wrap him or her in little sheets and blankets like a cloth cocoon, from which only a little wrinkled face will show. You'll stare mesmerised at that person born to be your child, absorbed into a trance. Something fundamental will stir within you, when our lives and last society took us beyond civility into a place that only fools presumed was better.

"Oblivious to your gaze, those closed eyes, soft nose, and little mouth won't be like those of any child or adult. They'll be the nascent forms of a person still to come. You'll stand there forever if you could, but I'll want you to bring him or her to me."

Brandon carried his lump of air to her. She accepted it, cradling it.

"I'll hold our child," she said. "My hair will be awry and face strained, but my smile will shine from my face and eyes. Love, without condition, will envelop me. People used to worry so much about being loved, but loving is better."

"You'll have never been more beautiful," said Brandon, hoping the words sounded better to her than they sounded to him, "nursing the new life you'd made." Their child would soften and strengthen both of them.

"If you ask me 'How was it?' I'll answer 'Terrible,' as I touch our baby's tender cheeks. That fresh flesh moving with my fingertips will rise readily back again. If our baby starts to cry, I'll hold him or her closer, but you: I need you to return to the end of our bed to see again from where our baby came."

Brandon returned to the end of the bed. Laura continued cradling empty air, her knees still up and legs apart.

"Still hanging from me will be the blood-drenched umbilical cord," said Laura. "Set the metal tray on the bloodied towel below me."

Brandon took the tray from the table. He placed it between her open legs.

"Holding the cord close to me as if you could accidentally break it, carefully pull the cord towards you. Unwinding it from me, through your reddening gloved or ungloved hands, it will become taut and more difficult to pull. If you tell me it's almost out, I'll contract the muscles in my pelvis to try to force from me the red wet meat placenta. You grip the coming edges to narrow it and drag it watchfully towards you, trying not to break it or leave any of it inside me. A final push from me and the lubricating blood and splashing juices should force the last of it to your hands and in the tray.

"Some foreign and ancient cultures revered that meal of human meat that fed our child, but we're English. We'll feed it later to the animals.

"What remains will be me. You'll take took another towel from the table, douse it in water, and gently dab my skin and hair to clean them of blood and anything else. You'll examine me for cuts or tears, telling me what you see as I'll tell you what I feel. Can you sew?"

Brandon shook his head. Any clothes that required sewing he'd replaced from the glut of clothes remaining.

"Before too long," Laura told him, "I'll teach you to sew thread through fabric like it was skin being spiked and separated. If I need you to be my tailor, you'll place our baby in the cradle and be more careful with that needle and thread in me than you've been about anything else in your life. Your last chore of the birth, that thread will tug me back together. I'd rather feel pain than die.

"I'll be expecting you to clean everything, take everything we need to wash outside, and make the room and our bed neat again. The house will be quiet again, and I'll tell you that you've done well, as you'll say the same of me. Our child will never know the moment of our meeting as you and I will not forget."

Laura closed her legs and laid them flat along the bed. She ceased cradling empty air.

"After you've done all you can do," she told him, "you can sit back in your chair, when the trauma of what we've done will catch you: you'd have cut two lives apart so both would live. Finally free to feel, dread and panic might well rain inside your flurried head. Your breath might shorten, pulse race, and skin flush, as you almost faint. Unable to think or see, you might feel frail and weak as you've never before felt.

"Gradually, your consciousness will regather, mind clear, and body settle. Without crisis, we're safe again."

Brandon sat back in that chair beside their bed, expecting her to resume her prophecy. He'd learned enough to believe Laura and her baby should survive, if the baby remained inside her womb for forty weeks and incurred no complications. If a new life in their image was a miracle, it was an ordinary miracle.

Laura stood up from their bed. She sat in Brandon's lap.

"If fate tempts us with chances to walk across the moon," she told him, "you will still never see anything more incredible, inspirational, or wonderful than the first unrepeatable moments of our child approaching you. A child gives a parent life as much as the parent gives it to the child."

"How do you know so well what I will think, six months from now?"

She kissed him, briefly. "My father told my mother what he thought when I was born," she told him, brushing loose hair from his forehead. "After he died, my mother told me."

16

SUMMERTIME

The dates that Laura marked off her calendar proceeded through June. Of an evening, she and Brandon had many rooms in which to sit; all the white sheets that once covered furniture had been removed.

Of a warm dry day, summer lit the land. They spent most of their time outdoors.

Slowly rising from the gardens they had planted were green rows of clumps of cabbages. Brandon cut one from the ground.

He loosened the soil around another tuft of leaves with his hands, grabbed the tuft, and gently pulled an ugly carrot from the ground. Small clumps and shreds of dirt fell from the jagged dull orange surfaces back to the broken earth. He and Laura reaped the vegetables from the fields for food and washed them in the creek, where the clear drops of hanging water shone better than did the fresh foodstuffs.

Keeping only themselves, there was never much to do. Whiffs of grass sometimes appeared in the courtyard. Brandon pulled them out and dropped them where grass was meant to be.

On the patio behind the house, Brandon set up a round white wrought-iron table and two of four matching chairs he'd found stored inside the house. There, he sat still. With a straight comb and pair of the sharpest steel scissors she'd brought with her,

Laura lifted his hair between the teeth of the comb and cut his long hair above it. Thick curls of his hair fell to the ground, as she cut the hair at the back and sides of his head. When she rested the cold scissors on his forehead and prepared to cut the hair there, Brandon closed his eyes and felt only the scissors against his skin. The slivers of his hair fell past his eyes.

Laura continued carefully thinning and trimming his hair. Finally, she combed his hair down. "There," she said, returning the comb and scissors to the table, "done."

She picked up two hand mirrors she'd brought down from her dressing table in their bedroom and offered one to him. With that mirror in his hand and the other she held behind his head, Brandon saw the back of his head in the reflections in two mirrors. "That's great," he said, "I think."

Laura returned the hand mirrors to the table. She then took a bottle and sprayed something on his hair.

"What's that?" asked Brandon.

"Never mind," she laughed.

Brandon stood up and out of the chair. He flexed his arms and legs.

Laura sat down where he had sat. "My turn now," she said, staring forward.

Her words surprised him, but he'd forgotten who they were. Her fair brown hair was already beautiful from her efforts washing and styling it that morning, but had grown past her shoulders since they met. "I don't know how to cut hair," said Brandon, reluctantly picking up the comb and scissors. "I'll only detract from you."

Laura reached over and retrieved a hand mirror. Studying the reflection cast in the mirror, she adjusted her head, as Brandon stood poised over her. "Don't worry," she said, her hair falling back as she stood up.

"Are you sure?"

"Sewing, I need to teach you."

Other times, they sat there with books, cups of tea, or both. Sometimes, they simply sat there.

"When I'm strong enough after our baby is born," said Laura, "we'll wheel our little infant in a pram to the church in Kirby

Knowle. After dipping a silver spoon in water, I'll rest the wet spoon on our sacred baby's forehead, leaving drops of water, pledging to protect our water baby and asking God to do so too. Only the arms of loved ones can carry our child into His arms."

Brandon didn't question things she did for all of them. "What more can you tell me about bearing babies and raising children? What more did your father tell your mother I should know?"

Laura carefully drew a long breath, before replying. "A newborn baby's eyes see only shades of light and dark," she told him. "To that tender brain, the senses meaning most are those of touch, so you'll rest your tactile father finger in those curling little digits.

"Those tiny blemishes and white dots at birth will fade, as our child's crimson skin clears and turns to pink during the coming weeks. Our child's skin will pale for life: to white whiter than you and I have come to be.

"Without language, there are no thoughts inside that head, but the instinctive needs of taste and hunger: the only dreams that sleeping mind can make. We'll feed him or her when he or she can't feed otherwise."

Laura sometimes paused between words, as if collating her thoughts. Brandon waited.

"Lying small and helpless," she resumed, "our child will sleep, wake, and sometimes cry. If those cries aren't for food, then we'll close the door to that room so we don't have to hear them. Our baby will vomit and possibly urinate or defecate on you, but the excrement that would've sickened you from any other person will be just another mess to clean.

"If our child sleeps too long, we'll listen closely to the silence for the sounds of breathing. Without knowing what neglect might kill or let our baby die, birth's fortune will continue every day our baby stays alive.

"More vulnerable to us than we are to him or her, that little life remains more vulnerable and for a longer time than do newborn animals in fields and pets in empty homes, before adults learn to think we're invulnerable or ought to be. Our child will be an onerous responsibility we'll cherish, needing us when no other person has. He or she might always need us, but we'd rather become comfortably redundant."

Sometimes Laura sounded so much the anthropologist she had studied to be. Other times, her voice could only have been her mother's passing through.

"Baby eyes will evolve enough to focus," she continued, "looking up at ceilings as we look up at skies. Smiles will ease into that little face, in recognition of parental smiles on show. You might twirl your finger in the air to see the child's eyes turn. The shining in those eyes will convince you our child is beginning to learn to smile.

"Baby cheeks and a chin, every limb, will slowly become stronger. Those baby fingers will strengthen enough to grip your finger coming near. Those eyes and hands will explore and examine everything to see and touch, without needing to understand. Our child will enjoy things we'd have called mundane and be impressed with things that long stopped impressing us, as if everything was brilliant and beautiful."

Sometimes Laura looked Brandon in the eyes, as if her words were most of all for him. Other times she looked past him towards the vale, as if her words were most of all for her to hear.

"The life to start the day we meet, if not before then, will come to feel and think, love and hate, laugh and cry," she said. "Its heart too small to contemplate will grow and might outgrow our tarnished souls.

"Time and age will harden those soft soles, palms, and muscles. Those feet and legs, which seem too fragile to learn to walk when first we see them, will grow strong enough for you to hold those hands, teaching our child to walk. You might even raise a son above your head looking up and throw him a short way in the air, but never too far from your hands catching him again. You'll be much gentler with a daughter.

"My father fretted that my soft baby head was askew, possibly distorted during the trauma of my birth. Looking down upon my ears, he saw one forward of the other. He'd have held my head to straighten it, but feared hurting me. So he studied other people's heads and faces to see they were no less asymmetrical than mine. Uniformity was important, in spite of every protestation otherwise.

"Every worry reminded him he loved me. He didn't need to worry for people he didn't love. You'll worry no less for a son."

When Laura and Brandon tired of sitting, they walked along the paths and around the courtyard. Laura continued imparting her memories.

"My parents saw such love and trust in my infant eyes as must once have been in theirs," she said, "without fear or doubt when they were there. Children smile and cry unabashed, but we learn too well to conceal. My parents found again unpleasant feelings and so the most profound of good feelings long lost in them. Together, we were spontaneous, playful and responsibly irresponsible.

"Consuming love, the senses my father previously knew of love were inadequate to measure the pervasive deep new love he felt for me in my young life. He loved my mother and would concede almost everything for her, but still mightn't sacrifice as much for her as he would surrender for me. He would try to save my mother from a danger, endangering his life to do so, but I think inadvertently forfeited his life to save her as he would unhesitatingly have forfeited it to save me.

"Dad couldn't explain the love he found inside himself; he couldn't have learned what he'd become. Without ego or pretence, my parents wanted more for my life than theirs: to live a childhood, adolescence, and life better than theirs had been. They wanted me to be a better person than either one of them had been, whatever that could mean. I was supposed to share the best moments my lost parents' lives had been, enjoying good things they knew and should've known. If love was innate to Englishmen, what else had always been within them?"

When Laura and Brandon tired of walking, they sat again. A starling rested near them.

"Dad had expected to teach me," she went on, "but hadn't expected to learn so much from me. With me, Dad learned to play again as he hadn't played since he was young. I think people always play, but most of them believe they're too important to realise it.

"He thought less often of the things he used to want, except to wonder why he ever wanted them. He thought less often of the people he used to know, including him. I made him laugh at who he once had been, before I came to make him better.

"My parents wondered when they'd stopped being like me. I made my parents young so they could never grow old again, but they did grow old.

"I too became older, hearing so many lies I dreaded the wrath of truth. We learned to take anything we wanted because no one gave it to us. My love corrupted, becoming unrecognisable from what it might've been, but in spite of everything I did and didn't do, I remained my loving father's daughter, my devoted mother's baby. For reasons vague but no less convincing for being so, my mother didn't want to die before I could cope without her."

Laura fell silent, this time looking at Brandon as if to say she couldn't think of anything more to say, not then anyway. He too had been a baby too small to know and work, at which a person staring couldn't have foretold the life he would experience. Nor could he imagine what his child's eyes would see.

The aged man, the tempered woman, was each a superficial transformation of the child that he or she once was. The transitions through the generations of their lives became no more comprehensible because they had occurred. Recalling Brandon's infant mind and heart could only soothe his adult life.

"Do you ever wonder how to reciprocate the love and help your parents gave you?" asked Brandon.

"I helped my mother as she aged and was glad to do so," said Laura, "without thought that I was recompensing my parents. I held her when she struggled to walk, as my parents once held me learning to do so. I cried with her when walking became too difficult. If I'd asked her what she wanted from me, I think she'd have said we can accord no greater gratitude to the people who brought us into the world than loving and taking care of their grandchildren."

"I still don't know how to be a father."

"I don't know how to be a mother. We can only do our best with what we know and try to know."

"What about the things we do wrongly?"

"They won't be as important as the things we do correctly."

Brandon had come to believe most things Laura said. In spite of Brandon's failings, his child would stumble through. He and Laura prospered and could do almost anything.

Mere knowledge was no reward without people to fulfil it. Much as Laura had taught him, so would they both teach their child. Their growing child mightn't need to know too much about sweet Laura and old him, but should know what Brandon knew for the journey of a life, without wasting time to learn it all afresh. His knowledge not imparted would lose its purpose when he died.

In a desk in the house lay reams of paper for diaries and letters never written. Before time dulled his fading recollections, Brandon began to write the story of the end of everybody else and the start of life with Laura. Leaving Brandon's memories behind let him think better thoughts to come, although Brandon didn't write to write but to be read. The names of authors were less important than their legacies in print.

Brandon and Laura wouldn't instil values by command but accidentally distil them by example, to paraphrase some wisdom he had heard. Their child should enjoy life, but pursue more than happiness. The meaning of success changes from time to time. A person should adopt useful technologies, but dismiss those not helping. A person needed to work and play to distinguish one from the other.

He would teach their child sports and other games, proud when first his child defeated him. They would try their best to win knowing that winning was unimportant, and stop playing if they ever stopped enjoying it.

An Englishman or woman should consider everything, but not concede life or livelihood to any thought or thing. England was the centre of his new philosophies and not mere adjuncts to any causes, consumption, or careers. If people served England, then England would serve them.

Humanity and compassion dictated loving only people a

person knows. Of paramount importance, Brandon's child should know of his and Laura's love.

He would read stories to their child, the last learning and leisure before being tucked into bed each night. His child would become a little like Laura and a little like Brandon in ways that weren't Brandon's to foresee, making choices like and unlike those he had made. His child would only know of other lives to the extent Brandon or Laura mentioned snippets of the lives they led, or his child draw inferences from the sad clues of old lives left behind.

Tilling fields and keeping house in order to survive weren't much to learn. Laura or Brandon could teach all that in one great day, or their child might learn from observations without them saying anything.

Brandon and Laura would replicate their formal schooling as best they could: teaching reading, writing, and mathematics. Old textbooks, wherever they found them, would teach the teachers principles they had forgotten as they taught them to their child innocent and ignorant. They would teach history, including theories for extinction. They had all much to learn, doing everything themselves.

His child would learn to think; that alone was more than Brandon learned to do. Brandon wanted his child to grow old enough to understand, although Brandon hadn't become that old.

Love and responsibilities might inspire Brandon to maintain aspects of his childhood for the next generation to enjoy. They might demand he leave them behind.

His child would learn lessons from him and Laura and choose what earnestly to believe. Each generation shouldn't make the mistakes the preceding generation made, and not make too many new ones.

The first great pleasures will be loves, from which the greatest sorrows flow. Sorrows shouldn't deter people from more feelings but prepare them for the revelry of the next pleasures to befall them, in every sense of being alive.

Learning would be for life in a world in which his child lived almost alone, without knowing what he or she had lost. Those things that Brandon and Laura missed would be no longer there. Knowledge of England gone needn't distract nor taint, but be aspects of an education. Films and books will reveal some things small about Europe's dead society. The politics, priorities, and preferences of a childless people would seem like the lies they were.

England had been good but never perfect; her second greatest failing her presumption she came so near to being perfect. The hearts of people who wouldn't love the little lives of sons and daughters had fallen hard and cold. All causes were hopeless that diminished their humanity and humanness. No crusades that anyone could feel or fight made righteous the unloving.

The people without love died long before their bodies did. Brandon and Laura might've been like them, near death, before their child's small life revived them. Much as artists loving art created works they cherished, men and women loving people created people.

Brandon couldn't reconcile parental love with love he bestowed upon a woman born a stranger. He didn't think he should. Nor would he bear the distraction of calling his new realm of service and long perspective a mere emotion. Self and liberty were crude and crass.

All that mattered were what helped the lives and lifestyles of people for whom he cared. The only people Brandon remembered being so generous were his parents.

Where the grass outside was not too long or where it was comfortably long, and free from the waste that animals excreted, Brandon sometimes lay on his back. Gazing through the sparkling spaces between the leaves of trees, he lost his thoughts in the white clouds and blue sky. The fresh air rolled into and through his lungs, cleaning them anew as they cleaned those of a born baby. Laura rested against an old rock wall or the trunk of a tree.

"So few people were parents in that last generation," said Brandon. "Why did your parents bear you?"

"I asked my mother that question, in the last months of her life. She said that she and my father were simply curious to be parents. She knew that curiosity wasn't a good reason to be a parent, but the reason wasn't important. The important thing was that they created me, and that their lives were immeasurably better for it."

"Most parents didn't say things like that to their children."

"My mother might've said them to me because she was dying. Her words might've made her unique among the rare, for English people now."

Brandon stretched out his chest and arms; lying too long on the ground discomforted him. "Your mother makes me wonder why your parents didn't have more children," he said.

"Her sister Mia was very mean to her when I was born. I don't think she meant anything personal, but she kept saying English people should have stopped having children, that my parents would regret it. My mother took everything personally, but she also saw little me taking it personally. I think Mia blamed my parents for bearing me more than she blamed me for being born, on the basis that children weren't responsible for anything, but I felt guilty. My mother saved a second child from feeling a pain I felt, but condemned me to sadness for the siblings I might've had."

"What were the husbands and fathers doing?" asked Brandon.

"Husbands never disagreed with their wives; only with their children."

Brandon laughed. "Your parents were rewarded with your companionship and support in their last years," he reminded her, becoming serious again.

"They hadn't thought so far ahead when I was born."

Brandon sat up on the grass. Instead of all the things at which he could have looked, he looked at Laura.

"Aunt Mia became older, richer, and lonelier," Laura resumed, "inside the comfort she thought she saw in a land fading away. She died alone, without any reason for having been alive. I didn't bury her; I suppose somebody did, or she might still be lying dead inside her empty house. I don't want to live like her, and I don't want to die like her."

Laura might've enjoyed a belated vindication. Nevertheless, her aunt left her alone.

"My greatest fear for our child is loneliness," said Laura.

"What else will matter to a person all alone? Knowing other people from our stories will never be enough."

Their child would sit alone in the same desk each day, quietly undertaking tasks without anyone with whom to pass messages between desks. The only educators and influencers will be the parents: the teachers in the classroom and the tutors after school, the sporting coaches and dieticians, the drama teachers and hygienists. Their child could not complain about a teacher to a parent or a parent to a friend.

He or she wouldn't marvel at the skills of other people: performers and scientists, engineers and artists. There'd be no stimulation of a conversation with a stranger at a party, learning something of other people's experiences. Ignorant of bliss and tragedy, there'd be no pursuit in love through the thrill and fear of chase, sometime succeeding. Brandon, Laura, and their child would be the best of friends and worst of friends, with nowhere left to go each day but home.

17

WHOLE LIVES FOR LITTLE PEOPLE

Of a morning, Laura often stood side-on before the mirror in their dressing room. Dressed for the day in another long dress, she rounded her hand over the arc in her stomach. Their child was slow to grow, but her coming fullness would mean the clothes that hugged her would become too tight. The larger dresses in the stores were designed for larger women and not for ordinary women in their pregnancies.

"Will I be ugly?" Laura asked him. "Will I look fat?"

"You will look pregnant." With Laura's belly becoming larger, Brandon's mind had more reason to dwell upon the person he would meet, come Christmastime.

She pulled her hand from her belly. "Might our child be England's final child?" she asked. "Might England be already dead?"

He, Laura, and their child would age. The sun would become lower in the sky each day and then higher again, as the seasons turn. The stars in constellation would traverse the sky again and again, marking the passages of years and lives. Their child was a new chance to be the last of a long kin, but without other children with whom to grow, there would be no England. Brandon had already achieved more than most recent Englishmen, but their child would come to little if England did not endure. The home they made and nurtured would end at the passing of their child's life.

"I thought so," said Laura. "Do you still want to break through a door with your axe?"

"No more banks."

"I didn't care at the time," she explained, moving around the room, "because people without children didn't pay much attention to the problems of parents, not English parents, but I've been thinking about it a lot lately. There's a restaurant in Bishop Thornton, a village north of Harrogate, heading into the Dales, in which I once ate with Ogden. The meal was all right, good even, but the restaurant prohibited kids under twelve years old from even being there. It was one thing not to have a kid's menu, but babies and children under twelve couldn't even sit and starve."

"The rule didn't just exclude children," said Brandon, "but parents too." People could've dispensed with the meals but were so keen to eat well, they dispensed with the children.

"A woman complained about it so loud that we couldn't help but overhear," continued Laura, "whereby the manager or someone said something about it being a carvery, but I don't know what that had to do with anything. Even if it had, the restaurant could have dealt with the problem, whatever it was. They were making excuses."

"I'm not much keen on excuses," said Brandon. "We haven't eaten out for a while."

With Laura directing, Brandon drove them south past Thirsk. They continued westward, towards the famously green Yorkshire Dales.

The tranquillity in green reminded Brandon that only he and Laura remained to appreciate them. "We saved the trees," he said, "but lost ourselves."

Along the way, signs directed them towards and welcomed them through empty villages. The slowly rusting metal and rotting wood were the fall of time, when Brandon and Laura's fertility were their families reborn. As much a birth, their baby would be England's rebirth. Their coming child made England beautiful again, filling the land as other relics of lives gone past could not. Wisdom was becoming young again.

Before reaching Bishop Thornton, at an intersection on which stood the derelict Drovers Inn, boarded up and behind rusting barricade fences, Laura directed Brandon right towards Fountains Abbey. Around them were more green trees and meadows on which stood lazy cows. Shortly up ahead were two white buildings two storeys high. Marked for no one left to see, at least one was the Chequers Inn free house.

As well as being a restaurant, it was a hotel with fourteen rooms, all of them with en-suite bathrooms, according to the sign dulling more than the buildings had. Brandon didn't doubt that all the rooms were still available.

Another sign, the hardest to read, declared caravans and motorhomes were welcome. No caravans or motorhomes were there.

Nor were there any cars where Brandon parked his car, in the courtyard off the road that several doors and four round-arched windows faced. The only interruption to the courtyard was a wooden table and benches midway along the building, much like those tables and benches scattered among the long grasses across the courtyard. "Do you think they're for children?" asked Laura.

"I'm in the mood to be inside today," said Brandon.

Laura stepped out, while Brandon removed his axe from the boot. They stood together before the white free house walls and windows.

"Do you see this?" Brandon called out to the inn, pointing his free hand to Laura's belly. "Do you see?" he called a little louder. "There's a child here, under twelve. We're here for lunch!"

"We haven't reserved a table," called out Laura.

"We know you have tables free," called out Brandon.

He could understand prohibiting children from a lounge bar for their health and well-being, so left that entrance alone. He led Laura to the door marked for the restaurant, beside which a small notice declared the hotel and restaurant closed and thanked people for their custom. They weren't the purpose of Brandon and Laura's visit.

The door was dark, solid timber, so probably thick and hard, like the hard-heartedness that almost murdered England. Standing before it, poised with his axe, Brandon slowly drew his axe back behind his shoulders. Drawing all the breath he could, he concentrated his energy in his muscles and his eyes on that door, as he had done at the bank in Harrogate.

"Have you tried the handle?" asked Laura. To the left side of the door was a single brass handle.

Releasing his long breath, Brandon slowly lowered his axe. He might only need to do so for a moment.

Laura stepped forward and turned the handle. She opened the door.

Brandon sighed, dropping his arms to his side. The axe struck the ground, as it had struck little else, before Brandon ambled back to his car and returned it to the boot.

Laura waited for him at the open door. When Brandon returned, he stood to the side of the door. Pointing his hand inside, he ushered Laura into the reopened restaurant. "Table for three, Madam?"

The cavern was cosy, with low vaulted ceilings, benches, and lots of wood and stone, but premises that children could've made charming had become another hole above the ground. In one space was a billiard table on which lay several billiard balls Brandon imagined Ogden playing. He left them alone. Scattered around the high parts of walls were antlers without the heads from which they had been cut.

The carvery counter was empty, left clean, as if it might be used again. The best remaining hints of food or wine were bunches of green plastic grapes hanging above it, around the boards on which were written the names of wines that might or might not still be available. Other blackboards were bare.

The kitchen area was just as clean. Opening a cupboard door, a brown cat leapt into Brandon's arms. He stumbled backwards with the shock, as the cat dropped through his arms onto the floor and ran away. Brandon looked into the cupboard, which was rather large but in which he could see no other ingress through which the cat could have come.

The pantry contained plenty of preserved foods, including tall glass jars of fruit, vegetables, jams, and marmalades. Brandon took a jar of cucumbers, a knife, and two forks from a drawer, which he took to Laura sitting at a table. She made theirs the best table in the house.

"I think this is where we sat when I last came," she said.

"Should I sit where Ogden sat," asked Brandon, placing the jar and forks on the table, "or not sit where Ogden sat?"

"The best thing is that I don't tell you where Ogden sat." She examined the jar before her. "We should get some plates."

Brandon brought two saucers from the kitchen. Covering the lid of the jar was a red checked cloth, which Brandon removed. "What was the purpose of that?" he asked. The lid was tightly sealed, but the strength he'd not used to enter the restaurant he used to remove the lid.

He cut a cucumber into several slices on Laura's plate. "Thank you," she said, "from both of us." He cut thicker slices for himself.

Brandon ate a slice or two, before sitting back in his chair; he wasn't really hungry. Sometime since they'd met, as he'd never before noticed, Laura's face had become radiant. "After our child is born," he said, "we three should return here; I don't know where we can get a babysitter."

"I might even ask for Pimm's," smiled Laura, "with lemonade."

"We won't need a children's menu, because you can feed our baby the natural way." The restaurant can't have ever before been so vibrant, elegant, and charming as it would be with Laura nursing their child. In the society they would compose, nobody would notice her child suckling at her breast because it would be so commonplace. Anybody who noticed would smile.

Laura wasn't looking at him but past him. Slowly, she stood, stepped away from her chair and the table. She proceeded across the room, between chairs and tables, towards an old dial clock affixed high on the wall. Brandon followed her, as she reached as close to the clock as the bench and table below it allowed. "The clock is ticking," she said.

Brandon stood near her. "A cat came at me from a cupboard in the kitchen," he said. "It can't have been there very long."

"I don't think we need fear a person who'd wind an English clock," said Laura, looking around. "Do we risk remaining here?"

Brandon listened; the carpeted floor ensured that not even he and Laura made a sound. They both stepped into more open parts of the restaurant and lounge bar. "Do we risk leaving?"

On a table by a window, looking out to the courtyard where Brandon's car stood, lay a single beer coaster. In a place where everything else was clean, it should have drawn his attention sooner, as should the billiard balls.

"Hello," he called out. "We won't hurt you. We're English."

He and Laura remained still for a minute or more, until a door slowly squeaked open. Soon standing before them was a man about sixty years of age, wearing a tweed cap above his black shirt and trousers. His nose was a little large, as noses could be in people getting old, with a crimson tinge not from the sun outside. In his hand was a glass pint mug of beer, partly drunk.

Sluggishly he moved towards the table with the cardboard coaster, on which he rested his mug. "Can I get each of you a drink?" he asked.

"I'm pregnant," said Laura.

"I heard you both outside."

He walked away from them to the bar counter, behind which he stepped, as might a barman. Brandon and Laura followed him, waiting for him outside the counter, as customers would.

"I have orange squash," said the man, slowly opening a bottle of Robinsons orange squash and pouring a portion in a glass. "I'm Alfie, everything's on the house now." Alfie opened a small bottle of tonic water, from which he filled the glass. He then held a mug at an angle under a beer tap and pulled the handle; Brandon had expected never to drink draught beer. "I hope your husband likes Theakston's." The brown beer flowed into the glass, against the side so as not to raise too much of a head, until Alfie pushed back the handle. "You might want to pick up some coasters."

On the counter was a pile of maybe half a dozen cardboard coasters, like the one on the table. Brandon picked up two, before he and Laura followed Alfie carrying the glass and mug to his table. There, Brandon placed his two coasters on the table facing the man's mug and coaster. He watched the man place Laura's glass on the coaster nearer the window and Brandon's mug on the other coaster. "You're now serving children under twelve?" asked Brandon.

"Dogs allowed, no children," he replied, sitting down. "How daft was that?"

Laura and Brandon sat facing him. Brandon sipped his beer, fresher than he would have expected beer from a long closed pub to be; perhaps it had reopened. Laura sipped her orange squash.

"You're the first people here this season," said Alfie, his lips returning to his beer. "Most days, I sit here alone, trying to remember what this place used to be, hoping some of my old customers come back, worrying about any car coming."

"Why didn't you allow children under twelve?" asked Laura.

"It was the mature place I wanted, that customers wanted. Consumers and crusaders, we were, opinion makers, people passing by. Don't blame me because English people stopped having children. I'm just a publican, a restauranteur."

Laura turned towards the window. Alfie's words played in Brandon's mind, as he knew they did in Laura's mind.

"People gone never resolved how to balance work and family," said Laura, looking through the glass, "but we asked the wrong questions. Work and family weren't equal, and work certainly wasn't more important. We should've facilitated men and women having families and organised the work we wanted to do around them."

Almost whimsically, Brandon reflected on an increasingly distant past. "School teachers told us that possessing a great skill or talent and not exploiting it to the full was a great waste," he said.

"Like selling dental products was so wonderful," laughed Laura, "or punching buttons on a computer keyboard because somewhere there's an assembly line making executive toys for people you'll never meet. Being able to bear children without doing so, raising them, playing with them, teaching them, was the waste."

"Leave the stupid things to people who can't do anything else, you think," said Alfie.

Laura turned back to him. "If I could take my knowledge now and go back in time to save society then I would," she told him. "I'd stand outside your pub and tell people coming in that each and all of them can enjoy all the good things they want – arts, beauty, roast beef and gravy – forgoing very little, if they knew what I've come to know."

"We can't change the past," replied Alfie, "even if we reconstruct it in the image of the future we desire. You're beginners, you two, taking up again what England lost. Germinate something better, without the craziness of last time, or we'll lose ourselves again."

"So," asked Laura, "what will you do if we sit here six months from now and our newborn baby becomes restless, pursing lips and making motions of swallowing food that isn't there? How will you react if I pull up my blouse, loosen the buttons, and feed our baby from my breast? I'll try to be inconspicuous, but can't promise I won't expose a white breast for anyone to see, before I set our baby's mouth against it, moving those baby lips around until they catch and hold my nipple. Bound to my breast will be our baby."

Brandon imagined horrified indignation from customers long gone, who'd have politely ignored people with disabilities but would scorn an Englishwoman functioning normally. If those customers weren't already in their graves, they'd taken England there.

Alfie maintained his weary tone. "I'll bring you another orange squash."

Laura sipped her drink. "I might ask for a Pimm's," she smiled. "If anyone had marketed children as businesses marketed drinks, then we'd have born our wealth in children, instead of bearing death without them. My Aunt Mia complained that motherhood treated women as incubators. She called men sperm banks with meat syringes. Europeans assumed that we alone among the people of the world chose what we did, with regard only to ourselves, but if we chose anything it was our infertility and other decline. I no longer value choice, but still we choose."

"Youth prevails over age," Alfie told her. "My parents saved us. You're saving us."

"We thought we had no parental instincts left," continued Laura, "no breath of paternity or maternity, but we never gave ourselves the chance to find what was always within us: to be what we could be. We should be ourselves to save ourselves, but were too often something else."

Brandon had become a listener to their conversation. He was much closer in age to her than Alfie was, but their dialogue of lives beyond anything he'd known left him feeling very young. He drank his beer getting lower in his mug. When he finished it he asked Alfie, "Can I please get another pint?"

"You're driving."

"Who'll know?"

"You'll know if you crash your car."

"I'll drive," said Laura.

Alfie took Brandon's mug, poured him another pint of Theakston's from the tap, and returned it to his coaster, as Laura finished her last mouthful of orange squash. Alfie took her glass and carried it and his mug back behind the bar. He soon returned with her glass and his mug full again.

"If you head from here into the village," Alfie sitting down again told Laura, "you'll see white lettering on a rock welcoming you; rocks last better than wood and steel. People here would have welcomed you, but I'm the only one left to say it. Come back any time."

"Why do you stay?" asked Laura.

"I went to the south-east, when others did. People are trying to rebuild in Cornwall, Devon; other places too, they say. With the understanding they've got now, there's community, children."

Brandon, Laura, and their child were but one family. They needed by good grace and miracle other remnants of their people procreating. Without other families like theirs, there could be no generations to come.

"Every adult's a parent who can be," continued Alfie, "growing back into something like England could be, reclaiming land my generation and recent generations lost, but I'm too old to father a child and, truth be known, I can't. All I had in my life since my wife died was this old pub: my England. We were decent people, who never understood we could save England until we couldn't anymore."

"Brandon was on his way to Cornwall," said Laura, "when I met him in Northallerton."

"They're admitting all the English people and only English people," replied Alfie, "since everyone else staked out their cities, boroughs, and towns. If you go there, you better keep to the bypasses along the way and avoid the London Orbital, but you'll like Devon, Cornwall. Someone said there's polygamy in some villages, but I never saw it. In St Austell, we had men and women in similar numbers so never had to consider it."

Laura looked at Brandon, involving him in their conversation as he rarely had been. She studied him, although she can hardly have seen anything new. More likely, she was thinking; she seemed to do a lot of thinking. If she was considering them headed to Cornwall, then she was taking up what he'd once wanted them to do. Since then, he'd become secure in their castle home.

"If fortune brings another English woman upon us," she said coolly, "and if you must father children through her with whom we can make our new society, then I hope you do so."

Laura spoke as England's guardian, the protector of their kind, the custodian of one generation. She was being clinical, when Brandon wanted them to be much more, but perhaps theirs was an era for being clinical if England was going to survive. Love and romance might have been indulgences more for other times than theirs.

"Would you bear the child of another man?" asked Brandon.

"Only if I can't bear another child with you."

"Would you love him?"

"Do you think that would mean I didn't love you?"

"Would you want me to love that other woman by whom I was fathering a child as much as I love you, or more so, if that were possible?"

She drank more of her orange squash, as she would when she wanted time to think. "You should love any woman with whom you bear a child," she said. "If you love her and her child, protect them, then she should love you."

Alfie had become obvious by his silence: the audience that Brandon had been. He drank the beer he had all day, every day, to drink.

"I think I'd feel jealous of you loving another man," said Brandon. "Why wouldn't I be able to father all your children?"

"I pray you can," said Laura. "Biological reality means we're more likely to want you to father children with other mothers than me to mother them with other men, but jealousy would be selfish. Jealousy harms the jealous, and we can't let envy affect us doing what we have to do. Our duties to each other are more precious than our rights."

"Sometimes," said Alfie, "I dream we again occupy the empty houses, towns, and farms, so that long after I've rolled my last keg across a floor there'll be in this old pub Englishmen drinking Theakston's and Englishwomen drinking Pimm's, or orange squash."

They were dreams in which Brandon was striving to believe. His unseen child might yet become a father to the fatherly or mother to the motherly.

18

OTHERS

Their child would inherit Brandon and Laura's castle house. Other castle houses would fall to ruin.

Standing at the bay window of their bedroom one morning much like any other, looking out across the Vale of York, a movement caught Brandon's eyes. It was along Whinmoor Hill, coming eastwards from Kirby Knowle, passing behind trees and then out again. The motion was there, then wasn't, then was again. "I think I can see a car," he said.

Laura hurried from their bed. She stood beside him, looking out.

"There," he pointed, as it disappeared behind greenery. "It was speeding as young people might, dark in colour." Brandon looked for any indication of the car coming up the driveway or of it continuing towards Upsall, but couldn't see it again.

"We have to be careful," said Laura.

Brandon stepped into the farthest reach of the bay window to see more of the driveway, but couldn't see it well enough. "The driver might be friendly."

"He might not."

Brandon rushed from the room onto the landing and into the bedroom he'd first occupied in the house. From the balcony off that en-suite bathroom, he looked onto the empty courtyard.

Laura soon stood at the open doorway. "You're hoping somebody will come, aren't you?" she said. "We can learn and train ourselves for whatever we need to do. Alfie will help us. I'm sure the people at the Friarage will help us if we need them."

No car appeared. As much as Brandon could see of the driveway, no car was coming.

"I like what we have here," said Laura. "I don't want to lose it. I don't want to make the mistakes England made again."

He turned back to Laura, their child showing through her face. The only lives he really knew were those of nearly three of them inside their castle home.

"We have a chance now," said Laura, in a voice as much of sombre as of hope, "a last chance possibly, to do everything better than we once did. We mightn't get another one."

Their castle house was visible between the trees from Whinmoor Hill to any person looking northward. Any visitor coming up the driveway should have no reason to believe anyone was there, with Brandon and Laura's cars in the basement garage and bicycles hidden.

"We have something else to keep in mind," said Laura, leading Brandon back through that bathroom, bedroom, and landing to their bedroom. From the drawer and table at her side of the bed, she removed another bedroom key. She held it out to Brandon.

That key had been out of his thinking since their first day in the house. He wasn't even sure how he realised what key it was, given all the room keys looked the same.

"We should be ready," she said.

Brandon took the key from her. "We will be," he said, putting the key back in the drawer and closing it. "I'm sure that wasn't the first car to drive past us, even here so near the Moors. It was the first car we noticed."

Laura and then Brandon showered and dressed for the day, glancing outside through the windows more often than they normally did. They ate their breakfast – the bread Laura baked from dough she'd learned to make and knead – speaking very little. "We should lock all the doors and windows," said Laura, walking from room to room, window to window, closing and locking them all.

"Aren't you being paranoid?" asked Brandon, following her.

"Aren't you being naïve?"

Brandon felt at loose ends, as he hadn't on other days with so few tasks to undertake. "If you want to keep lookout," he told Laura, "we are in a castle."

He led them back upstairs and upstairs again to the highest part of their home: the tower. At the highest parapet they stood, looking out on a sunny day that seemed a little less sunny than other days had been.

There suddenly seemed many roads through the vale, although what lined a road and what was simply a line of trees or hedges could be hard to tell. Only the driveway coming up the hill towards them was obvious. Brandon kept an eye out, most of all eastward to where the car had gone, for a reflection or movement, without expecting to see one.

Laura closed her eyes. "Please God," she whispered, loud enough for him to hear, "keep watch over our child, family, and all English people, always."

Brandon closed his eyes in deference to her prayer. The changes inside her might've made believing in Him easier, but her faith remained too personal for Brandon to ask. He might've feared dissuading her if he talked about it, or feared her persuading him. In silence, except to God, Brandon prayed their child would speak freely of the things that he and Laura didn't.

"By the grace of God," she whispered, "help us bring our child a better life than we will have had."

When Brandon knew she'd finished her prayer, he opened his eyes. Her eyes remained closed a little longer, before opening.

Standing there, even leaning against the stone parapet, could be tiring. The sun became warmer and breeze became cooler the longer they stood there. Struggling a little with the stairs, Brandon brought up two chairs on which they sat. Laura brought up bottles of soft drink and cider. They became leisurely there, looking out without really looking out, drinking and talking. They sat where they could best see the driveway and entrance courtyard, while looking less often at them.

"I want nice people to come," said Laura, "like Alfie, but deciding who is nice can be difficult, even impossible."

"I would like Doctor Hendricks to come, even Niamh."

"They're not coming."

"If they knew you needed them and we couldn't get you to Northallerton," Brandon told her, "I think they would."

She looked away from him, back towards the landscape they'd come there to see. Slowly she leant forward, without standing any more than she needed to stand.

Brandon turned to where she looked, as a dark car, possibly the car he'd seen that morning, came up the driveway. They crouched where the occupants of the car couldn't see them, as it entered the courtyard and approached the house, driving out of their sight.

Laura and Brandon were silent, listening for any sound. A car door opened, and then another, or perhaps two or three more doors. They heard voices, too far away to understand.

"Are they speaking English?" whispered Laura.

"I can't tell."

Laura reached her hand down to where her empty bottle of mineral water stood. From behind it, she pulled the key that Brandon had earlier returned to her bedside table. She offered it to him.

He hesitated, as a thud came from the front of the house. "It's a thick door," said Brandon. "They're thick walls."

"They're thin windows."

"Aren't they double-glazed?" asked Brandon.

"They're not sealing a bank."

"Should we try to escape?"

Laura moved the key she offered him closer to his face. Brandon took the key.

The stairs and floorboards had never before creaked as they creaked then, although the people outside couldn't have heard them. Fearful of the sound they made, listening for other people's sounds, Brandon and then Laura crept back to the room locked since that first day there. Brandon unlocked that door. Laura followed him.

As they would, the rifles remained on the wall and the bullet cartridges on the table. Identifying the rifle he and Laura handled last time they were there, Brandon hesitated, until another thud from downstairs shuddered through the house.

"How many doors are there?" asked Brandon.

"They're trying them all."

He stepped across the room and took the rifle in his hands. With Laura watching his every move, Brandon examined the rifle trying to recall what he'd done the last time he was there. If she thought of hurrying him along, she didn't need to. He managed again to open the barrel. Beside the bullet he'd inserted last time from the box on the table, he inserted a second.

"We don't know how many of them are there," said Laura, looking at the rifles on the wall. If she was wondering whether to take one for herself, then Brandon let her wonder. She took one from the wall.

After a quiet patch, came the loudest thud. Brandon turned around; it would have come from the door atop the fire stairs outside the games room, on the floor on which they stood.

Laura opened the rifle in her hands. She loaded it with two bullets.

"Now, what do we do?" asked Brandon.

They were two floors up. Outside the open door of the room in which they stood was a landing by the stairs. Everything on the floor below them seemed suddenly unimportant, except the materials for Laura giving birth might be irreplaceable. On the ground floor and in the basement were all their foodstuffs.

A lesser thud sounded from below, perhaps three storeys below, in the basement. Around the last side of the house, obscured from the courtyard, the garage door was probably harder to breach than other doors.

Laura stepped back across the room. Taking the box of bullets and another rifle, she sat on the floor, against a wall, facing the open door. She started to load her second rifle with bullets.

Brandon also took a second rifle, the fourth and last on the wall, and sat beside her. From where they sat, they could see through the open door to where the trespassers might come up the stairs, unless those intruders came up other stairs when they would appear on the landing. He too loaded his second rifle, with bullets from the box on the floor between them.

When they both finished, they each sat with their knees upright, on which they each rested loaded rifles pointed towards the open doorway, at which they stared. Their arms held steady rifles while their fingers itched close to the triggers. Lying on the floor between them were two more loaded rifles, also pointing to the door. In the box were more bullets than they would get the chance to use.

The light from the windows behind them illuminated the open doorway for them. It might also have illuminated them for the intruders. A window by the top of the stairs would illuminate anybody coming up.

"We should let them have what they want if they then leave us alone," said Brandon.

"Then they'll eventually take everything," said Laura, "and still mightn't leave us alone."

If the next thud from the basement signalled their ingress into the house, then it wasn't obvious at the time. Voices gradually sounded from below: loud voices, from men unconcerned about being heard. Brazen footsteps pounded on wooden floors. If they didn't think the house was empty, they didn't care that it wasn't. Only the two floors between them and Brandon and Laura stifled their impact.

"They are speaking English, I think, sometimes," whispered Laura, her voice muffled, "but not as English people do. Some of those words aren't our English."

The intruders moved around downstairs: the ground floor, Brandon was certain. Somebody laughed; a male, perhaps more than one person. "We should try to speak to them," whispered Brandon. "We're not shooting anyone unless we know he's hostile."

Downstairs was a heavy thump; Brandon tensed, Laura jolted a little. Soon after, there came the crisper crash of heavy glass breaking and then another crash, and another, and another. There were four crashes: the four crystal decanters in the drawing room, Brandon guessed.

"Now we know," whispered Brandon.

He adjusted his rifle a little higher. Staring through the open door, as Laura was, Brandon listened.

The footsteps across the floor two storeys below became a little louder. They then became softer again, moving through the rooms. Brandon tried differentiating pairs of footsteps to decipher how many people were there. One set of steps might have been lighter than another, or others; a woman might have been among them. Brandon listened most of all for the intruders starting up the stairs.

"I'm grateful you came to Northallerton," whispered Laura. "I'm glad I waited. I'm not glad for everything that brought us together, but I'm glad for that."

Another floorboard or what might have been a stair under foot creaked, louder than previous creaks had been. Somebody was coming upstairs, if only to the first floor of bedrooms still a floor below where Brandon and Laura sat. Their rifles pointed through the open door towards what might be the chests of ordinary-heighted men, without Brandon knowing what might be the ordinary heights of the men prowling about downstairs.

"I love you, Brandon," Laura whispered.

"You tell me, now?" replied Brandon, his voice remaining very soft, continuing to study the space outside the room.

"You've never said you love me."

"I didn't think I needed to."

"Neither did I."

More laughter came from the floor of bedrooms below Brandon and Laura, more footsteps. All the invaders might be heading up through the house, doing whatever it was they did. The invaders would slowly realise there was nothing for them among the bedrooms, unless they'd come to stay. There wasn't much for them to break among the beds and bedroom furniture.

"Who will save our child when we no longer can?" whispered Laura. "This isn't a world for someone alone, no world is. Our child should have brothers and sisters."

"Aren't you daunted?"

"Child bearing will get easier. Threats like this might not."

The creaks of stairs again were unmistakable, coming further upwards, to the floor on which Brandon and Laura sat, up the stairs immediately beyond the landing. His breath stopping and heart thumping in his chest, Brandon and Laura again adjusted their rifles; to the space atop the stairs where a person would soon come. The steps on the stairs slowed from what they'd been; the intruder might have lost his enthusiasm, or he might be wary venturing any further.

Perfectly silently, as Laura was, Brandon listened for any voice to reassure him they needn't be afraid. The steps continued. Never before had Brandon realised how many stairs there were on that flight from one floor of bedrooms to the next.

A voice bellowed out, further from them downstairs than was the person on the stairs, Brandon thought; he couldn't understand the words. The steps towards them continued, as did another pair of steps beneath them, until in the space atop the stairs a dark shirt appeared.

Laura shot; the explosion much more than a single rifle should make. Brandon tensed further still, closing to pulling the trigger on his rifle without doing so. The shirt disappeared, back down the stairs, running even. Voices yelled from below, as all the feet that had previously stepped towards them seemed to run away.

Brandon and Laura remained silent, listening to the rush of retreat below: to yells and running feet. Both became less loud, muffled again, as the intruders hurtled down more stairs and across floors away, quietening until there was only silence.

The silence remained: a silence of escape, relief. Brandon listened for the sounds of them leaving: reopening their car doors, driving away. The walls thick enough to keep out their car battering into them were also thick enough to keep out the sounds.

Slowly Brandon stood. He turned and faced a window behind them, hiding as best he could from anyone outside. From the windows in that room, he couldn't see the courtyard, but he leant close enough to the glass to see as much as he could of the driveway back to Whinmoor Hill.

The intruders mightn't leave. They might have weapons in their car they'd gone to get. They might be planning their assault having learnt a person; perhaps only one person, they might think, defended the house with a solitary gun.

Brandon looked down at Laura, at the top of her head. She remained sitting on the floor, holding her rifle rested on her upright knees as she'd held it when she fired it, staring at the place she'd shot.

"Are you all right?" Brandon asked her.

"You should have fired," she said. "I shouldn't have had to fire."

"I wanted to see his face."

"I saw his hand."

Brandon looked back through the window, at the car speeding back down the driveway and away. "They're going now," he said.

She stood up and returned the rifle she hadn't fired to the wall, where Brandon returned his rifles. She returned the box of bullets to the table, when she removed one from the box and loaded it into her first rifle, replacing the bullet she'd fired. When they'd finished, all four rifles hung loaded on the wall.

They left the room, when Brandon started to remove the key from the lock. "Leave it there," said Laura.

At the top of the stairs, where the shirt had appeared, lay a single drop of blood. Laura found the towel to wipe it clean, leaving no record it had been there. She kept the towel with her.

Downstairs, they found their bedroom a mess. They found the baby's bedroom even messier, with everything for their child upturned or strewn about.

"Why would they do this?" asked Brandon.

"I'm more interested in the fact they did," said Laura, starting to put everything back where it had been. Brandon did the same, in their room as well. "We'll wash the linen," she said, "and the towel. We'll clean everything."

Fallen over in the drawing room on the ground floor was a small table, not for any reason it seemed except that the trespassers could push it over. The mantelpiece was empty. All around the floor were cuts and slivers of shattered crystal, spread out from central points like the decanters had been deliberately thrown down with all the force the person or people throwing them could call upon.

Laura and Brandon tiptoed around the glass. Brandon stood the table upright again.

In the kitchen were several empty packets of food. A packet of dried apples had been opened and then dumped on the floor. "All the food they touched," said Laura, "we feed to the animals."

In the basement, they found the open door through which the intruders had come and gone. Brandon had locked the door, but the intruders had broken through the lock.

"It's easier to repair than a broken window would be," said Laura examining the lock.

They collected dustpans and brushes and returned to the drawing room. Laura and then Brandon copying her brushed clean the floor. Kneeling carefully where it was safe to do so, they carefully picked up the largest pieces of broken crystal and placed them in her dustpan.

Laura's three clay towers and other European keepsakes stood inviolate in the display cabinet. "I wonder why they didn't push the cabinet over," she said, as she cleaned.

"We have three towers and two more candles," Brandon reminded her, as he cleaned.

"We have whole boxes of candles," replied Laura.

Brandon looked at her. She stopped cleaning and smiled. Brandon also stopped cleaning.

"I want our child to have brothers and sisters not just for their protection," said Laura, "but for them to know each other and be known better than you and I know anyone, to never be alone. Two children are a couple replicating themselves. It's neat, but we saw today what can happen to neatness. Three children is procreation, the next generation larger than the preceding one had been, making the world better, strengthening us in our small land. What else but children could fill our lives, or theirs? We've every reason to raise an entourage of children, replenishing our people. We have no greater mission or career."

"How can we love so many?" asked Brandon. "I don't want so many children that we can't love each of them.

Laura laughed. "Love isn't a sum game," she explained, putting down her dustpan beside her brush on the floor.

Tenderly, she reached out her hand and stroked the back of her fingers along the skin of Brandon's face. "Love isn't finite. Everything plus everything equals everything. We will never exhaust the love we feel for each one of all our children. Love spreads its wings and makes you fly, long after you can't see it anymore."

She smiled again, before brushing more crystal glass from the floor into the dustpan. When she'd filled the pan, although more glass remained on the floor, she stood up. Brandon too stood.

"We should bury the broken glass by a garden wall," said Laura, resting the dustpan on the display cabinet.

Brandon did the same, closely examining the cabinet's contents. "Did you know that among the ornaments that Ogden's family left in here," he asked, "the little animals and birds, there's a pig?"

Laura examined the same ornaments: the same pig. "We should bring up some tin cans of ham from the cellar stores and set them in prominent places around the house, where they're obvious to see through the windows."

"That won't worry everyone out there," said Brandon.

"It might worry some, I hope."

"Will they return with guns?"

"Will they return with more people?"

"We can't stay here," he told her.

"What would you have us do: keep retreating to our shrinking bits of England? Europeans have been retreating for decades, longer even, without admitting it, even to ourselves."

"Cornwall isn't shrinking, or Devon. We can't survive just the two, three, or even a few more of us. Our child will need than just a mother and poor father for the education and inspiration to be better than we are. Our children alone can't sustain our people."

19

DEPARTURE

Parked again in the courtyard outside the front of the castle house, Brandon and Laura packed Brandon's car with everything to equip them to travel south. They filled it much as Brandon filled it leaving his childhood home, however many months earlier that was, but with most of his more men's things giving way to more pregnant women's things and the books and materials they'd obtained from the Friarage Hospital. He knew only they were leaving better than they'd arrived, in a land no worse for more months of neglect. Their coming child was all the world of difference since they'd come.

"Should we cover the furniture?" asked Laura, standing with Brandon in the drawing room. The sheets they'd removed from the armchairs their first day there were in a cupboard.

"An occupied house might scare away bad people but invite good ones," replied Brandon.

"It didn't scare away the last bad ones."

Brandon pulled aside a sheet of writing paper. "*We're headed to St Austell*," he wrote. "*We'll be here again on the first day of September.*"

"Will we?" asked Laura. "If we say we'll be here, we must be here."

Brandon took a Bible from a shelf. He slipped the message

inside the front cover and laid the Bible on the coffee table. "We need only visit."

On her wrist, Laura again wore her watch. Brandon returned the watch he'd found in the Northallerton public library to its small box, safeguarding it for its journey.

"We're the watch's custodians," he reminded her, "until our child's call for it is greater than ours and he or she takes custody." Their child's time would always be his or her own.

"We can't give our child enough material possessions to demonstrate our love," said Laura. "Don't even try."

Laura's three fragile clay towers and other ornaments remained in the display cabinet. "Aren't you bringing your souvenirs?" asked Brandon.

"I'll decide in September."

"We might be unable to return."

"This house might prove more secure than a car; I've not forgotten the men we saw in York. We'll know in September."

Brandon returned the watch to the cabinet. He and Laura left their photographs upstairs.

They checked that nothing remained inside the house they wanted to take with them that day. They would take petrol from tanks below the filling stations and other resources to the last of each repository and proceed to the next. Brandon's home was anywhere he lived with Laura and their child.

In the basement of the castle house, Brandon switched off the boiler. Conserving gas, he wouldn't exhaust their scant resource.

He and Laura remained with the crackling cooling metal to see and feel the last of its warmth. Brandon imagined a daughter someday standing beside a fireplace upstairs, wearing winter pyjamas and dressing gown, holding a small doll. He imagined a son kicking a plastic ball along the floor towards him. Warm clothes and central heating, summer clothes and air conditioning, made the seasons inside houses mere lengths of days. They might live inside that house throughout nights of winter cold, while outside the creek froze over.

Their travel tasks completed, Brandon closed the doors and windows of their home. He locked all of them but the basement door he couldn't lock, since the intruders broke through it. The keys were again on the floor in the reception hall, where he and Laura found them the first day he entered the house.

"If I could find more of anything," he told Laura, walking with her towards his car, "I would find more medicines."

When they reached the car and Laura was about to open the front passenger door, she stopped. "I know one place we might find medications," she said, talking across the roof of the car. "Aunt Mia stocked in her home everything she wanted and thought she might yet need. She could live another hundred years without using it, and she wasn't the sort of person to give away anything she wanted. She gave away a lot she didn't want and raised her head further in the air for being so benevolent, but she never gave anything away she might want for herself. She hid it all in boxes under her bed, where she thought burglars wouldn't look."

"Aren't your worried about finding her dead in there?"

"I'd only be worried about the smell. She didn't smell very nice when she was alive."

Nothing had changed since they last they visited Northallerton, beyond the seasons of the year and more leaves rotten on the ground. The leaves of new seasons would fall, but nothing else would change. Laura directed Brandon driving to the north side of town and Quaker Lane.

Seeing those two young faces, an old man slowly clapped his hands in a welcome home parade for two. Grinning broadly, he slowly raised his right leg a short way from the ground, recreating an old dance, but he was too weak to hold it there. If he had anything to say to them, he would've waved his arm to flag them down.

Laura stopped them outside one particular house. The grass around the house already long might grow until it subsumed the house. Brandon didn't know how tall green grass could be.

At the end of a thinning path, the wooden door to her Aunt Mia's home included leaded lights. The door was locked. All the windows were also locked, as were the doors at the rear of the house.

A long, satisfied smile slowly spread across Brandon's face. "Wait here," he said.

Brandon returned to their car, opened the boot, and removed his axe. Laura, starting to smile, stepped back.

Standing before the door, Brandon slowly dragged the axe high behind his shoulder, laying all his weight through his outstretched arms into it. Feeling power, loyalty, and vengeance, he protected Laura, their child, and all the people who might've been. All muscle and virulence swelled within him until, expending them through his swinging arms and hands, Brandon struck the axe against the locked handle.

The door smashed open, splaying shreds of wood, jettisoning the buckled lock and handle across the air. The cracked door thumped against a wall, before bouncing back again.

Brandon's axe pushed aside the dangling broken door. He then stepped back, motioning Laura inside. "After you," he said.

The interior of the house was dark, without the power of the castle house. The air was cool, stale, and stuffy. Without hands or breeze to make it fall, a vase stood on a tabletop, frozen in a moment of life alone. A trace of dust had settled everywhere, although no person or other life could've left it there. Patches of black mould had formed on the shower recess in the bathroom.

Brandon and Laura took all the medicines they found to the car. Not even ghosts remained.

Before leaving the house, Laura stopped and turned around. She stood silently for a minute or more, before speaking. "If our child is another chance at immortality for us, our parents, and our grandparents," she said, "then what was my aunt? Was she any less my mother's parents' daughter than was my mother?"

She started edging back into the living room, with its big bay window and thin white curtains. She drew open the curtains, breathing a little more light inside.

"We wouldn't be here now, collecting medicines, but for her, would we?" she asked. "Did my mother need to let her prevent me from having any siblings?"

Like and unlike England, her aunt's significance lay not in what she and Laura felt but what they were. Their opinions of each other were less important than the facts of their existence.

They had become disparate long before they ceased to be important to each other.

"I'm not saying I like my aunt," said Laura. "I'm simply saying she was my aunt."

She made Brandon believe that he was part of all his relatives and they were parts of him. His ancestors and other kin were aspects of each other: not strangers. They were no less his family for any traits distinguishing them as they were for the most important trait they shared: their backgrounds in biology. They survived in him. He would have been less alone had he been all of them.

They would survive in his and Laura's child: a child of their ancestors. His parents had always been such children.

Brandon stood beside Laura in the centre of her aunt's living room, when she placed her arm around him. Brandon kissed her forehead, before he put his arm around her. She rested her head against his chest.

They were parents of all their descendants. Each generation needed only to be short moments in the journey of a people. Each generation coming could make each generation past immortal, links in a chain of life through centuries that ought to last forever. Their lives would be more instants in the continuum: the eternity of procreating lives.

Being moments in the journeys of their long line of families could make the pains of any single life less gruelling. They could accentuate every pleasure as one shared with lives long dead and lives not yet conceived.

Each generation could be bold enough to be proud of family past: prouder than the people newly dead had been. Greater than any pride for what their family used to be, would be an aspiration to be better in a better land than had been the preceding generation, which had let their family fade away to one. They could then be proud of what their family coming after them would do. Instead of living for a present quickly past, condemning themselves to vanish in a distant ancient past, they would be living for the future.

"I love my family," said Laura, "without loving, liking, or even knowing every one of them." All they needed to know about their ancestors was that those ancestors had brought them to be, without further recognition. All they needed to know about their descendants was that those descendants would come.

"Can we say the same of England?" asked Brandon.

"England is our most extended family."

The failings in a life remained each person's to make and overcome as much as were the triumphs, but the powers of their people exceeded any that a person could make alone. Great men and women were never greater than they were being their forebears' children and descendants' parents. The greatest achievement of most people was to contribute to a population among which were great men and women, when all of them were great.

Laura slowly pulled away from him, out of the room. With her and Brandon still in the house, she pushed the broken front door closed. "Without a lock," she said, "a gust of wind could blow it open." The leaded lights remained intact.

Together, they carried the heaviest armchair in the living room to the entrance hall and pushed it hard against the front door, securing it from wind and other weather. She then led them through the door at the rear of the house, closing it behind them and leaving it unlocked. "I'm still pleased you broke the front door," she told Brandon, as they walked around the house. "Our child should know what you did."

He recovered his axe from outside the front door and returned it to his car. Watching them from across the street was the old man who'd already clapped them in.

"Thank you," Brandon called to him.

"Thank you." The old man waved them away.

Headed south again, Brandon drove back along High Street towards All Saints Church. "We never returned to the Buck Inn," said Laura. "You said we would."

Brandon parked the car much where he had parked it the first time he visited Northallerton. The words Brandon wrote on the wall beside the Buck Inn door beckoned Laura and so him towards it, as it had been supposed to beckon people. The letters once shining indelibly black had faded into matte and almost grey with time and rain. "*We will return.*"

She opened the inn door and went inside. The lounge bar, eating areas, and function room were empty, the billiard table idle. Out back, no one sat at the long timber seats and tables. No cars or bicycles were parked.

Brandon followed her upstairs, into one of the rooms, and to a window, at which she must have stood when first she saw him. This time, they gazed together through the glass upon High Street.

Northallerton was as pretty as any town on earth, but the world could fall away without concerning Brandon, if his precious family survived. Nothing material was important without them to enjoy it.

Laura rested her hand against a handprint on the otherwise clean glass, her palm and fingers touching the impressed palm and fingers as if they were touching a bare cold hand. Her fingers didn't reach the tips of the fingerprints, and she checked her palm against the marks. She carefully adjusted them, but couldn't reconcile them. The imprint in the glass was larger than her hand.

Brandon looked at the imprint and at her smaller hand. He rested his hand against Laura's on the glass. She warmed his hand when the glass would have made it cold.

"This window was clean," she said. "That handprint on the glass isn't mine."

She pulled her hand and so Brandon's hand away from the window, as she turned around to face the room. Anybody there had left the inn neat, although Brandon couldn't know if anything had gone. On the table beside the bed lay a piece of paper, to which Laura walked. She picked it up and read it, before giving it to Brandon.

"*I came but you had gone,*" said the strong and steady hand. "*I will keep looking, I will come back later, Rufus.*"

"He could've been here at any time since the day we left," said Laura. "He might've come this morning."

Another Englishman might've made them less alone for having come, or made them more alone for having gone away. "I should've returned sooner," said Brandon.

Rufus might've driven a car or ridden a bicycle. He might've ridden a tall white horse that Brandon never learned to ride. Beyond the hand whose imprint Laura touched, might've been a face she recognised.

Laura took back the paper and picked up a pen from the desk. She tried to write with it, but the pen was dry. She opened the drawer of the bedside table and removed a pencil. After writing her message, she passed the paper to Brandon. "*We're headed to St Austell*," she'd written. "*We'll be here again on the first day of September.*"

When he'd finished reading, she folded the paper to conceal the message. She placed it back on the table, drew a large Christian Cross on it, and left it there.

Stepping outside again, Brandon looked to the left of him and to the right of him. "We're back!" he yelled.

A dog barked. No human being replied.

Brandon listened for the sounds of a car engine, bicycle, or other noise that people made. The dog again barked. Brandon wondered what it might've told him.

They took up again the journey they'd started south the day they'd met. This time, Brandon drove them in his car.

"I want our sons to fall in love with women much like you," said Brandon as he drove, "born to people we've not yet found, and our daughters to become much like you." Their child would make the choices he or she needed, nay, wanted to make, but should love as he and Laura loved.

"If not St Austell," Brandon continued, "we will travel to every town and village of our once great country, knocking on the door of every lonely cottage and estate, searching for the men and women who would become grandparents of our grandchildren. If we can't find Englishmen and women in the land of our blood then we will search for them in Wales and Scotland. We will use our lives to scour every reach of Britain.

"I would expend every day forever searching without regret, if I knew young England was there to find. We owe too much to the land of our slow births to abandon her; whatever we surrender to save England, England confers more on us. We owe it to ourselves and to the earth somehow to survive and prosper. We can survive huddled around log fires trying to be warm at night and on cooler days, but we can't survive as strangers lost before crowds of other people." The pasts before them implied chances for many different futures.

"We can drive around York," said Laura, as they neared the city.

"I know."

Returning to York, scrawny dogs in packs and cats alone watched them in their rolling car like they were food to eat. Malnourished animals were too weak to chase them. A group of small monkeys occupied a park. The relic of old stone and darkened glass was a maze of antiquated caverns in a dilapidated town museum.

Ahead of them in the centre of a street stood several men, perhaps the same men they'd seen when last they ventured through the city. "They're faces you see," said Laura, "not balaclavas."

Brandon sped past them, whereby one man waved a cricket bat at them. "That's better," he said.

The street on which they drove ended abruptly. Brandon thrust his foot onto the brakes to stop the car, glanced at the rear-vision mirror, and saw the men walking slowly towards them, holding several cricket bats in the air.

The buildings beside them filled the blocks without lanes between them, trapping Brandon and his family in their car. Any pedestrian walkways were too thin for their car to enter.

"What's that?" asked Laura.

Brandon looked past her to a crumpled heap of clothes in a corner of the pavement. The battered body of an Englishman lay bloodied on grey ground, with his eyes half open in the blood. "We can't help him now," said Brandon.

He hurriedly turned the car towards the heap, reversed the car from the kerb before stopping, and faced the men walking towards them, their faces shaded. Brandon changed the direction of the gears as he prepared to drive forward back along the street from which they'd come.

The men's eyes glared at Brandon and Laura in their car, with most of them brandishing cricket bats ready to swing them. The men didn't need to run, stalking their prey in their confinement.

"Please God," said Laura, holding her hands in front of her face in fear and prayer. The rest of her words she said to Him alone.

Brandon locked the car doors. He checked that all windows were closed. The car was their armour.

The men dragged their cricket bats above their heads as they approached them. Those bats might've been the weapons with which they'd killed the man lying dead on the pavement, for no more or less reason than they wanted to kill Laura and Brandon.

Perhaps the men before them didn't kill that man lying dead. Perhaps other people like them did.

Any number of people like them could've been watching the spectacle from building windows above them, preparing to join it. "Look around and tell me if you see anyone," said Brandon, watching the men coming towards them, obstructing them.

Brandon fastened his seat belt around him. He glanced at Laura to see that hers was still fastened around her. "I once vowed never to kill anyone," said Brandon, gripping the steering wheel.

"Killing is better than being killed."

"We can kill in self-defence."

"Practice is much more difficult than principle."

One of the men threw his head forward with the roar of a battle cry. The rest soon followed, racing together towards Brandon and his family.

Brandon's arms and legs prepared themselves. "Hang on," he told Laura, before suddenly he turned the steering wheel and thrust his foot on the accelerator pedal. The car surged forward towards the side of the street, trying to pass the men, but one man rushed towards the space into which Brandon's car sped. Brandon veered the car over the kerb just shy of a wall so that half the car was on the pavement, but the man moved further into their path.

If Brandon stopped the car to save the stranger's life then the strangers might then kill him and his family. He continued driving at the man in front of them. The man didn't flinch as he began to raise the bat again, before the car struck him. Laura screamed, her hands gripping her face, as the man bounced on the bonnet of their car and crashed into the windscreen. The shattered glass obscured Brandon's vision but he continued driving, as the man's body fell into the gutter behind them. Their car leapt back across the kerb, bouncing him and Laura in their seats, speeding away.

The shattered windscreen made driving difficult and everything ahead of them ugly, as Brandon drove fast towards the sanctuary of countryside. His life until that day might've been no different to that of the murdered Englishman whose battered body lay dead in a crumpled heap, until each of them chanced upon the men usurping rule in York.

"I can't help it," said Brandon, slowing the car for the drive to Cornwall, "but I feel safer thinking that any man who would have harmed us is dead."

Turned to her side and with her cheek against the cushioned seat, Laura gazed past him through the clear side window. "We can get another car."

ABOUT THE AUTHOR

Simon Lennon has lived, worked, and travelled throughout Europe, America, Australasia, Asia, and the South Pacific. He is married with six children. He is the author of the following books.

Fiction
The King of a Vacant City
Swansong of a Childless People
A Young Man's Tale

Non-Fiction
Western Individualism
The End of Natural Selection
The Need for Nations
People's Identity
Of Whom We're Born
Biological Us
A Land to Belong
The Failure of Multiculturalism
Reclaiming Western Cultures
Christendom Lost
Aiding Islam